YULETIDE
HOMICIDE

Also by Jennifer David Hesse

MIDSUMMER NIGHT'S MISCHIEF

BELL, BOOK & CANDLEMAS

YULETIDE HOMICIDE

JENNIFER DAVID HESSE

KENSINGTON PUBLISHING CORP.

http://www.kensingtonbooks.com

KENSINGTON BOOKS are published by

Kensington Publishing Corp.
119 West 40th Street
New York, NY 10018

All Kensington Titles, Imprints, and Distributed Lines are available at special quantity discounts for bulk purchases for sales promotions, premiums, fund-raising, and educational or institutional use. Special book excerpts or customized printings can also be created to fit specific needs. For details, write or phone the office of the Kensington special sales manager: Kensington Publishing Corp., 119 West 40th Street, New York, NY 10018, attn: Special Sales Department, Phone: 1-800-221-2647.

Kensington and the K logo Reg. U.S. Pat & TM Off.

ISBN-13: 978-1-4967-0496-2
ISBN-10: 1-4967-0496-7
First Kensington Mass Market Edition: October 2017

eISBN-13: 978-1-4967-0497-9
eISBN-10: 1-4967-0497-5
First Kensington Electronic Edition: October 2017

10 9 8 7 6 5 4 3 2 1

Printed in the United States of America

For my beautiful sisters, Jana and Jill:
strong, smart, and savvy, like the best of heroines

Chapter 1

"Blackmail? Really? Someone is blackmailing Edgar?"

Now there was something you didn't hear every day. Before I could stop myself, an image flashed to mind: Edindale's most prominent silver-haired citizen engaged in a steamy, salacious affair. Scandalous! But with whom? I shifted in my leather seat and smoothed my pencil skirt, as I waited for my boss to continue.

Beverly cast a sharp glance at the door to her dark-paneled inner office. It was still closed.

"Let's not use that word from here on out," she said. She pressed her lips together, a visible demonstration that *mum*, not *blackmail*, was the word.

"Right. Sorry," I said quickly, though I still wasn't clear as to why Beverly was telling me this—well, me and my colleague, Crenshaw Davenport III.

Crenshaw cleared his throat from the chair next to me. His long legs were crossed in an elegantly relaxed pose, but I could tell he was just as intrigued as I was.

He thrust his bearded chin forward slightly more than usual.

"It's understandable that Mr. Harrison desires discretion in this matter," he said, "especially given his recent announcement." Crenshaw turned toward me and looked down his nose. "Monday was the filing deadline for anyone interested in running for mayor next fall. Edgar Harrison announced his candidacy, along with half a dozen other Edindale residents."

"I know," I said evenly, biting back the snarky comment on the tip of my tongue. Crenshaw took every opportunity he could to school me in front of Beverly. It was one of his more annoying habits—one of many. We had both been with the firm for about six and a half years, and lately Beverly kept hinting that someone might be making partner soon. This only served to ramp up the competitive wedge between us.

Beverly removed her red-framed glasses and rubbed the bridge of her nose before responding. It had been a long week at the law firm, as everyone tried to finish up as much work as possible before the holidays. Of course, Beverly still looked impeccable in her designer pantsuit and expensive makeup, even if her eyes bore telltale hints of exhaustion.

"As I said, he was contacted by an unknown person who claims to have some information that Edgar would not like to be made public. This person has demanded a large sum of money in exchange for his or her silence. Edgar has until Tuesday to produce the cash." Beverly paused and looked from Crenshaw to me with a deadpan gaze. "Obviously, the information is not true. Edgar assured me that the person manufactured their so-called evidence. However, they must have done a convincing enough job that it could still damage Edgar's reputation should it be released."

I glanced at Crenshaw and saw him raise one eyebrow. He must have been wondering the same thing as me: *Why worry about what a blackmailer might reveal if the information is not true?*

Beverly held up her palm. "I know what you're thinking. Don't. I've known Edgar a long time. He has no reason to be involved in anything illegal. His businesses are all doing extremely well."

That was no surprise. Edgar seemed to have a knack for investing in only the most lucrative projects. He owned Edindale's only riverboat casino, its fanciest hotel, and its trendiest residential developments—among other holdings. But did that necessarily mean everything was on the up and up? Evidently, the blackmailer had information that might indicate otherwise. So much for my steamy affair theory.

"Here's the deal," said Beverly, twisting the silver rings on her left hand. She appeared to be choosing her words carefully. "Edgar is convinced that someone hacked into his computer. This person accessed some confidential financial records about some of Edgar's investments . . . and found a way to twist the truth about the records in a manner that might portray Edgar in a less than favorable light. While Edgar has done nothing illegal, the intricacies of business law are not always easy to explain to the layperson."

Out of the corner of my eye, I saw Crenshaw nod his head and steeple his fingers under his lips. *Oh, sure. As if he already knows what Beverly means, even though she's being extremely vague.* I cleared my throat. "Is that why Edgar came to you instead of the police? Because even the police might have a hard time understanding the legalities?"

Beverly frowned. "Not exactly. It's more that the information might make Edgar look bad, in spite of the fact that his dealings were technically legal. In any event, Edgar fully intends to go to the police as soon as he has evidence. He already has a couple of suspects in mind . . . which brings me to why I asked the two of you into my office this afternoon."

"How can I help?" asked Crenshaw.

"How can we help?" I asked, at the same time. I narrowed my eyes and glared at Crenshaw, before turning back to Beverly.

"As Edgar's attorney and close friend, I agreed to help him figure out who is doing this." Beverly stood and paced to her window where she paused and looked outside. Snow was falling in slow, lazy swirls. She walked back to us and remained standing. "Of course, I immediately thought of you, Keli, because of your detecting skills. You seem to have a knack for recovering stolen objects and ferreting out criminals. As for you, Crenshaw, in addition to being one of my most trusted lawyers, I believe your acting skills may be useful in this case." Crenshaw nodded his whole upper body in a seated bow, as if thanking her for a well-deserved compliment. I fought the urge to roll my eyes.

I looked up at Beverly. "How can we possibly figure out who is blackmail—I mean, who is threatening Edgar?"

"The logical place to start is at Edgar's main office. Harrison Properties has a new IT support specialist, a young, tech-savvy guy named Zeke Marshal. Edgar thinks that if anyone could hack into his secured, password-protected files, this fellow would be the one. The only problem is, Edgar can't imagine why he would do it. The young man was just hired. He has a bright future ahead of him, in a career that will compensate him well. It doesn't make sense."

I nodded, beginning to feel more and more curious myself.

"I've arranged for the two of you to set up shop in Edgar's office for a few days. The ostensible purpose will be to conduct a thorough legal audit of his corporation's files. In fact, Edgar will be paying you to do just that. His staff will be told this is a proactive measure to ensure the company is in compliance with all relevant business laws. At the same time, you will keep your eyes and ears open, and see what you can learn about Zeke. You'll start right away. The sooner we can end this headache for Edgar, the better."

After leaving Beverly's office I headed to my own, much smaller office to gather my coat and purse. Crenshaw and I had agreed to meet downstairs in the lobby in ten minutes and then walk over to Harrison Properties to get started on our strange assignment. Shaking my head, I pushed open my office door and stopped short when I saw what was sitting on my desk: a large gold-colored box, topped with a golden ribbon.

"A delivery guy brought it while you were with Beverly," said a voice behind me. I turned to see Julie, our twenty-something front desk receptionist, peering over her trendy glasses toward the gold box. "There's a card, too."

I smiled at Julie's eagerness, then walked over to my

desk to check out the package. Right away, I noticed the word *Godiva* embossed on the lid of the box.

"Did someone say chocolate?" I looked up to see Pammy Sullivan standing in my doorway next to Julie. Pammy was a fellow associate with heavily sprayed hair and a stylish, if somewhat gaudy, wardrobe. Today she wore a salmon-pink skirt suit, which matched her lipstick and fingernails. The buttons of her blazer strained ever so slightly across her plump figure.

"Come on in," I said, laughing. Pammy must have known about the delivery and was just waiting for me to return to my office.

"Ooh, Godiva," said Pammy, squeezing between the two guest chairs facing my desk to get a look at the gift box. "The nearest Godiva shop is in St. Louis. Someone must have ordered this online, unless they brought it in from out of town. Is it from a client?"

Shrugging, I slipped the small plain card out of the white envelope and furrowed my brow. "I don't think so," I said, in answer to Pammy's question. The card simply said *Missed you*. It was unsigned.

"Aw," said Julie, looking over my shoulder. "It must be from that hunky boyfriend of yours. Hasn't he been out of town?"

"Yeah, for a week. Wes helped his brother move to Seattle. He's supposed to get back later today. I'll see him tonight."

"Well, maybe he came back early," said Pammy, her eyes still on the gold box.

"Maybe," I agreed. I lifted the lid and tore off the protective plastic covering to reveal an assortment of fancy chocolate candies. It was a somewhat odd gift, coming from Wes. He knew I wouldn't eat milk chocolate because I'm vegan. On the other hand, he would also know I'd share the candy.

I replaced the lid and handed the box to Julie. "Would you take this up front and leave it on your desk for all to share? I've got to get going."

Pammy followed Julie out of my office, while I slipped on my long black coat and tied the belt. I grabbed my shoulder bag and hurried to the elevator. It was a short ride, four flights to the ground floor lobby. I pulled on my gloves as I walked over to join Crenshaw where he waited for me by the revolving door. I almost laughed when I saw what he was wearing.

In a Victorian-style overcoat, long scarf, and short top hat, Crenshaw looked like a character straight out of Dickens's *A Christmas Carol*. In fact, as an amateur actor, he probably was. Outside his law practice, Crenshaw was active in the local theater circuit.

"Nice outfit," I said. "Where are you performing?"

"I beg your pardon?"

"The caroler getup," I said, gesturing toward his coat. "Aren't you . . . Never mind."

With Crenshaw, it was sometimes hard to know when he was being serious and what he was really thinking. At times, he could be incredibly sweet. More often than not, he was just obnoxious. My best friend, Farrah, called him the "original pompous ass."

We stepped outside into the crisp, breezy air and made our way down the sidewalk toward Main Street. We walked carefully, knowing there could be slick spots in spite of the rock salt sprinkled like breadcrumbs in our path. Snowflakes stuck to every surface, from the cars parked along the curb to the tops of signs and the large red bows decorating every light post. The bows had been up since Thanksgiving, but it was the fresh snowfall that really made the scene look a lot like Christmas. It ought to, I thought, since the holiday was only a week away.

We turned right at the corner and continued down Main Street, walking past downtown shops with cheerfully decked-out storefronts. When we passed Moonstone Treasures, I slowed down to admire the window display: gracefully draped garland and glittery five-pointed stars framed an artful arrangement of red and gold candles. Just then, the door opened and the store owner herself hurried out, raising her hand in greeting.

"I had a feeling I would see you today, Keli," she said. She approached us and gave me a hug, enveloping me in the scent of rosemary, patchouli, and orange blossoms. I smiled in return. I had known Mila Douglas for years, but we had become closer friends last February when I had helped catch the criminal who had been harassing her and breaking into her shop.

Crenshaw regarded Mila with a raised eyebrow. With her white velvet tunic over black leggings and the strands of silvery ribbons crowning her brunette shag, she looked like a cross between a snow queen and rocker Joan Jett. I ignored Crenshaw and complimented Mila on her window display.

"Thank you, dear," she said. "I can hardly believe Yule is only four days away. I still hope you'll join—" She stopped mid-sentence at my warning look. Mila was forever trying to coax me into joining her coven, but I preferred to follow a solitary spiritual practice. Only a small number of people knew I was Wiccan. Crenshaw was not one of them.

"Will you stop by later?" she asked. "I have something important to tell you."

"Um, is tomorrow okay? I'm not sure what time I'll get off today, and Wes is coming by tonight."

Crenshaw crossed his arms and tapped his foot on the snow-covered sidewalk.

"Oh, I'll just tell you now," said Mila. She took my hand and spoke quickly, her breath forming puffs of fog in the cold air. "I had a vision this morning," she said, "and you were in it. So was Mercury, the messenger god." She paused, and squeezed my hand. "There are two things you need to know. One: You will soon have a visitor from your past. Two: Someone in your midst is going to die."

Chapter 2

Upon hearing Mila's remarkable message, I gasped and Crenshaw swore. Only he seemed to be more irritated than alarmed. "Keli, can we go now?" he demanded. "We really don't have time for any more fortune cookie prophecies. If you want to hear your lucky numbers, you'll have to come back on your own dime." He turned on his heels and headed down the sidewalk.

I bid Mila a hasty good-bye and jogged to catch up with Crenshaw. I had nearly reached him when my foot slipped on a patch of ice, causing me to grab his arm for balance. "Whoa!" I said, as we tussled for our footing. "Sorry about that."

Crenshaw scowled but helped steady me, and then offered me his arm. I held on to him as we continued three more blocks to Edgar's office. On the way, I tried not to freak out about Mila's dire message. I didn't doubt for one minute that she had really had the vision as she stated. The fact was, Mila was a gifted psychic. I tried to comfort myself with the knowledge that psychic predictions were often symbolic and subject to more than one interpretation. Perhaps the death she mentioned was not meant to be taken literally. Still, the whole incident made me shiver.

"Here we are," said Crenshaw, holding the door open for me. "Out of the cold at last."

We entered the six-story office building, which housed a bank on the ground level, and took the elevator to the top floor. Passing through frosted double doors bearing the words HARRISON PROPERTIES, INC., we found ourselves in a nicely appointed lobby, complete with plush carpet, leather sofas, and Impressionist paintings on the walls. Several large poinsettias occupied every end table in the room.

Crenshaw strode up to the reception desk and asked for Edgar's assistant, Allison Mandrake. The receptionist, a pleasant, soft-spoken woman, told us Allison would be with us shortly and asked us to have a seat. Crenshaw thanked her and wandered over to study the paintings, while I sat on one of the sofas and glanced at the only other person in the room, a middle-aged man with thinning hair and an ill-fitting suit. He had his nose to his phone and didn't even look up when I sat down a few feet away from him. He looked familiar, but I couldn't place him.

Before long, the door next to the reception desk opened and a tall woman entered the lobby. I guessed she was probably in her late thirties, though she carried herself with the confidence of someone older. Or maybe it was her tailored business suit, short, slicked-back hair, and burgundy lipstick that made her seem more important than a mere assistant.

She smiled at Crenshaw and me and held up one

finger, then turned to the man on the sofa. "Mr. Treat, I'm sorry to keep you waiting."

Ah, so that's who he is. Lonnie Treat. I knew I recognized him. He was a mattress salesman who often appeared in local television commercials to promote his store, Treat Mattresses. Immediately, I could hear the catchy jingle in my head: *"What a treat is a good night's sleep!"*

Lonnie Treat stood up quickly, grabbing the worn brown briefcase at his feet and the brown coat on the seat next to him. The tall woman raised her hand to halt him in his tracks. Speaking smoothly, she said, "I'm sorry, Mr. Treat. It turns out Edgar's train from Chicago was delayed, so he won't be coming into the office this afternoon. I'll tell him you dropped by."

Mr. Treat's face fell. "This is the fourth time I've been here!"

"Yes, I know. But Mr. Harrison is a very busy man. You understand." With that, she took Mr. Treat by his elbow and deftly ushered him to the exit, murmuring a firm good-bye as she did.

When he was gone, she turned to Crenshaw and me and shook her head. "Ever since Edgar announced his candidacy for mayor, he's more popular than ever. Everyone wants a piece of his time."

"Perfectly understandable," said Crenshaw, smoothing the front of his jacket.

The woman smiled. "I'm Allison Mandrake, Edgar's executive assistant. I assume you're the lawyers from Olsen, Sykes, and Rafferty?"

"Indeed, we are," said Crenshaw, with a half bow. "Crenshaw Davenport III, at your service."

"I'm Keli Milanni," I said, offering my hand to Allison.

"Wonderful. Follow me, and I'll show you where the files are."

Allison led us down a quiet hall to a spacious conference room. I was happy to see the wall of windows overlooking the boulevard below. I could never bear the idea of being cooped up in a windowless room, a quirk that only worsened a number of months ago when I found myself lost in the tunnels that ran beneath town. Brushing off that memory, I turned my attention to the large oval table dominating the center of the room. It was piled high with file boxes and stacks of folders and ledgers.

"Edgar is old-school, as you can see," said Allison, pointing at the boxes. "I keep trying to get him to switch to electronic systems, but he does love his paper."

"Hmm," said Crenshaw. He stared at the boxes, clearly not relishing the job we had before us.

I cleared my throat. "I understand the company recently hired an IT specialist. So, Edgar must be coming around, right?" *Of course, if someone really hacked into his computer, he's probably ready to ditch the digital system once and for all.*

Allison chuckled. "The IT specialist was my idea. I had to twist Edgar's arm, and he's still skeptical, but I'm sure he'll see I'm right before long. He has to join us in the twenty-first century eventually, right?"

"Not necessarily," said Crenshaw. "His way seems to have served him well so far." I wanted to kick Crenshaw for his lack of tact, but Allison was unfazed.

"Make yourself comfortable," she said. "There's bottled water and fruit there on the credenza. If you'd like coffee, we almost always have a pot brewing near the workstations. Just go through the double doors opposite the conference room, and you'll find yourself in the central work area. Feel free to help yourself. If you need me, I'll be in my office at the end of this hall."

Crenshaw and I thanked her and began to remove our coats. She was halfway out the door when I stopped her. "Oh, Allison?"

"Yes?"

"Do you expect Edgar to come into the office at all today?" I was hoping to question Edgar about the anonymous notes he had received. Beverly had told us he destroyed them, so unfortunately, I couldn't see them for myself.

Allison lifted a slender shoulder and shook her head. "It's hard to say. But don't worry. He explained to me why you're here. These files cover the past three years and include tax documents, corporate filings, customer contracts and correspondences, advertising records, and employee files. If you need investment portfolios or anything else, just let me know." With that, she waved her fingers and took off down the hall.

I looked at the piles of paper on the table and sighed. "You know, this isn't exactly our area of expertise." Though Olsen, Sykes, and Rafferty was a general practice law firm, I was more accustomed to representing individuals and families than corporations. "I think we should outsource this part of the job."

Crenshaw lifted the lid off one of the file boxes and winced when he saw how crammed it was with paper. "I'm inclined to agree. However, we must keep up pretenses." He pulled out a manila folder and sat down at the table to review its contents. "Who knows?" he continued. "We might actually learn something."

I wasn't sure if he meant we would learn something

to help us suss out the blackmailer, or we'd learn a new area of law. With Crenshaw, it was hard to tell. Slowly, I walked around the table, lightly touching stacks of paper as I skimmed the top documents. I was used to reviewing tax records for my divorce clients, but corporate filings were a whole other beast. Now, if I could find the employee records, I might learn something useful.

The ping of ice pellets hitting glass drew my attention away from the table. I walked over to the window to have a look, but a wintry mix obscured the view. "This isn't going to help those slick sidewalks," I remarked. Crenshaw only grunted in return. "I think I'll go find that coffee," I said.

I slipped out of the conference room and made my way to the open central work area, which featured half a dozen cubicles surrounded by lines of filing cabinets along each wall. Someone had taped silver and gold tinsel and construction-paper chains along the tops of the cubicles, but all the desks were empty. That is, all but one. Perched on the edge of one of the office chairs, with his back toward me, a young man tapped frenetically on a black keyboard. His head swiveled back and forth between two large computer monitors set at right angles on the corner of his L-shaped desk. This had to be Zeke, the IT guy.

I watched him for a moment. What could possibly be so fascinating about all those rows of numbers? My eyes wandered from the screens to Zeke himself, whose appearance was much more interesting than his spreadsheets. In tight, cuffed jeans, and a crisp black T-shirt, he was kind of cute, in a scruffy, boy-band kind of way. He was slender, but not soft, and his light brown hair curled endearingly around his ears. I had a strange urge to wind a lock of it around my finger.

"Like what you see, Miss Milanni?"

I jumped at his words. He swiveled in his chair and faced me with an impish grin. "The new version of Excel," he said, cocking his head toward the computer screens.

My eyes flicked to the screens, and I shrugged. "I haven't used it. What are you working on?"

"It's a real estate profit-loss analysis. I'm entering all the handwritten data into the computer to confirm the calculations and look for trends."

I nodded and took a seat at a nearby desk. "You must be Zeke. I was going to introduce myself, but you seem to know who I am already. I guess Edgar told you about the legal audit?"

"Allison did," said Zeke. He glanced at his watch, a complicated-looking piece that might as well have been developed by NASA. Then he looked up into my eyes. "But she didn't mention how pretty you are."

Why would she? I thought, blushing in spite of myself. This kid was smooth.

I was saved from coming up with a reply by Crenshaw, who moseyed in with his hands in his pockets. He affected a purposefully casual air. "Thought I'd partake in a cup of coffee as well," he said.

"Pot's there in the corner," said Zeke, as he sized up Crenshaw. "The clean mugs are in the cabinet below."

I gazed around the room, taking in all the empty, cleared-off desks. "It sure is quiet in here," I said.

Zeke looked away from Crenshaw and gave me a smile. "Lots of people take off the week before Christmas.

They gotta finish their shopping, bake their cookies, you know. Do you bake cookies, Miss Milanni?"

Was this kid flirting with me? More to the point, why was it so disconcerting? "Um, sure. Sometimes."

Crenshaw brought me a cup of coffee and pursed his lips. "I'm not sure if what you make qualifies as cookies. They would undoubtedly be vegan, gluten-free, sugar-free . . . tasteless. Am I right?"

"Hey, don't knock 'em till you try 'em," I said, warming my hands on the mug. "In fact, you can try them next week. I'm bringing date-nut oatmeal cookies to the office holiday party. They're quite delicious, if I do say so myself."

"Hmph," said Crenshaw, just as the door opened and Allison came in.

"There you are," she said. "I have something for you." She handed me a white envelope. "It's two tickets to the holiday ball tomorrow night, courtesy of Edgar. For you and a date."

"Oh, wow. Thank you!" I had heard about Edgar's annual holiday balls at the venerable Harrison Hotel. Beverly and the other partners went every year, as well as all the town's VIPs. I had never been. "Did you say for me and a date? What about Crenshaw?"

"I'm flattered you would ask," said Crenshaw dryly. "But I already have tickets. *And* a date."

"I wasn't asking—wait. Who are you taking?" We worked in a small office, and Pammy and Julie liked to gossip. If Crenshaw was dating someone, surely I would have heard about it.

"It's someone you know, I believe. Sheana Starwalt."

"The reporter? When did you start dating her?"

"Don't look so shocked. I have dated before, you know. Not that it's any of your business, but I met Ms. Starwalt—Sheana—last fall. She wrote a piece for the *Edindale Gazette* in which she covered my performance in *Arsenic and Old Lace.* When she interviewed me, we discovered we share an ardent affection for all things theater."

For some reason, I had a hard time picturing the pretty, but hard-nosed reporter as a theater lover. *Oh, well. Good for Crenshaw.*

Allison excused herself and retreated to her office. Zeke glanced at his watch again, then hopped up and stretched. He grabbed a hoodie from the back of his chair and put it on as he approached me. He nodded at the envelope in my hand. "All the employees got tickets. I wasn't gonna go, but maybe I will now. If there's any chance you'll save me a dance . . . ?"

On that note, I smiled and stood up. Some questions were better left unanswered.

For the rest of the afternoon, Crenshaw and I pored over documents in the conference room. First, we inventoried the files, organizing them by date and subject matter. Then we divided the bunch and began systematically reviewing each record for our dual purpose. We used a compliance checklist to ensure the records met all legal requirements, and a yellow legal pad to note any clues to the anonymous blackmailer. At the end of three hours, our yellow pads were still empty.

I slapped my pen on the table and looked out the window. The precipitation had let up, but it was still overcast. The waning daylight filtered weakly into the room.

"Are you having any luck?" I asked Crenshaw.

He shrugged and set down the paper he had been reading. "It's hard to know at this point what's relevant and what's not," he admitted.

"Exactly," I said. "I now know about all the property Edgar owns in Edindale—which is quite a lot. But I have no idea how or if any of it relates to the problem Beverly told us about."

Crenshaw unscrewed a bottle of water and took a sip. "Well, you're the illustrious detective. What do you suggest?"

Ignoring his dig, I pushed back from the table. "I think we should go talk to Allison. We need to learn more about the people who work here. The employee files she gave us are pretty slim, basically just a list of names and titles. There has to be more. I'll go ask her if we can have the HR files."

As I headed for the door, Crenshaw stood up and walked around the table. "I'll join you," he said. "I need to stretch my legs anyway."

We followed the carpeted hallway to the end and turned left. The first closed door on the right bore a brass plate with Allison's name. A little farther down the hall I could see elegantly carved double doors—clearly the boss's office. I raised my hand to knock on Allison's door, but hesitated when I heard a raised voice on the other side. I tilted my head and listened. It sounded like Allison's voice, and she did not sound happy.

"Are you kidding me?" she shouted. "I don't believe

it!" There was a pause, and I realized she must be on the telephone. "That's outrageous. Absolutely outrageous!"

Crenshaw and I looked at each other. "What should we do?" I whispered.

Suddenly, a piercing alarm blared throughout the hallway, drowning out Crenshaw's response to my question. I clapped my hands over my ears. Just then, the door flew open and Allison rushed out. "That's the fire alarm!" she said. "I wasn't informed of any drill scheduled for today. We need to evacuate!"

Chapter 3

"Just take the blasted jacket," said Crenshaw. For the third time, he tried to hand me his suit jacket.

"No," I said, through chattering teeth. "Thank you, but I'm fine."

We huddled on the sidewalk across the street from Harrison Properties, waiting for the Edindale Fire Department to give us permission to return inside. Between the bank employees and customers, and all the workers from the upper-floor businesses, there had to be at least thirty other coatless people shivering right alongside us. I didn't need any special treatment from Crenshaw, gallant as he wanted to be.

"Didn't anyone ever tell you that stubbornness is not an attractive trait?" he said, shrugging back into his jacket.

I sucked in my breath. "Didn't anyone ever tell you—"

"All clear! Watch your step, people. Careful now." A firefighter approached us and began herding the office workers back across the street, thus interrupting my chance to chide Crenshaw for his sexist remark. *Oh well, I'm sure I'll have another opportunity before too long.*

Once we were finally inside the lobby, I rubbed my arms and looked around. A small crowd was gathering in front of the elevators, and I overheard more than one person grumble that they just needed to collect their coat and belongings so they could go home for the day. Crenshaw maneuvered through the people to stake his spot in line, but I held back. I noticed Allison speaking to the firefighter, and I wanted to find out what she learned. However, before I could join her, someone grabbed my arm.

"Psst. Follow me."

Startled, I whipped around to see Zeke, grinning at me like a mischievous schoolkid.

"I know where the interior stairs are," he said. "And you're obviously in shape. We don't need to wait for the elevators."

"Oh. Okay," I said. I figured a climb up six flights of stairs ought to warm me up.

I followed Zeke past the bank entrance to a small side hallway. We passed a service elevator bearing an OUT OF ORDER sign and stopped at a nondescript metal door. "Here we are," he said, opening the door.

"You sure this is okay?" When we evacuated the building, we had taken an emergency exit, which led downstairs and out into the alley behind the building.

"Why not?" he responded.

"All right, then. After you." I wasn't too worried about being alone in the stairwell with the young IT guy, but I wasn't about to have him looking at my butt for six flights. I would be the caboose on this train. On our way up, I tried to make small talk. "Where'd you go to college, Zeke?"

"SCIU, here in town," he said. "But I've been out for a few years. I worked at Green Elf Energy Company before taking this job."

"That's cool. So, how old are you?"

Zeke looked at me over his shoulder. "Twenty-five. More than old enough."

I snickered. Only six years my junior, yet so much less mature. Wasn't that often the way with boys? I was suddenly even more eager to see Wes in a few hours. He was my age and, unquestionably, all man.

When we reached the top floor, we emerged from the stairwell into a dimly lit hallway. I followed Zeke past a mailroom and some restrooms, then down another hall, which led back to the cubicles.

"How long have you worked here?" I asked.

"Just a couple months."

"Do you like working for Edgar?"

"Absolutely. Edgar's great. And generous with his employees. He throws his lavish holiday ball every winter, and a huge picnic at his ranch every summer." Zeke sat down at his desk and shook his computer mouse to wake up the matching monitors. "Edgar never forgets the little people."

"That's nice," I said. *Was there a tinge of sarcasm in Zeke's voice?* I didn't know him well enough to tell. And since he had begun typing, I guessed he didn't feel like talking anymore. Like everyone else, he probably wanted to hurry up and finish his work so he could get out of there and get started on his weekend. I returned to the conference room. Crenshaw wasn't back yet, and the mountains of paper didn't look any less daunting. I sighed. *Maybe Allison's back now.*

I checked her office, but it was empty. She had left her door open and the lights on. Part of me wanted to sneak in and look around, but I knew that wasn't a good idea. She would surely show up any minute now. I glanced down the hall. Beyond Edgar's office, the hallway turned left, and I realized it must lead to the restrooms and the other entrance to the cubicles.

I took a few steps forward when something caught my eye on the floor in front of Edgar's office doors. *Is that a wet footprint?* I leaned down and touched the floor. It was wet all right. A speck of snow melted under my fingers. *Hmm.* I tried Edgar's door, but it was locked. I wandered down the hall and looked around. There were no other visibly wet spots. Someone must have stood in front of Edgar's door just long enough for a piece of snow to fall off the person's shoe. Immediately, I thought of Zeke. I had seen him leave the building with everyone else, but I hadn't paid attention to where he was the whole time we were outside trying to keep warm. *Did he come back up here while everyone was outside? If so, why?*

Voices from the lobby drew my attention, so I jogged back toward the front of the suite. I met up with Crenshaw and Allison in front of the conference room. Crenshaw appeared startled to see me. Before he could ask how I got upstairs ahead of him, I turned to Allison. "Was there a fire in the building?"

She shook her head. "False alarm." She checked her phone. "Listen, it's almost five o'clock. We're going to be closing up here soon. You can stay as long as you'd like. The front door will lock behind you when you leave."

Crenshaw and I took our places at the conference room table and picked up where we had left off. A few minutes later, Allison and Zeke breezed by, calling out good-night. As soon as we heard the front door click shut, we looked at each other and spoke at the same time.

"Shall we go?" said Crenshaw.

"Shall we snoop?" I said. Then I grimaced. We really were not on the same wave length.

Crenshaw stood up and grabbed his coat and scarf. "I don't know about you, but I have other clients to attend to. I'm going back to the office."

"Right," I said. "Actually, I have something to do at home, so I'm not going back to the office tonight. You go ahead. I'll leave soon."

For a moment, Crenshaw stared at me. Then he donned his Scrooge hat, tossed his scarf over his shoulder, and grunted, "Farewell."

Alone in the conference room, I tidied up, stacking the files we had already reviewed and pushing them to one end of the table. It was too bad we weren't able to speak to Edgar today. How did he expect us to help him when we still didn't know exactly what the blackmailer had found? Plus, if it was electronic files the black-mailer had accessed, shouldn't we be reviewing those instead of all these hard copies?

I wandered out into the hallway and thought about poking around Zeke's cubicle. After all, he was the only suspect Edgar had identified so far. I also couldn't help wondering if Zeke had had something to do with the fire alarm. But when I tried opening the door to the workstations, it was locked.

Oh, well. The snooping could wait. I had higher priorities right now anyway. I had a date to get ready for.

After leaving Harrison Properties, Inc., I walked to the parking lot near the law firm and retrieved my car, a silver-blue Ford Fusion. Carefully navigating the dark streets, I drove the few short blocks to my brick town house on Springfield Lane. As I fumbled with my keys, I heard the front door open at my neighbor's place to the right.

"Yoo-hoo! Hi, there!"

"Hello, Mrs. St. John," I said, smiling at my gray-haired neighbor.

"Home early tonight?" she called from her stoop.

"A little bit."

"It's a good thing. I hear the roads are nasty."

"They're pretty well salted downtown," I said, opening my door. "Well, have a nice—"

"Hold on, I have something for you," she said. "It arrived this afternoon. I knew it wouldn't do to leave it outside, not in this weather." She disappeared into her home. I dropped my bag on the floor inside my house and grabbed the shovel I kept in the foyer. Quickly, I shoveled off my stoop and front steps, then cleared a path on the walkway and up the steps to the St. Johns' front door. As soon as I reached their doorstep, I heard a spastic yapping from the other side of the door.

"Chompy, hush!" said Mrs. St. John, as she came outside again. Then she glanced at the shoveled steps. "Oh, how nice. Now Oscar doesn't have to get dressed."

She handed me a tall rectangular box. "Here's your flowers. I'd invite you in for cocoa, but we're about to sit down to supper."

"That's okay," I said, taking the package. "Thanks for holding these for me." I was kind of surprised she didn't insist I open the box and read the card in her presence, but when I got home I saw why. The tape on the box had been pulled up. *She already had a peek, the Nosy Nellie.* Chuckling, I found some scissors in the kitchen and cut through several layers of plastic to reveal a lovely bouquet of red and yellow tulips in a green metal vase.

"Pretty," I murmured. *But . . . tulips? In December?* Wes usually made a point to bring me flowers that were in season. I opened the card and read the message: *See you soon.* Like the card with the chocolates, this one was unsigned. It had to be from Wes, though. I'd be seeing him soon—really soon, in fact. He was due to arrive in little more than an hour. I needed to hurry.

I set the flowers in the center of my dining room table, then ran upstairs and took a fast shower. After putting on makeup and drying my hair, I pulled on a soft blue knit dress and lacy black tights. Finally, I slipped on my silver pentagram necklace. I usually wore this particular necklace under my clothes, hidden from view, but that wasn't necessary tonight. With Wes I could be myself.

I walked over to the table under my bedroom window and looked outside. The backyard was dark, except for a small patch of light from the St. Johns' patio to the right of my yard. My neighbors to the left were out of town for the holidays. I closed the blinds and focused on the objects on the table: two pillar candles, one green and one red; a silver chalice; a gold-colored wooden wand; a mortar and pestle; and several sprigs of holly, mistletoe, and pine.

This was my altar, the symbolic focal point of my spiritual practice and a constant reminder to be present within my own spirituality. It was the place where I cast spells, honored the God and Goddess, and accessed the sacred. As a Wiccan, I didn't need a priest to act as an intermediary between me and the Divine—I could be my own priestess. Wicca was an experiential religion. No leap of faith required.

I lit the candles and took a slow, deep breath. I didn't have time for a full ritual right now, but I could still set an intention for my date. My relationship with Wes was going strong. We had been dating for about a year and a half and were growing closer all the time. I had even invited him to fly home with me to Nebraska to visit my family over the holidays. He would have come, except he had already booked a job shooting wedding photos the day after Christmas. Still, I loved it that we were at the point where it was natural to spend holidays together.

In the beginning, things were a little uncertain—I wasn't entirely sure of his true feelings, and he had some insecurities of his own to work through. Then, earlier this year, we finally opened up to each other, and that sealed the deal. Turns out communication really is the key to a successful relationship.

However, there was one thing Wes didn't know. He didn't know we were about to reach an important milestone. In just a few days, Wes would officially be my longest-term boyfriend. Previously, most guys never lasted more than a few months—largely because I couldn't bring myself to share with them my deepest, most personal secret. I once went out with a guy for more than a year without so much as hinting at my Wiccan leanings. That was way back in college, nearly a decade ago. The relationship had fizzled when I decided to move to Illinois for law school, and he went another direction. In hindsight, I knew we probably wouldn't have lasted much longer anyway. Wes and I were a much better fit.

The question was, where were Wes and I headed? We were an exclusive couple, but we rarely talked about the future. Every time I thought about bringing it up, I became tongue-tied. What I needed was some courage. I needed to be open with Wes again, just like when I first admitted my feelings for him.

Closing my eyes, I whispered a prayer to the Goddess Aphrodite and vowed to be honest and forthcoming. No sooner had I finished when the doorbell rang. *Right on time.* I smiled, extinguished the candles, and went downstairs to let Wes inside.

"Wow!" he said. "You look amazing, as always. Was I gone only a week? I feel like I haven't seen you in ages."

I laughed and took the bottle of wine and gift bag from his hands. "Why, Wesley Callahan. It's great to see you, too." With his sparkling eyes and rugged good looks, Wes still took my breath away. He leaned in for a kiss, and I instinctively wrapped my arms around him. In spite of the wintery cold outside, the kiss was hot enough to melt ice. We pulled back and gazed at each other for a second.

"I am one lucky guy," Wes said.

"You took the words right out of my mouth," I said. "Except for the 'guy' part."

Wes chuckled and took off his coat. "Want me to open the wine?"

"That would be great. Dinner will be ready soon. I made the soup last night, so I just need to heat it up on the stove."

Wes followed me into the kitchen and found the corkscrew. "Is it that delicious vegetable soup with butternut squash and coconut cream?"

"Yep. Over brown rice."

"Mmm. I've been thinking about that soup ever since the last time you made it."

"I know," I said, smiling. "That's why I made it." Wes wasn't a vegetarian, but he always gamely went along with my food choices.

I put the soup on the stove and took some bowls from the cabinet. "How was Seattle?" I asked, as I set the table.

"Chilly and wet, but still pretty cool. Rob is excited to be there."

"I'd love to go with you to visit him sometime. Maybe next summer?"

Wes brought me a glass of wine. "Definitely. Let's plan on it." He took a sip from his own glass, then set it on the table. "I brought you something from this neat little chocolate shop in Rob's new neighborhood." He handed me the gift bag. "It's cacao nibs. I think you like to bake with these, right?"

"Awesome," I said, inhaling the luscious chocolate aroma from the bag. As I did so, I realized my original doubts about the Godiva candy had to be right. They weren't from Wes.

At that same moment, Wes noticed the tulips. "Nice flowers," he said. "Where'd they come from?"

I hesitated. "I'm not sure." I showed Wes the card. "Maybe there was a mix-up at the flower shop. Lots of people are sending gifts at this time of year. Maybe this message wasn't intended for me at all."

"Could be," said Wes. He shrugged and walked over to stir the soup.

Yeah, I thought. It was entirely *possible* that both deliveries weren't meant for me. But I didn't really believe that. One was sent to my office and one to my home. And the messages were too similar to be a mistake. Someone was being deliberately mysterious.

For some reason, I found this to be very disconcerting.

Chapter 4

By the next day, I had put my secret admirer out of my mind. Wes and I had spent a lovely evening catching up. In fact, I enjoyed my time with him so much, I failed to bring up the question of our future. Again. At least I had suggested that trip to Seattle in the summer. I supposed that was something.

Saturday morning I went to a yoga class with my best bud, Farrah Anderson. We had become fast friends in law school and stayed close after graduation. She had worked for a couple years in a large law firm, then left the traditional path to become a legal software salesperson. It better suited her vivacious personality and gave her more freedom for extracurricular pursuits. Some of my most fun times were with Farrah. Besides Wes, Farrah was the only other non-Pagan to know about my secret Wiccan identity.

"Did you hear my stomach growling in there?" she asked, as we rolled up our mats. "All I could think about for the past ten minutes was the Hungry Farmer Platter at the Cozy Café."

I wrinkled my nose. "Oh, God, you wouldn't really eat that, would you? Isn't it, like, two of everything on the menu? Bacon, sausage, ham, eggs . . . a vegan's nightmare."

Farrah snorted. "I could try."

A short time later, we sat across from each other in a red vinyl booth at one of our favorite restaurants in downtown Edindale. Farrah ended up ordering an omelet with a side of bacon, while I chose a black bean burger with French fries. While we ate, I told her about my invitation to Edgar Harrison's holiday ball.

"Lucky!" she said. "I got to go one year, back when I was dating that mortgage broker. He turned out to be a bore, but the ball was great. I've always wanted to go again."

I had a sudden thought. "You know, I could actually give you a ticket. I have two, but Wes doesn't need one. He has to take photos of the event for the newspaper, so he can use his press pass to get in."

Farrah's eyes lit up. "Really? But . . . solo? Do I dare show up without a date?"

"Of course! You can keep me company when Wes is working. Plus, I'm sure you'll know some of the other guests."

"Ooh, I wonder if Tucker Brinkley will be there." Farrah finished her bacon and licked her lips.

"Why does that name sound familiar?" I asked.

"He's been on various city commissions over the years, and he just announced he's running for mayor. He's probably Harrison's most viable opponent."

"Right. I must have read about him in the paper." I took a sip of lemon water and tried to recall what I had read. "'Tucker Brinkley. Doesn't he own a hunting lodge or something?"

Farrah nodded. "Stag Creek Hunting Club. They have a lodge at Diamond Point Lake. It's quite nice, actually. Decent restaurant."

"And this guy wants to be mayor?"

"Apparently so."

"Hmm. So, why would he be at Edgar's holiday ball?" I paused and narrowed my eyes. "More importantly, why do you care?"

Farrah grinned. "Oh, I don't know. He's kind of a known guy in certain circles, involved in local politics and such. He also happens to be one of Edindale's most sought-after eligible bachelors . . . probably because he's got this cool, Sam Elliott–cowboy vibe going on." Farrah paused and looked wistful. "He asked me out once, but I was with Jake at the time."

"Ahh, I see. Speaking of—"

"Don't ask," Farrah said.

I shook my head. "Okay. If you say so." Farrah was on the outs again with her longtime on-again, off-again boyfriend, Jake. Last time they were together, I had really thought they'd make it work. Then Farrah backed away again. Maybe they weren't compatible after all.

Suddenly, Farrah slapped the table, causing me to jump. "What is it?" I asked, alarmed.

"Look at the time! Come on, Cinderella! We have a ball to prepare for."

The Harrison Hotel was Edindale's version of The Plaza, only on a smaller, slightly less opulent scale. Stress the *slightly*. Built in the 1920s, it retained much of its classic charm. The lobby was an open, elegant affair featuring marble columns, an oversize fireplace, and a crystal chandelier. Beyond the check-in counter and through an arched doorway, the lobby opened into a spacious balcony-ringed atrium complete with gurgling fountain. On the far end of the atrium, a majestic ten-foot spruce tree took center stage, surrounded by a cluster of smaller silver and white trees. Through another doorway was the grand ballroom, a favorite space for weddings, parties, and galas of all sorts.

Farrah and I oohed and ahhed our way through the hotel, from the gaily decorated lobby all the way to the wine bar set up in the back of the ballroom. A five-piece jazz band played upbeat Christmas tunes, while dolled-up guests laughed and mingled.

I helped myself to a glass of pinot grigio and surveyed the room. In some ways, the festive scene reminded me of an adults-only wedding reception. Many folks wore formal attire, like a bridal party would—or prom-goers, for that matter. Other guests wore less fancy versions of their Sunday best. Based on a few familiar faces, I gathered that the latter group included some of Edgar's employees. I spotted Zeke, wearing a nice trim suit with a skinny red paisley tie. He was chatting with a group of people that included the receptionist at Edgar's office. Zeke must have sensed me staring at him. He looked straight at me and winked.

Nice. I raised my glass in acknowledgment and looked away. *He is a cutie*, I thought. *But I don't trust him as far as I could throw him.* The wink didn't help. I once knew a young lawyer who had a habit of winking at me, and he turned out to be up to no good.

Farrah nudged me. "Check out Fred Astaire over

there." She nodded toward Crenshaw, who soared across the dance floor in time to the band's hopping version of "Jingle Bell Rock." With coattails flying, he swung his partner so rapidly her hair came loose from its complicated updo.

"Whoa," I said, then laughed. "Poor Sheana. I wonder if she had any idea what she was getting into."

"I doubt it," said Farrah. "Who woulda thought your buddy could be so light on his feet?"

We moved along the perimeter of the dance floor, saying hello to fellow attorneys and acquaintances along the way. At one point, I noticed my boss, Beverly, head-to-head with Edgar Harrison. They seemed to be engaged in a serious dialogue. *I wonder if they're discussing the blackmailer. Maybe there's been another threat.* I thought about going over to find out, when another couple approached them and they drifted apart. I watched as Edgar joined his wife, Gretta, near the side wall. She was wheelchair-bound during a months-long recovery from hip replacement surgery, but she still looked elegant with her silver-blond hair and emerald gown.

Just then I spied Wes across the room. He had come early so he could take lots of photos before I arrived. Our eyes met and my heart did a little flip. His smoldering gaze heated me up from ten paces away. I had never seen him in a tux before.

"My, he cleans up nicely, doesn't he?" said Farrah, at my elbow.

"Mm-hmm," I murmured in agreement. I fanned myself with my free hand. "Is it warm in here, or is it just me?"

Farrah snickered and took my empty wineglass. She grabbed two more glasses from a passing waiter and

handed one to me. As we made our way toward Wes, I
heard Farrah whistle softly beside me.

"Hey," I joked. "You're not still eyeing my boyfriend,
are you?"

"Huh-uh. Take a look. My cowboy is here."

I turned to see who had captured her attention. No
one was wearing a cowboy hat, boots, or Western wear,
but I still knew exactly who she meant. Maybe it was
the thick mustache. Or perhaps it was the permanent
squint on his tanned face, as if he had stared into the
sunset on too many a lonely evening.

"So that's Tucker Brinkley," I said. "He looks like
he'd be more at home on the range than behind a desk
at City Hall."

"Yeah." Farrah sighed. "But he could be good for
Edindale. He actually has support from a diverse cross-
section of townspeople. Conservationists like him
because he believes in protecting land from development. Businessmen like him because of his hunting
lodge. Women like him because . . . well, for obvious
reasons." Now it was Farrah's turn to fan herself.

I took another sip of wine and pondered the rivalry
between Tucker and Edgar. I had thought they were
friends and sometime business partners, which would
explain why Tucker was welcome at Edgar's ball. But if
Tucker was against new property developments, I could
see how the two men would have plenty of opportunities to butt heads. Of course, now they were political
opponents as well.

Farrah pulled a tube of shimmer gloss from her clutch
and dabbed some on her lips. "Who is he talking to?"
she asked. "Do you think she's his date? They don't
exactly look cozy."

I looked over and recognized the tall, short-haired woman standing next to Tucker. "That's Allison Mandrake. She's Edgar's executive assistant. It would be strange for her to be with Tucker, considering the election."

I felt a hand on my waist and turned to see Wes, who had finally made it through the crowd. "Hey, babe," he said, then leaned over and stole a quick kiss. "You look incredible. Is that a new dress?"

I smiled. "New to me. It's Farrah's dress." Farrah and I had raided each other's closets as we often did. Tonight, she wore my short red cocktail dress, and I wore her long gold sequined evening gown. We had agreed that red better suited her blond coloring, while the gold went well with my brunette hair.

"How about a picture?" asked Wes. He lifted the camera that hung from a strap on his arm. He carried it with him so often, it was like another appendage.

Farrah linked her arm in mine, and we posed for a few snapshots. When Wes lowered his camera, Farrah kept ahold of me. "Before you and Wes go dancing off into the moonlight, walk with me over to Tucker's little group. Since you know Allison, you're my way in."

"Okay," I agreed. Wes tagged along as we made our way over to the growing cluster of people surrounding "Cowboy Tuck," as I'd begun to call him in my mind. As soon as we approached, Tucker's eyes fell upon Farrah, and I knew she didn't need any introduction. I said a quick hello to Allison, then slipped away with Wes. He took my hand and guided me to the dance floor.

Carefully draping his camera across his back, Wes took the lead and we danced to the band's rendition of "Walking in a Winter Wonderland." I pressed close to him and inhaled his spicy, masculine scent. He paused mid-step and stroked my hair, then brought his lips close to my ear. "I'm not usually much of a dancer," he admitted. "But this gives me a nice excuse to hold you in my arms."

"I think you're a fine dancer," I said.

He laughed, then pulled back and gave me a whirl. We danced for another two songs, then decided to take a walk.

We had barely left the dance floor when Allison stopped us. She nodded at me and spoke to Wes. "I have a favor to ask," she said. "I know you're here for the *Gazette* tonight, but would you mind taking some photos of Edgar? I need some pictures for his campaign. We'll pay you, of course."

"Oh. Well . . ."

"It's okay," I interjected. "I don't mind." In fact, I thought, I could go along and watch. *Then maybe I'll finally have a chance to speak to Edgar.*

"All righty then." Wes turned to Allison. "Just give me a minute. Then I'll go track him down."

"Wonderful." Allison pivoted on her stilettos and headed off to speak to someone else. *That is one efficient woman.*

Wes touched my arm. "Thank you for understanding. I actually need to take a few more pictures for the paper, too. I'm supposed to capture as many guests as possible. Is Farrah around here somewhere?"

I scanned the growing crowd and noticed Farrah was still where I had left her earlier, rubbing elbows with Tucker Brinkley. So to speak. The group around him had shrunk, but there were still a few other women vying for his attention—one of whom was Sheana Starwalt. Crenshaw's date.

"Huh," I said.

Wes saw her, too. "Uh-oh, looks like Sheana ditched Crenshaw. He probably overwhelmed her with his enthusiasm."

"Poor guy," I said. I spotted Crenshaw sitting by himself on a bench against the wall. He tapped his foot in time to the music and avidly watched the few couples who actually seemed to know what they were doing on the dance floor.

"Hey, you should go ask him to dance," said Wes.

"What?" I looked at Wes in surprise.

Wes grinned. "Maybe it's the holiday spirit, but I'm feeling kind of sorry for the guy. Plus I feel bad about leaving you."

I waved away Wes's apology and told him I'd be fine. After he left, I glanced over at Crenshaw again. He had stopped tapping his foot and was now examining his fingernails. I sighed.

Oh well. This will give us a chance to talk about Edgar. Maybe Crenshaw had learned something more from Beverly.

When he saw me walking toward him, Crenshaw popped up from his seat. "Greetings. That's a . . . lovely gown you have on."

"Why, thank you, sir," I said. "Care to dance?" I gestured toward the dance floor.

"I beg your pardon?"

"Would you like to dance? With me?"

"Oh. Certainly. I'd be delighted." Crenshaw held out his hand and led me to the center of the floor. Fortunately, the band played a slower song than before, so I didn't have too much trouble keeping up with him. We engaged in a passable foxtrot to the tune of "Santa Baby."

"So, have you found out anything more about . . . you know," I asked him.

Crenshaw stared at me for a moment. "Our assignment?"

"Yes. I think we need more information. I was hoping to catch Beverly tonight, and maybe Edgar, too."

"This isn't exactly the time or place for such discussions," he said. "But I agree. We need to know more. I'll see if I can schedule a meeting with Beverly early Monday morning."

I nodded and would have said more, but we had somehow managed to slow-slow-quick-quick our way next to the band's speakers. It was too loud for further conversation.

After one song finished and another began, I decided I had done my duty. I was about to tell Crenshaw I needed a break, when I felt a tap on my shoulder. Crenshaw looked at the person behind me and narrowed his eyes, evidently annoyed at the intrusion. I turned, expecting to see Wes.

I gasped. It wasn't Wes. Just as Mila had predicted: *It was someone from my past.*

Chapter 5

"Mick!"

"Hello, Keli." He grinned at me, then glanced at Crenshaw. "Mind if I cut in? Keli and I go way back."

Without waiting for a response, Mick encircled my waist and swept me off into the crowd of dancers. Gripping my hand tightly, he swung me sharply in time to the music. At first, I was too stunned to say anything. I hadn't heard a word from my old college boyfriend since I left Nebraska nearly ten years ago.

At first, I tried to keep up. Then I came to my senses. *This is crazy. I don't want to dance with this guy.* I halted and pulled away. "What are we doing?" I said. "Let's go sit down and catch up. I'm tired of dancing anyway."

"Love to." He grasped my arm to guide me off the dance floor, and I sped up to free myself. Who did he think he was, anyway? He had no right to act possessive of me.

As we left the ballroom, I kept an eye out for Wes. I finally spotted him in the atrium, where he was taking photos of couples in front of the fountain. I didn't want to interrupt his work, but I wished I could get his attention.

"Let's go to the lounge upstairs," said Mick. "I'll buy you a drink."

"Fine."

As we climbed the steps to the upstairs bar, I glanced over at Wes again. This time he caught sight of me. He raised his eyebrows, and I gave him a weak wave. At least now he'd know where I'd gotten off to.

Mick snagged a small round table near the railing and held out a chair for me. "Keli, you look fantastic. You haven't aged a day since college. What's your secret?"

I lifted my shoulders and gave him a small smile. I couldn't bring myself to return the compliment, even though he didn't look too bad. Sure, he was a little thicker around the middle and thinner at his hairline, but he still had those dimples and long eyelashes I'd found so charming once upon a time. And as he removed his tuxedo jacket and draped it across the back of his chair, I noticed he still had quite impressive biceps. Still, as much as I had once loved him, the thrill was now, most definitely, gone.

"Mick, this is such a surprise. What brings you to Edindale?"

"Business. I remembered you came here and decided to look you up. Did you get the flowers and chocolate?"

"Yeah. I did. That was very nice. But why didn't you sign your name?"

He leaned back in his chair, looking smug. "Where's the fun in that? Besides, I thought you'd figure it out." He puckered his lips in a mock pout. "Are you telling me you don't remember?"

"Remember what?"

"Spring break? We went to that park, and I picked you tulips? And we joked about Lady Godiva because of that horse statue?"

Huh? I stared at Mick as I racked my brain for any memory of what he was talking about. I decided to change the subject.

"So, what have you been up to? Last I heard, you were moving to Washington, DC."

"I did," he affirmed. "I live in Arlington now." He went on to describe his job running a political action committee devoted to supporting up-and-coming local politicians. He was in Edindale to vet Edgar as someone his PAC might support. This surprised me, for as far as I knew, Edgar had never been in politics before his current run for mayor. "Tell me about you," Mick said. "I know where you work already. What do you do for fun?"

I proceeded to list off some of the activities I enjoyed: running, gardening, seeing concerts with friends. In my head, I groaned. I had no connection with this guy anymore. I wasn't about to reveal any personal details about my life.

For that matter, I noticed he didn't ask if I was married or seeing anyone. Apparently, it was obvious Crenshaw and I weren't a couple. I wondered if Mick had ever settled down with anyone after college. Would it be rude to ask? He didn't have on a wedding ring, but that didn't prove anything.

On the other hand, I wasn't really that interested. In fact, I was tired of his company already. I wanted to go back to the party. As Mick droned on about some sports team, I cast around the bar to see if there was anyone I knew—anyone I could call over to rescue me.

Raucous laughter erupted from the back of the lounge. I looked over and saw a group of people crowded around a table, some sitting and some standing. I recognized at least one of them: Lonnie Treat, the mattress salesman. He appeared to be angling for a seat at the table. When the group shifted, I saw why. It was Edgar. Seated in a captain's chair, with his back to the wall, he was clearly the center of attention. He appeared to be relating an entertaining story to his rapt audience. Or maybe, like Allison had said, people were drawn to him because he might be the future mayor. Either way, they hung on his every word.

"He certainly is popular," said Mick, who was now watching Edgar, too.

"Yeah," I agreed. "I think he's generally well liked around town. Of course, throwing parties like this doesn't hurt."

Mick scooted his chair back. "I guess the waitress isn't going to come by. I'll go order our drinks at the bar." Instead of standing up, Mick leaned forward and waggled his eyebrows. "How about a purple hooter shooter, for old time's sake?"

Just then, a shadow fell across our table. We both looked up to see Wes standing there, scowling.

"Hey, Wes! All done taking pictures?" Finally, an excuse to get away from Mick. I glanced between the two men. "Mick, this is my boyfriend, Wes. Wes, this is—"

Mick stood up and stuck out his hand. "Mick MacIntyre, Keli's old college flame. Talk about awkward. I'm sorry if this looks bad. She didn't tell me she was dating anyone."

I gaped at Mick. The situation didn't have to be

awkward, but his clumsy explanation made it so. Luckily, Wes only looked bemused. He shook Mick's hand, then turned to me.

"I'm just going to shoot a couple more photos of Edgar, then I'm done for the night."

"Terrific. I'll come with you." I stood up and linked my arm through his. To Mick, I said, "It was nice seeing you again, Mick. I hope you enjoy your stay in Edindale."

Wes and I danced to one more song, then walked hand in hand around the hotel's atrium. We stopped next to the tall Christmas tree to admire the shiny ornaments. I had given up on trying to speak to Edgar that night. After Wes had taken a couple of candid shots in the lounge, he put his camera away. It was obvious he wouldn't get any pictures appropriate for an election campaign. I didn't know how many glasses of scotch Edgar had downed, but his cheeks were ruddy, his eyes were bloodshot, and his loosened tie was crooked. He was clearly drunk.

Now all I cared about was being with Wes. I had repeatedly assured him that I didn't have any lingering romantic feelings for Mick, and he seemed satisfied. Still, it couldn't hurt to demonstrate my devoted affection for Wes. I moved closer to his side.

"Look at that," said Wes, pointing up at the tree. "Isn't that mistletoe?"

I didn't bother looking. I simply turned to Wes and smiled. "Yeah. It definitely is."

He drew me near and kissed me. I closed my eyes and allowed myself to melt into him, oblivious to the other party guests strolling and chattering around us. After a moment, we drew back, slightly breathless.

"Shall we go?" I asked.

Wes nodded, and we headed to the cloakroom. Farrah had already told us good-bye after we had left the lounge and returned to the ballroom. She had decided to join a group of people who were leaving the party to check out a rock band playing at a nightclub down the street from the hotel.

There was no attendant in the cloakroom, so we decided to climb over the counter to look for our coats. Wes bounded over first, then held out his hand to help me over. I hopped onto the edge and tried to swing my legs over without falling off. It didn't work. I blamed the long dress, but perhaps I was a little tipsier than I thought. I fell into Wes's arms, knocking him off balance. We ended up on the floor and in an instant, Wes pulled me close and we began making out under the coats. We pulled back, laughed, then started kissing again. I moved my hand to brace myself on the floor and it met with something sharp. "Ouch!"

"You okay, babe?" said Wes, his voice husky. He sat up, and I showed him my hand. He lifted it to his lips and kissed my palm.

"Ahem." We looked up to see someone standing on the other side of the counter, with arms crossed. It was Crenshaw.

Wes stood first and helped me to my feet. "Hey," said Wes. "There was no attendant, so we had to climb over. Lost our footing."

Without a word, Crenshaw walked to the end of the counter and swung open a door. *Oops*. Wes and I started laughing again. Crenshaw walked past us, retrieved his coat and hat, then swept out of the room. Wes found our coats and helped me on with mine.

Before we left, I glanced at the floor to see what had pricked my hand. It was a piece of a broken buckle, with a distinctive bead pattern that looked familiar. I scooped it up and held on to it as we hurried out of the cloakroom and made our way to the hotel's exit.

Two hours later, Wes and I were snuggled up on his couch looking at the photos he had taken at the ball. I wore one of his old flannel shirts as a nightgown, while he wore pajama bottoms and a T-shirt. I leaned up against him as he scrolled through the photos on his camera, making comments about which ones he would probably submit to his editor at the newspaper. He had taken a lot of pictures before I arrived at the hotel, including some of Edgar greeting guests in the lobby and a few of Edgar with his wife, Gretta, and their two daughters. From what Beverly had mentioned, I knew Edgar's elder daughter was a surgeon and his younger daughter had just started college. Gretta was involved in horticulture and philanthropy, though her hip surgery had probably slowed her down in recent months.

"Looks like you got some good pictures of Edgar after all," I said. "You should show these to Allison."

"Yeah," said Wes. "Technically, these belong to the paper, but I'm sure they'd be willing to sell a few."

"Oh, then I guess you can't charge for them," I said. "That's too bad."

Wes shrugged. "That's not why I was there in the first place. If they still want more campaign pictures, I can offer to set up a photo shoot in Edgar's office."

"That's a great idea." I rested my head on Wes's shoulder. In the past, he had struggled to make ends meet as a photographer. I wasn't sure how much he earned at the newspaper, but I had the impression he was still a little sensitive about his income, especially as it compared to mine.

Wes chuckled. "I don't think we'll be sharing this one with Allison." I looked at the photo on his camera. It showed Allison glaring at Edgar, who was apparently speaking to someone off-camera.

"Wow, I wonder what Edgar did to make her look at him like that."

"Maybe nothing," said Wes. "That's the thing with photos. You never really know the full context. Like any other art form, once it's out there, it's no longer about the original meaning. It becomes open to the viewer's interpretation."

I pondered this and realized Wes was right. Allison's expression could have been caused by anything, from a story someone had relayed to a bad reaction from something she ate. Still, it sure looked like she was aiming daggers directly at Edgar. This made me recall the argument I had overheard in her office.

Before I could give it any more thought, my cell phone rang. I fished it out of my purse and stared at the unfamiliar number. Who would be calling me at one o'clock in the morning? Only one way to find out.

"Hello?"

"Hey, Keli. You're still up. I thought you would be. You always were a night owl."

"Mick? What's up?" I brushed off his attempt to act like he still knew me. Sure, I stayed up late in college, but usually only when I was out partying with friends—or if I had a paper to finish or a test to study for. But that was a long time ago.

"I didn't get a chance to tell you before. I have something of yours. If you come by the hotel, I'll return it to you."

My mind flashed to half a dozen things I had given Mick that I wouldn't mind having back. I hadn't thought of them in ages, but at the time of our breakup it had really bothered me that he still had them. Most of the items didn't have any real value, but there was a nice print that had hung in my dorm. It was the first piece of original artwork I had ever bought for myself, and I really liked it. I had given it to Mick during a period when I was spending more time at his place than at mine. More importantly, I had also let him borrow a book that had belonged to my long-lost aunt Josephine.

Josephine O'Malley was my mother's older sister who had run away from home when she was seventeen to join a commune right here in Edindale. As bad as that was, from her parents' perspective, it got even worse when she left the commune, never to be seen again. She had sent an obscure letter saying she was leaving on a "secret mission" and not to worry about her. *Yeah, right.* After that, she sent postcards from various places around the country, but she never came home. This was way back in the 1970s, before I was born. Although I had never met her, I always felt a special connection with my free-spirited aunt. I had tried to find out what had happened to her by researching her old commune, the Happy Hills Homestead. I even tracked down a woman who had known my aunt back when they both lived there. The woman, Fern Lopez, still lived in the area and was nice enough to meet with me and share her memories of "Josie," as my aunt was known back then. But Fern was also a little bit odd, and, much to my disappointment, she claimed not to know why Josie left or where she went.

Nevertheless, I still held out hope that I might find Aunt Josephine someday. She had to be somewhere—she was still sending postcards! I had even received one from her on my thirtieth birthday a couple summers ago.

It had always galled me that Mick never returned Aunt Josephine's book.

"What is it?" I asked Mick now. "What do you have to return?"

"It's a surprise. You *haf* to meet me in person." Mick slurred his words, and I sighed.

"Okay," I said. "I'll stop by tomorrow."

"No, that's too late," said Mick. "I'm leaving early in the a.m. You need to come now."

Irritation bubbled to the surface, but I gritted my teeth and tamped it down. "It's late, Mick. How about if I meet you for an early breakfast?"

Wes, who had been watching me throughout the call, narrowed his eyes. I tried to give him a reassuring look.

"No can do," said Mick. "I'll be gone by then. Just come over now. I'm in room 418." He hung up, and I made a face at the phone.

"Unbelievable," I muttered. I checked the time and saw that it was 1:15 a.m. Well, I supposed it actually wasn't that late for a Saturday night. I stood up and grabbed a pair of jeans from the backpack I'd tossed on the floor earlier.

"What are you doing?" asked Wes.

"Mick says he has something of mine. He wants to give it to me tonight, since he's leaving early tomorrow.

I really kind of want to know what it is, so I'm just gonna run over to the hotel. I'll be back in—"

"I'm coming with you."

I didn't argue. A short time later, Wes drove into the porte cochere at the Harrison Hotel and pulled up in front of the main entrance. He hopped out of the driver's side and met me as I stepped out of the car. "Oh," I said. "I don't think you should leave the car here. Why don't you wait and I'll be right back."

"No way," said Wes. He closed my door, then turned as a valet came outside and approached us.

"Really," I insisted. "I won't be more than five minutes. It's not worth having the valet take the car." Before Wes could protest, I dashed inside and scurried past the unoccupied front desk. Through an open door behind the desk, I saw a young guy playing a computer game. There was no one else in the lobby. As I waited for the elevator, I peered through the now-closed glass doors to the atrium. The party was long over, but twinkling lights still lit up the trees and the garland along the bannister leading up to the second-floor lounge.

What's taking the elevator so long? I tapped my fingertips together impatiently. I really wanted to get this over with and get back to Wes. Then I remembered that there was another set of elevators near the bar upstairs. I pushed open the doors to the atrium and ran across the darkened floor.

At the bottom of the stairs, I hesitated. Maybe it was the quiet stillness of the empty, cavernous room, but I suddenly recalled how strangely Mick had acted. It was almost creepy, now that I thought about it. What was he up to with those anonymous gifts sent to my office and home? Come to think of it, how did he get my personal cell phone number?

I shivered. I was pretty sure Mick was harmless. Wasn't I? Still, why take any chances? I decided it would be wiser to have Wes accompany me after all.

I turned to head back to the lobby. That was when I noticed something amiss near the towering Christmas tree. One of the smaller trees next to it appeared to have been knocked over. Frowning, I walked toward them. I couldn't believe the cleaning crew would have left it like this after the party. As I drew near, I could see bits of broken ornaments scattered like glitter all over the floor. It was an overcast night, so not much light shone through the glass roof of the atrium.

I decided I would tell the guy at the front desk about the tree. It could be a fire hazard, considering all the electric twinkle lights.

Just then, the clouds parted, letting in a small ray of moonlight. It fell upon something against the wall. Something I hadn't noticed before. Something far worse than broken ornaments.

It was a body. Crumpled and contorted in a most unnatural way, as if it had tumbled off a balcony high above. I shrieked, horrified, as I recognized who it was.

Edgar Harrison. Dead.

Chapter 6

I couldn't stop screaming. The sight of Edgar's broken body was too horrible to comprehend. Then the lights in the atrium flashed on, and people came running from all directions. A woman in a housekeeping uniform was one of the first to arrive at my side. When she saw Edgar, she began screaming, too. That's when I came to my senses and shut my mouth. I pulled her away and briefly squeezed both of her hands.

"Go call nine-one-one," I said.

She nodded and ran away. Only then did it occur to me that I could have pulled out my own cell phone. On the other hand, my hands were trembling so hard, I probably wouldn't have been able to push the numbers anyway.

"Jesus Christ!" It was the young guy from the front desk. He clapped his hand over his mouth and looked like he might vomit. A security guard yelled at him to come and help keep people away. Guests had begun streaming down the stairs to see what was going on.

Worse, some of them were peering over the edge of the railings above.

I backed away from the scene in a daze, weaving my way through the chaos. I wanted to put as much distance between myself and Edgar's body as I could—as if distance could somehow reverse the horrible thing that had happened. Was still happening.

Halfway to the exit, I bumped straight into the hard, muscular frame of a tall man. I whipped around, then threw myself into his arms.

"Oh, Wes," I sobbed.

"Hey," he said, his voice full of concern. "Are you okay? What happened?" He smoothed my hair and held me tight.

I didn't know how to answer him. I had no idea what had happened. Suddenly, though, I felt a lot less freaked out. As much as I hated to admit it, I felt stronger now that Wes was here. His presence soothed me.

We made our way to a bench in the lobby where we could observe the action from a safe distance and wait for the police to arrive. We watched people come and go and listened in on hushed, incredulous conversations. Between the twinkling Christmas lights draped throughout the lobby and the red and blue police lights flashing outside the sliding glass doors, I felt like I was at a weird laser light show. Or in a movie. A sad, surreal movie. Either way, it was all too hard to believe.

The next morning, I woke up in the cold, dark predawn hours and rolled out of bed. It had been a fitful night. No matter how many relaxation techniques I tried, how many breathing exercises, mantras, or transcendental tricks, I just couldn't quiet the noise in my head. Images crowded my mind, too, but it was the sounds that kept me awake: the scream of the hotel maid, the blaring sirens, and the questions. So many questions. Everyone demanded answers: the police, the hotel staff and guests, Edgar's family and friends who had descended upon the scene with surprising speed.

And Beverly.

Wes and I had run into her in the lobby talking with Allison. Or, more accurately, she was *weeping* with Allison. I had never seen my boss so distraught. She was the most unflappable person I knew, the epitome of calm, cool, and collected. But not last night. Last night she was a hot mess. She was coatless, and her ball gown was rumpled, as if she had fallen asleep in it. Her makeup was smeared, and, I swear, she shed more tears than Edgar's wife. Gretta had appeared more shell-shocked than anything. I overheard her tell the police she hadn't even heard Edgar leave again after they'd returned home from the party.

When Beverly finally brought her sobs under control, she joined Allison in plying me with questions. They all began with one word: *Why*. Why had Edgar come back to the hotel? Why was he upstairs by himself? Why had he fallen? Why hadn't someone helped him? Why was he dead?

I didn't have any of those answers. I comforted Beverly and Allison as best as I could, then, after giving my statement to the police, I fled the hotel with Wes.

Now I shivered in my chilly bedroom and wrapped myself in a fluffy robe. I stepped into my faux-fur slippers and padded downstairs to put on the tea kettle. I could always sleep later. In theory.

As I puttered about, switching on the twinkle lights that framed my front window and turning the thermostat up a notch, my foggy head started to clear. I realized there was another reason I had had trouble sleeping last night. Something else was bothering me besides the distressing sights and sounds in the aftermath of finding Edgar's body. It was the conclusion everyone had jumped to. In subdued tones, so many people had said the same thing: "It was an accident. A tragic accident."

Even the police sergeant had said it to Edgar's family. "It appears to have been an accident," he had said. "It looks like Mr. Harrison fell over the balcony." To ease their worried minds at least a little bit, he had added, "There was no note on his person." *No suicide note* was what everyone knew he had meant.

Allison apparently agreed with the police. "He'd had so much to drink," she had said, wringing her hands. "He was stumbling when I last saw him toward the end of the night." She had shaken her head and looked around helplessly. "I can't believe this is how it ends. A stupid, senseless accident."

An accident? I supposed that was the most logical explanation. The railing was low, the hallway dark. Edgar had clearly been inebriated last night.

So why did this conclusion make me so uneasy?

Maybe it was because of the secret that only Beverly, Crenshaw, and I knew: that Edgar was being blackmailed. It couldn't be a coincidence, could it? Wasn't it too strange that he died within days of being threatened by some creepy, anonymous crook?

My tea kettle whistled and I shook myself out of my brooding daydreams. I was tilting at windmills. Blackmailers weren't killers, were they? Not that I

knew any blackmailers, but it just didn't make sense.
The blackmailer wanted money from Edgar. *You can't
extort money from a dead man.*

I sipped my tea and checked the time. Five-thirty
a.m. I wondered what Wes was doing. Probably sleeping. His editor had called in all the staff as soon as word
of the incident came through on his police scanner. The
Gazette wanted to break the story, and then run a full-
page spread on Edgar in the morning edition. Wes had
to search the newspaper archives for the best photos of
Edgar over the years, as well as quickly sort through
and process the ones he had just taken at the ball.

Of course, Wes had wanted to stay with me last
night. But I had told him it was okay for him to leave.
He needed to do his job, and I was perfectly fine on
my own. Which was mostly true, even though I was
secretly sorry to see him go.

Clutching my mug of tea, I stepped out on my deck
to feel the bracing air on my skin and breathe in its
cleansing coolness. In the pale morning light, I could
still tell the backyard was a pristine blanket of snow
capped by a layer of glistening ice. At least, it was pristine behind my house and in the parkland beyond. The
St. Johns' backyard looked as if it had been chewed up
by a garden tiller. I smiled. I knew their rambunctious
pug, Chompy, was responsible for the wreckage.

As the darkness faded, I looked to the east. Watching the sun rise, I felt moved to say a prayer for Edgar.
I didn't know him very well personally, but I knew he
touched a lot of lives in Edindale. And I knew he was
Beverly's close friend. With my eyes to the sky and my

thoughts on the goodness in the man, I murmured a few words from my heart:

> *May you find peace, rest, and understanding in the*
> *Summerland.*
> *May the Goddess comfort your loved ones, and the*
> *God give them strength.*
> *You lived well in this life. May the lessons you*
> *learned serve you well in the next.*
> *Blessed be.*

I spent the rest of my Sunday morning on ordinary household chores and mundane errands. There was nothing like the repetitive routine of laundry to make a person feel normal again. At some point in the middle of folding my underwear, I suddenly remembered Mick. I hadn't seen him in the crowd of people milling about behind the police tape last night, but that didn't mean he wasn't there someplace. I was disappointed I didn't get to find out what it was he was going to return. On the other hand, I didn't regret not seeing him again. By now, he was probably already back in DC, and that was just fine with me.

After a fortifying lunch of beans and rice, I gathered up some holiday CDs and headed over to Farrah's place. She had asked me to come over and help decorate her Christmas tree—and to fill her in on the excitement she had missed last night. I would have much preferred to hear about her post-ball evening than relive mine, but she insisted I go first. True to our friendship, I spared no detail.

"Oh, honey!" she exclaimed. "You poor thing. I can't believe you're the one who found him. What are the odds?"

"I know." I shuddered. "Right place, right time? Or wrong time, if you think about it."

"Well, at least you didn't see it happen. That would've been way worse."

"You're telling me. Ugh." I reached over for my glass of warm spiced wine and took a sip. Then I returned to the task at hand—stringing popcorn and cranberries. Farrah had gotten a notion to go all old-fashioned this year, which I found amusingly ironic. Farrah was anything but old-fashioned.

"Ouch! Dang it." Farrah sucked on her finger where she had pricked it with her needle for at least the fifth time. "I wish I had one of those whatchamacallits for your finger."

"A thimble?"

"Yeah. A thimble. I wonder where you can buy one of those?"

"Lots of places, silly. I could've brought one over if I would've thought of it."

Farrah waved away the idea. "You've been preoccupied. I wouldn't expect you to think of such things."

"I suppose." I stared at the flickering candles Farrah had arranged in her fireplace, and my mind flashed back to the hotel atrium again. After a moment, I looked up. "What were we talking about before? The time of the fall? You know, it probably happened just minutes before I got there. I overheard the hotel manager tell the police that the last party guest left at midnight, which is when the hotel bar closed. Then a cleaning crew came in, did their job, and clocked out at twelve-fifty."

Farrah shook her head. "It just goes to show you, having a bar with a balcony is a really bad idea. In a way, I'm surprised someone hasn't tumbled over the railing before this."

I looked over at her. "Oh, I don't think he fell from the second-floor bar. I think he fell from one of the upper levels where the rooms are." I grimaced at the thought. "I wonder why he was up there in the first place."

"He probably got confused," said Farrah. "I heard he got smashed at the party." She saw me cringe and slapped her forehead. "Poor word choice. Sorry. He got really drunk," she amended.

"Who did you hear that from?" I asked. I remembered how Edgar had appeared when I last saw him in the hotel bar. There was no doubt he'd been drinking, but I wouldn't have called him falling-down drunk. Plus, he seemed like the sort of man who ought to be able to hold his liquor.

"From Tucker," said Farrah. "Before we left, he went and found Edgar to say good-bye."

Another thought occurred to me. "Jeez, if he was that drunk, it's a wonder he didn't kill himself on the drive back to the hotel from his ranch. Or worse, kill someone else."

"Maybe he didn't drive," said Farrah. "He probably had his driver bring him."

"What makes you think so?"

"Well, that's how he left the hotel after the ball. Tucker and I walked back to the hotel parking lot where he had left his truck, and we saw Edgar come out of the hotel with the last of the guests. A uniformed chauffeur held open the car door for him." She grinned. "The chauffeur was kinda cute, too, that's why I noticed. What is it about men in uniforms?"

I smiled. "You're incorrigible. You still have to tell me about your evening with Tucker, by the way. But first, before I forget, how did Edgar look when you saw him leaving the hotel? And did he leave alone?"

Farrah scrunched her brow in thought. "He was alone. I saw his wife board a wheelchair van earlier, when we left for the nightclub. As for how he looked? I'd say he looked like someone who had stayed until the end of a party. I guess he was sort of disheveled and red in the face." She shrugged. "I didn't exactly study him."

I chewed my popcorn thoughtfully, overlooking the fact that the last several pieces I'd grabbed had ended up in my mouth instead of on the thread. I was still thinking about Edgar. "So, if he did have his driver bring him back to the hotel an hour or so later, the driver might know *why* he came back."

"Yeah, maybe," said Farrah, reaching over to help herself to some popcorn. "But what does it matter anyway?" She made a face. "This popcorn needs salt."

I leaned over to grab my purse from where I'd left it on the floor. "You know me," I said, in response to Farrah's question. "I like to have answers. Plus, I was the one to find him. Maybe I need closure."

Farrah watched me curiously as I pulled out my phone and scrolled through my contacts. "I'm going to call Edgar's assistant," I told her.

Allison picked up on the first ring. After expressing my condolences, I asked her if Harrison Properties would be closed for a few days.

"No, I don't think so," she said. "We still have a business to run. We'll probably just close on Thursday for the funeral. And maybe we'll close early on Wednesday for the visitation." She told me the name of the funeral home, which I jotted down. Then I cleared my throat and prepared to employ one of the oldest tricks in the book: act like you already have more information than you really do.

"I feel so bad for Edgar's family," I said. "There were so many unanswered questions last night. Do you know if Edgar's driver was able to at least tell them why Edgar went back to the hotel?"

"I spoke with Bob myself," she said without hesitation. "He said Edgar didn't call him for a ride last night. Bob didn't bring him back to the hotel. Edgar must have driven himself."

"Oh," I said. "You don't think Edgar called a cab?"

"No. Edindale cabs won't usually drive that far out of town, especially in the middle of the night. Anyway, Edgar's BMW is still in the hotel lot. It will probably remain there for a while, until Gretta decides what to do with it."

I repeated my sympathies and ended the call. When I relayed our conversation, Farrah had one word to say: "Baloney."

"What do you mean?"

"I mean baloney. Edgar didn't drive his BMW back to the hotel, because his car was already there in the parking lot. Tucker and I walked right past it on our way to his truck. I even pointed it out and asked Tucker if he would ever drive something so luxurious. He drives a Ford pickup, so, of course, he just laughed. A deep, throaty, toe-tingling laugh, I might add."

I rolled my eyes. "You really *must* tell me everything about your date with Cowboy Tuck. But . . . this is so strange. If Edgar's BMW never left the parking lot, then he either drove something else from the ranch, or someone else picked him up. Both scenarios seem unlikely. If Edgar had another vehicle, you'd think Allison would have seen it in the parking lot. And—"

"There is another possibility," said Farrah. "Maybe his driver—"

"Lied." I finished her sentence, grabbed my phone, and hit REDIAL. When Allison answered, I spoke carefully. "I'm sorry to bother you again, but I have a quick question. Could you give me Bob's phone number? It occurred to me that he's out of a job now, and I might be able to throw some work his way." I crossed my fingers and silently vowed to find a way to turn my fib into the truth.

After a moment's silence, Allison told me to hold on. A few minutes later, she came back with the number. When I hung up, Farrah handed me one end of the cranberry garland she had just tied off. "Help me with this," she said. "And while you're at it, explain to me why the driver would lie . . . and why we care."

We walked around her Christmas tree, a nice, fat white pine, and draped the garland from the top to the bottom. I decided to answer Farrah's first question and stall on the second. "Maybe he felt guilty about driving Edgar to the scene of his death," I suggested. "Maybe Edgar was in no condition to leave the house again, and the driver felt bad?"

"If that's the case, how are you going to get him to tell you anything different?"

"I have my ways."

Farrah froze, her eyes wide. "Wiccan ways? Are you going to cast a spell on him? Can I watch?"

I laughed. "I've told you before, we don't cast spells on other people. Usually. However, I might just cast a teeny tiny spell on myself, to help me be more persuasive. And, you know, give me confidence."

"Oh," Farrah said, "that's not as fun," before she threw some popcorn at me.

Chapter 7

Monday morning, I left home extra early so I would have time to stop at Moonstone Treasures before work. I liked to visit the occult gift shop before Mila opened to the public, and thus avoid being seen by anyone who might recognize me. As clean and charming as the shop was, some of my more old-fashioned clients would definitely raise an eyebrow to find out their lawyer frequented the place.

Leaving my car in the municipal lot, I cut through the alley in back of the shop and tapped on the steel door. It swung open even before I lowered my arm.

"Good morning," Mila sang out. "I've been expecting you."

I followed her inside, through a storage room lined with boxes of inventory, and into Mila's exotically adorned divination parlor. A teapot, two cups and saucers, and a plate of cookies sat in the center of the cloth-covered round table. Mila waved me toward one of the chairs and poured me a cup of tea.

"How are you, Mila?" I didn't bother asking how she

knew I'd be stopping by this morning. It could have been her intuition, or a premonition, or perhaps just an educated guess based on the news of Edgar's death. It didn't really matter. What mattered was I was grateful to be having tea with a sympathetic friend.

"I'm fantastic," she said. "I just completed my year-end accounting, and I'm happy to say we made up for all the lost days and bad publicity at the beginning of the year. We are firmly, happily, in the black—which, as you know, is a great color to represent a reversal in fortunes."

I smiled and took a sip of tea. "I'm happy to hear it."

Ten months ago, around the February holiday, Candlemas, Mila had almost lost her business when vandals repeatedly broke in and left threatening notes. Recalling the anonymous notes reminded me of the blackmail threats Edgar had received. I wondered if there was a way I could seek Mila's counsel about that mystery without breeching my confidentiality obligation.

Before I could pursue the matter, Mila leaned forward and took my hand. "There's something I need to tell you," she said.

Uh-oh. Not again.

The alarm must have shown in my face, because Mila's expression took on a note of concern. She peered at me closely. "What's the matter? Have you had a premonition?"

I laughed. "Not me. It's your premonitions that have me worried. Those two messages you gave me Friday morning came to pass already. In less than forty-eight hours!"

"Oh, that," said Mila, relaxing. "I'd love to hear

how Mercury's communications helped you, if you don't mind sharing. But that's not the kind of news I have now."

"News?"

"Yes." She withdrew her hand and clapped her palms together as she bit back a smile. "I've decided to take the next step in my spiritual evolution," she said.

"You have?"

She nodded. "For some time now, the other members of Magic Circle have been pressing me to step up and become High Priestess of our coven. I've resisted, preferring to maintain our group as a collective without a single leader. Then, a couple months ago, something shifted. I felt the winds of change and noticed signs cropping up everywhere I looked. The Goddess is calling me to enter into a new role."

I smiled. "Then you have to answer." I had received signs and omens myself over the years. I knew it was futile to ignore them—they would only grow bigger and more persistent.

"And so I have," she said. "My initiation is scheduled for New Year's Eve. I would be honored if you would attend."

"Oh! Gosh. Wow." I hadn't seen that coming. For as long as I had known Mila, I had politely declined all her offers to attend rituals and meetings with her coven. Mine was a private religious practice, and I liked to keep it that way. Swigging my tea, I tried to think of a plausible excuse without appearing so flustered.

Mila smiled kindly and sipped her own tea. "Think about it," she said. "You wouldn't be committing to anything if you attend. We won't make you sign a blood oath and pledge your undying allegiance to our cause."

I chuckled softly and looked down at my hands.

"An-d," said Mila, drawing out the word until I looked up. "I won't be offended if you don't come. Nor will I be offended if you don't come to our Yule celebration tomorrow night. You know you have a standing invitation."

"I know. And thank you for that," I said. "Speaking of Yule, that's one of the reasons I stopped by. I was thinking of treating myself to a new ceremonial robe. Something for indoors."

"Ooh, I've got just the thing. Let me show you what we have." Mila hopped up and disappeared through the gauzy purple curtain that separated her divination parlor from the main shop. I followed her, and we climbed upstairs to the second-floor clothing section. We passed several racks filled with colorful arrays of blouses and skirts, dresses and trousers, until we reached the back wall, which featured a wide variety of robes, cloaks, and capes. Some were dramatic, such as the full-length hooded capes with cascading folds of velvet. And some were simpler, made from cotton or wool. Mila selected an elegant white gown with a matching satin-lined cloak and held them out for me to see.

"Lovely," I said, touching the soft, loose sleeves.

"With the plain, unadorned neckline, you can change the look by wearing different necklaces. You can also add different colored belts, if you'd like, to suit the occasion."

"It's perfect," I said. "I'll take it."

Back downstairs, as Mila boxed my package behind the counter, I browsed the shelves of herbs and tonics. "If you're looking for Yule plants," Mila called, "they're over here. I've got fresh juniper berries, bayberries, and holly berries."

I joined her at the cash register. "Actually, I'm looking for something else. Something to help draw out the truth from someone who might be inclined to lie."

Mila looked up from the shopping bag she had just opened. "Someone is lying to you?"

"Not yet. I plan on asking someone a question, and I'd like to do whatever I can to encourage a truthful answer."

"Hmm. Is this related to your law practice?"

"No, but . . ." I trailed off, uncertain how to explain what I was up to. I wasn't even sure how to rationalize it to myself. It was just a feeling I had that there was more to Edgar's death than a drunken accident.

"Say no more," said Mila. "I do have something, only it's not on the shelves. I'll have to mix it up in the back room. Can you come back later?"

A rap on the front door drew our attention. "Oh, gosh, it's time for you to open," I said. "I'll come back this evening, if that's okay."

"That would be fine," she said. "I'll have it ready by closing time. If you don't make it, then I'll take it home and you can stop by my house tonight."

"Wonderful. Thank you, Mila." I gave her cash for my purchase and slipped out the back.

The law office buzzed with talk of Edgar's untimely death. Half of my colleagues hadn't even made it past the lobby. They gathered around the reception desk reading the online version of the *Edindale Gazette* over

Julie's shoulder. As soon as I joined them, all eyes turned to me.

"Oh, Keli! You poor thing," said Pammy. "We heard you were the first on the scene after Edgar fell."

"That must have been awful," said Julie. "Isn't this, like, the second time you've found a dead body this year?"

"Yeah. Lucky me," I said. "Wait. The newspaper didn't say that, did it?"

Kris Rafferty, one of the firm's partners, patted my shoulder and shook her silky bobbed hair. "No, the paper didn't mention you. Beverly called me yesterday and filled me in. How are you holding up?"

"It was quite a shock, but I'm okay." I looked around. "Is Beverly in yet?"

Before anyone could answer, the office door opened and Crenshaw entered with the firm's third partner, Randall Sykes. They had been laughing about something, but they each sobered quickly when they saw me. Randall gave me an arch look. "Hey there, Keli. Are we going to have to start calling you the Grim Reaper?"

Pammy gasped. "Randall! That's not nice."

I pursed my lips. "Please don't," I said to Randall.

"Aw, I'm just kidding," he said. "I was sorry to hear about your experience."

Crenshaw gazed at me in an uncharacteristic silence. I stared back, then said, "Um. Did you make that appointment with Beverly? So we can discuss our special assignment?"

"Oh," said Kris. "I was about to tell you. Beverly isn't coming in to the office today."

"I know," said Crenshaw. "I spoke with her, too."

"Okay," I said. "Well, I think Crenshaw and I should go on over to Harrison Properties then, and work on—"

"Ms. Milanni," Crenshaw interrupted. "May I have a word with you in my office?"

I frowned at him. Why did he always have to act like he was my superior? "Sure, *Mr. Davenport*. Just as soon as I check my messages." I brushed past him and headed to my office. As I opened the door, I saw him come down the hall after me.

"Sorry," he said contritely. "I didn't mean to sound so rude."

"Thank you," I said. "So, what's the big deal? Don't you agree we still have a job to do at Harrison Properties? I already spoke with Allison, and she told me they'll be open today."

Crenshaw gently pushed me into my office and closed the door behind us. "Actually, no. I don't agree. With Edgar's tragic demise, I think it's safe to say he will no longer be receiving any demands for hush money."

"But, what about—"

"As for the audit, I've already contacted a commercial lawyer I know at another firm. We often make referrals to each other. He agreed to take the job for the same fee Edgar planned to pay us."

"I see." I bristled at Crenshaw's taking the lead without at least consulting me. "Don't you think that should be Beverly's decision?"

Crenshaw glanced away. His eyes fell absently upon the row of crystals I had arranged on my desk in front of the window. He looked back at me with a somber expression. "Beverly's in no condition to make decisions right now. She's still quite upset at the loss of her friend."

"Understandably," I said. "All the more reason why we shouldn't make any hasty decisions right now."

He crossed his arms and gave me a dour look.

I hitched my purse onto my shoulder. "I mean, I agree with you about passing on the audit to another firm. But don't you think we should still look into the matter of the blackmail threats? That was our real job."

Crenshaw shook his head. "Unless someone else receives a blackmail letter, we have no client."

I sighed. This man might be the most stubborn person I knew. "Fine. But I'm going back to Edgar's office one last time. I'll straighten up the files we left and write a note for the new attorney."

Crenshaw hesitated, then acquiesced. "Very well. I don't think it's necessary, but if it makes you feel better, then by all means."

Now that I knew this might be my last time at Harrison Properties, I was anxious to get over there. I locked up my office and returned to the lobby. As I passed by the reception desk, Julie stopped me.

"Keli, are you leaving? I thought you'd be in the office today."

"I'll be back later. Why?"

"Didn't you check your e-mail? I made an appointment for you at ten-thirty. A couple wants to come in and update their will. They called this morning and requested you specifically. I thought your calendar was free. Did I mess up?"

"No. That's okay." I checked the time. It was just past 9:30. "I'll be back by then."

Before anyone else could stop me, I hurried out of the office. I had less than an hour to get to Harrison Properties, find some answers, and get back to the law firm.

If only I knew what I was looking for.

Chapter 8

The atmosphere at Harrison Properties was heavy and subdued. When I entered the lobby, I saw that the receptionist was speaking quietly on the telephone, so I used my cell phone to call Allison. She came out shortly and led me to the conference room.

"You're on your own today?" she asked.

"Yes, and I won't be here long." I explained about the new attorney taking over. I wondered if she would think it was odd that we were handing over the project to a different firm.

She clenched her jaw. "Well, let's hope the auditor finds everything in order. Because it sure won't be for long." With that, she stormed out of the room.

I stared after her, perplexed. *Well, that wasn't the reaction I expected.*

Shaking my head, I looked over at the stacks of files on the table. I realized there wasn't much I could do to make them any more orderly or more sensible. I grabbed a yellow notepad and scribbled some labels for the broad categories Crenshaw and I had identified.

On the piles we hadn't gotten to yet, I slapped on a sheet of paper and wrote *Not Yet Reviewed*. That done, I scurried on over to the workroom.

This time there were two other employees besides Zeke: a motherly looking woman and a heavyset young man who appeared to be about Zeke's age. All three had swiveled their chairs to face one another, with their backs to their computers. When I entered they looked my way.

"Well, there she is," said Zeke. "The prettiest lawyer in town."

The older woman cast her eyes heavenward, then smiled at me and turned to her computer. The heavyset guy gave me a curious stare.

"Uh, good morning," I said. "Any coffee left? Or shall I start another pot?"

Zeke stood up and strolled over to the table by the window, where he lifted the carafe and shook it. "Come and get it," he said. When I joined him, his eyes took on a mischievous twinkle. "How do you like it? Hot and sweet?"

I snorted. It was impossible to hide my amusement around this guy. "Just hot, please."

He poured me a mug and held it out. As I reached for it, he pulled his hand back. "You know, I never got my dance with you at the ball. Every time I looked for you, you were dancing with a different guy. Was it something I said?"

I spread my palms wide. "What can I say? You snooze, you lose."

"Ouch," he said, handing me the mug. "You wound me."

I smiled and lightly touched his arm. "On a more

serious note, I'd like to extend my condolences to you and the rest of the staff. I'm sure this must be a really difficult time."

"Thanks," said Zeke, bowing his head. Then he turned to help himself to some coffee. I took a sip of mine and studied him. He didn't appear to be overly distraught. Of course, he was new to the office, so he probably hadn't had an opportunity to grow close to Edgar. On the other hand, if he was the blackmailer, he didn't seem to be upset at the loss of his cash cow, either. Maybe Edgar had been wrong to suspect him after all.

Casually I sauntered down the aisle along the windows and pretended to look at the Christmas cards someone had displayed on top of the cabinets. As I did, I thought back to what Beverly had told Crenshaw and me in her office last week. If I recalled correctly, she had said Edgar had "a couple" of suspects in mind. Not just Zeke. *Who else did he suspect?*

I glanced over at the other two workers. The heavy guy was eating cookies from a gift box while scrolling through Facebook on his computer. The woman appeared to be typing a text message on her cell phone. Evidently, not much work was going to happen today.

Zeke came up behind me and lowered his voice. "These poor saps have no idea what's in store," he said, jerking a thumb toward his coworkers.

I widened my eyes. "What do you mean?"

He leaned in conspiratorially. "Do you know Annabelle?"

I thought for a moment. "Annabelle Harrison? Edgar's daughter?"

Zeke tipped his chin in a subtle nod. "Edgar's younger

daughter. Eighteen years old. Rumor has it he was gonna hand over control of this office to her if he won the election. And now? I guess it depends on what his will says." He gave me a questioning look.

I smiled tightly. "My boss handled his will. I suppose we'll all know soon enough."

Zeke looked over his shoulder, then back at me. "Either way, things are going to get messy around here. Allison won't give up the helm without a fight."

"Allison? Are you saying she wants to run the office?"

"She practically does already. She just doesn't have the title."

I took a step back to regain a bit of my personal space. Apparently, Zeke just wanted to gossip, and I didn't have time for that. "I'm sure it will all get worked out," I said. "Beverly will make sure Edgar's last wishes are honored."

Zeke flashed a doubtful smile and stuffed his hands in his pockets. "Well, I'm not gonna hang around and watch. I've got another job lined up."

I looked at him in surprise. "You're quitting already?"

"Soon." He put his fingers to his lips and retreated to his cubicle.

Hmm. I wasn't sure what to make of the information Zeke had shared, but I didn't have time to dwell on it. According to the wall clock, I had only twenty more minutes to spare before I had to head back for my appointment. *Dang it.*

Without any other ideas, I left the work area and wandered down the back hallway to use the restroom. Afterward, I passed the mailroom and noticed a stack of mail in a bin just inside the door. On a hunch, I ducked inside the room and pulled the door closed partway behind me.

Moving quickly, I thumbed through the envelopes and noted that they were postmarked late last week. I assumed last week's shortage of staff was to blame for the undistributed mail. A lot of it was addressed to Edgar, but nothing appeared to be out of the ordinary— that is, until I came to a plain white envelope with no return address. *Could it be?*

I held the envelope up to the light. Nothing. Tapping the edge of the envelope on my palm, I argued with myself about what to do. It's a federal offense to open someone else's mail. However, this envelope could very well contain a letter from the blackmailer. And blackmail was a crime, too. No matter what Crenshaw said, I still thought our original assignment was worth pursuing.

The sound of a door opening down the hall made me flinch. *That's it*, I thought. *I'll let Beverly decide.* I hastily tucked the envelope in the waistband of my trousers under my blazer, and stood quietly behind the door. Peering between the hinges, I saw Allison walk by toward the restrooms. I waited a second, then slipped out and dashed back to the conference room, where I stashed the envelope in my purse. Then I pulled on my coat. I needed to get back to my own office and my real job. Until I could talk with Beverly, there wasn't much more I could do here.

With a last wistful glance at the untouched files, I started to leave the conference room. That's when my eye fell upon a turquoise bead on the table. *Did I drop that?* I did a quick scan of my simple jewelry and confirmed I wasn't wearing any beads today. It certainly didn't match Crenshaw's style. Still, there was something familiar about the pretty, marble-sized piece. I snatched it up, tossed it in my purse, and sped out of the room—bumping smack-dab into Zeke.

"Oh, sorry!" I said.

He grinned and grabbed my arm for balance. "Guess I got my dance after all."

I chuckled politely and made a move for the door to the lobby. "I have an appointment, so—"

"Wait a minute," he said. "I heard I might not be seeing you again. Allison told us another firm is taking over the audit."

"Mm-hmm." I didn't feel the need to elaborate. I didn't owe Zeke any explanations.

"So, I figured I better give you your Christmas card now." He handed me a large red envelope.

"Oh," I said, surprised. "That's really sweet of you. Thank you." I slipped the card in my purse and gave Zeke a more genuine smile than I had before. "Who knows?" I said. "Maybe I'll see you around sometime."

After my morning appointment, I thought about taking a break, but then my phone rang. And it pretty much didn't stop ringing all day. Between work-related calls and all the friends and acquaintances who wanted my firsthand account of finding Edgar's body, my day flew by like the flock of blackbirds outside my window.

It was dark when I finally left the office. Moonstone Treasures was already closed, so I called Mila and told her I'd stop by her house a bit later, after dinner. First, I headed to the gym for a quick workout. After sitting at my desk for so many hours, I wanted to get my blood pumping on the treadmill and shake off all the stress of the day.

The gym was only a few blocks from my office, so I decided to walk. Halfway there, I began to regret that decision. The temperature had plummeted throughout the afternoon, and the frigid wind stung my face. On top of that, the weather had driven everyone inside, leaving the streets dark and deserted. With my head down and my hands clutching the scarf at my face, I scuffled down the sidewalk as fast as I could without falling.

A sound behind me caught my ear. It was hard to make out through the whistling wind, but it might have been a footstep. For no good reason, my heart beat faster. I craned over my shoulder and peered into the misty gloom. There was no one there.

I continued onward, but a few seconds later, I heard it again—a shuffling, scraping noise. Before I could react, the nearest streetlight burned out, shrouding the path in darkness.

Chapter 9

With a tiny yelp, I whipped around to confront the source of the noise behind me. Again, the sidewalk was empty. Suddenly, a clatter echoed from the adjacent alleyway. Utterly spooked, I took off running—and sliding—the rest of the way to the fitness center.

Who needed a treadmill to increase blood flow? My own jumpy nerves could do the trick.

By the time I changed and joined the other exercisers in the brightly lit gym, I was able to laugh away my jitters. I spent the next forty minutes on the aerobic machines, and another ten minutes of gentle floor stretches. Then I showered and changed into the clean jeans and sweatshirt I kept in my assigned locker, and hit the center's café for a post-workout protein smoothie. As I sipped the thick, filling shake, I texted Wes and Farrah, making plans to see each of them the following day.

It was nearly 8:30 when I finally left the fitness center. The weather outside hadn't improved. I shivered at the prospect of another dark, lonely walk all the way back to the parking lot near my office building. Recalling Edgar's driver, I realized it really would be nice to have a car service at my disposal. Not having that option now, I bundled up and took the long, but more-traveled, way back. When I reached my car, I drove straight to Mila's house.

Mila and her husband owned a charming redbrick bungalow in an established subdivision on the edge of town. As I made my way up the shoveled path to their front porch, I admired their Yuletide décor. Twinkling lights in the trees reflected in a series of red gazing balls in the front yard, while wreaths of holly and pine brightened the front door. Mila came out to meet me and ushered me inside.

"Come on into the kitchen," she said. "I just took a loaf of banana bread out of the oven. And don't worry—it's vegan."

I kicked off my shoes on the doormat and followed Mila into her spacious, country-style kitchen. Her plush gray cat, Drishti, sauntered into the room and rubbed up against my legs. I was fond of the friendly kitty, especially after our shared adventure in the Edindale tunnels last winter. I reached down and petted her smooth fur before tossing my coat over a chair.

"It smells marvelous in here," I said, taking a seat at the square wooden table.

"I'll slice the banana bread as soon as it cools off a bit. In the meantime, have some fruit salad. Alex made it earlier tonight."

"I would love some. I actually didn't have much of a dinner," I admitted.

"I figured as much." Mila smiled, and set a bowl and fork in front of me, as well as a cup of hot herbal tea.

"Where is Alex?" I asked.

"Getting ready for bed. He's on the renovation crew for the old civic center, so he was up at the crack of dawn today and will be again tomorrow."

I put down my fork. "I shouldn't have come over so late. I won't stay."

"Don't be silly," said Mila, sitting down across from me. "It's not that late and, anyway, Alex always goes to bed before I do. You relax and tell me what's going on in your life."

We chatted for a while as I polished off my bowl of fruit. Then she sliced the banana bread, and I helped myself to a generous piece. While we talked, Mila absently played with an assortment of smooth flat stones that were lying on the table.

"Are those runes?" I asked.

"They are," she affirmed. "I'm brushing up on the symbols for a client of mine."

"I've always wanted to learn rune symbology, but I'm not sure I have the patience. It seems like something you'd have to study for years to become really adept at them."

Mila smiled. "You and I are a lot alike. The Goddess usually speaks to me in visual images, so I'm most comfortable with tarot cards. I also like palm reading, because of the personal contact. Of course, palmistry employs your sense of vision as well as touch."

I considered my own experiences communicating with the Divine. "You're right. I do tend to receive messages from the Universe most often through imagery, especially dreams and visions. Although, sometimes I hear them, too, through random songs on the radio or directly from another person—like the messages you delivered to me on Friday."

"Ah, yes," said Mila. "That was an interesting vision. I don't often receive messages for other people when I'm not directly working with them, but I saw you so clearly. Then again, my intention was to be of service, so hopefully I was."

"Hmm. The Universe does work in mysterious ways, doesn't it?" I took a sip of tea and thought about a question I had been wanting to ask. "Mila, those two messages, about the visitor and the death, were they connected? Was Edgar's death connected to the visitor from my past? To Mick MacIntyre?"

Mila furrowed her brow. "Not necessarily. Or . . . maybe. But the connection may not be direct."

I must have looked confused, because Mila gave me an apologetic smile. "I don't mean to be vague. What I mean is that the two events may not necessarily be connected to each other, but they are both connected to you. *You* are the common denominator."

"Oh. I suppose that's true, in a way. If I hadn't been going to meet Mick that night, I wouldn't have been the one to find Edgar's body."

"Precisely."

I reached for a second piece of banana bread. "I guess I was meant to find him," I mused. "And now I have this sense of responsibility . . . or, at least, curiosity. I want to know why he fell, and why he was even there. That's why I want to talk to his driver. Other than Edgar's wife, whom I wouldn't dream of questioning, the driver was probably one of the last people to see him alive."

"Do you think so?"

"Well, I know he drove Edgar home, because Farrah

saw Edgar get into the car. I also think there's a good possibility the driver brought him back to the hotel later that same night. The only problem is, I'm not so sure he'll be forthcoming with me."

Mila stood up and retrieved something from the counter. When she placed it on the table in front of me, I saw that it was a clear glass vial with a stopper made of cork. It was filled to the brim with a cloudy amber liquid. "Here's the 'truth serum' you ordered. A couple of drops ought to loosen your driver's lips." Mila chuckled at her own joke, but I was beginning to feel a little nervous.

"What exactly is in this, Mila? And do I need to drink it, too? You know, to open the lines of communication between myself and . . . my subject?"

"Well, it won't harm you, but I wouldn't drink it unless you're with someone you trust. Otherwise, you might wind up revealing secrets you didn't plan on telling."

I lifted the vial and held it up to the light. "Um. There's not actually a narcotic in here, is there?"

"Heavens, no. It's only stinging nettle, powdered caraway, and vanilla. Besides, it won't work until you say a spell over it. I can give you some suggestions, but your own intention will be the key."

"Got it," I said, breathing a little easier.

"Now then, can you arrange to have tea with this driver fellow?"

"Tea? I don't know about that. Will alcohol work?"

Mila smiled. "It depends on the person. For many people, chamomile tea is the most relaxing beverage. For others, a nice wine or even a cold beer will do the trick."

Trick *is an interesting word choice,* I thought sardonically. The question was, could I pull it off?

The next morning I woke up bright and early, threw on a coat, and headed out to my backyard to fill the bird feeders and greet the morning sun. Today was the winter Solstice, the shortest day of the year. For Wiccans, it was also known as Yule. According to the old mythologies, the sun had completed its cycle and would be born of the Goddess once again after the longest night. Ultimately, this was a day of hope and comfort. As cold and dark as the season might seem, this day marked a turning point. Little by little, the sun's rays would lengthen every day, and the warmth would return. *After death, there is rebirth.*

Contemplating these truths, I took a handful of birdseed and walked slowly around the fir tree near my dormant garden. As I scattered the seeds on the snow-covered ground, I murmured a chant under my breath:

> Though the earth slumbers, it is not dead
> Though the Goddess labors, she is not sad
> Though the night lingers, 'tis not the end
> The wheel turns, the light returns,
> The God is born anew

After circling the tree three times, I became aware of the sounds of my neighborhood waking up. A door slammed after someone had retrieved the newspaper. Down the block, someone's ride honked impatiently on the street. And from the St. Johns' yard, I heard Chompy tear out of his doggy door, yipping ferociously at a squirrel. I took this as my cue to go inside. My fingers and toes had begun to feel numb anyway, so I went in and prepared a nourishing bowl of oatmeal with walnuts, flax, and raisins. As I was getting ready for work, my doorbell rang. It was Mila.

Before I left her home the night before, Mila had mentioned she was in a bit of a bind. Her sister-in-law was coming to visit and the woman suffered from terrible allergies. Being the sweetheart that she was, Mila decided to find a cat sitter for Drishti. However, her usual helpers were either out of town or busy with company of their own, and her assistant, Catrina, lived in a strict pet-free apartment. The minute I heard about Mila's predicament, I volunteered to host Drishti. I thought it might be nice to have a pet around the house, at least for a couple of days.

"Good morning!" Mila said, as I let her inside. She set down a pet crate, then hurried back to her car for a box full of supplies: cat food, water dish, toys, litter box, and a scratching post. "Drishti isn't a terrible scratcher," she said, unpacking the bag, "but she's wearing temporary nail caps to be on the safe side."

"Aww, let's see." I reached down to unlatch the crate, but Mila stopped me.

"Mind if we do a quick walk-through first?" she asked.

"Not at all." I wondered if she intended to cast a spell or perform an enchantment to make Drishti feel more at home. Instead, she examined all my house plants.

"This is the only one I'm worried about," she said, handing me a potted peace lily. "It's toxic to cats."

"I'll take it to my office," I said, placing it by the door. She then moved my vase of tulips to a small shelf on the wall, tied up my window cords, and hung my holly and mistletoe out of reach. "The poinsettia plants are fine. She's not likely to chew them, but if she does, they're not lethal."

After letting Drishti out to explore, Mila gave me some quick instructions. Then we left together. I headed to work in high spirits.

For most people, this was just the Tuesday before Christmas. They didn't know the Solstice was a holy day for some religions. That was okay. I had already arranged to take off early from work, telling everyone I needed to run errands and complete my holiday shopping. Besides, like the rest of Western culture, I recognized that the winter holiday was really a season-long celebration. It wasn't limited to a single day. I would still make merry with my friends and family on December twenty-fifth. In fact, I would be having Christmas Eve dinner with Wes and his parents, and then flying home to Nebraska later that night. I would wake up on Christmas morning in my childhood home, just like old times.

As soon as I dropped off my coat and purse, I made a beeline for Beverly's office. I had several things I wanted to discuss with her, not least of which was the mysterious white envelope burning a hole in my purse. I tried her outer door and found it to be locked. *Darn it. She's still out?* Even though I didn't think she was in there, I knocked anyway.

Crenshaw came down the hall, carrying his briefcase and coat. "She's not coming in today," he said. "She's still too upset."

I frowned. "Do you speak to her every morning, or what? Why do you know these things?"

He glared at me without responding. I sighed. "Well, I know something you might not know." I stepped closer to him and lowered my voice. "Did you know Allison Mandrake wants to take over management of Harrison Properties? And that Edgar had planned to appoint his younger daughter to that role? Apparently, Allison is not very happy about that." I snapped my fingers. "Maybe that's what she was yelling about when we overheard her in her office last Friday!"

Crenshaw sucked in his cheeks and shook his head. "When will you stop playing detective, Milanni? There's no case here. The police ruled Edgar's death an accident. Remember?"

"I know, but—"

Crenshaw turned on his heels and stalked off without letting me finish.

I growled under my breath and headed to Kris's office. Crenshaw liked to fancy himself Beverly's right-hand man, but the fact was he was just an associate like me. I would speak to the real number two person in charge.

"Come in," called Kris, after I tapped on her door. "Have a seat, Keli."

"Good morning, Kris. If you have a minute, I'd like to run something by you."

I explained to her my idea of having the firm retain a private driver. I also pointed out that the time was ripe, since Edgar's chauffeur was now out of a job. She tilted her head from side to side, indicating her ambivalence about the idea.

"I suppose it might come in handy," she said. "But, as far as I know, you're the only one who tends to find herself without a car because she walked to work."

She gave me a teasing grin and took a sip from her coffee mug.

"True," I admitted. "But there are evenings when others go out for happy hour or dinner. At one time or another, I think we've all found ourselves in a situation where we'd rather not drive ourselves home. And you know how small Edindale's taxi fleet is. If we had a private driver on call, it could be a life saver."

Kris smiled. "Fair point. All right. Go ahead and reach out to the man. Find out if he's interested and how much he would charge. After you have the info, I'll bring it up with Beverly."

Beaming, I stood up. "Thanks, Kris. Speaking of Beverly, do you know how she's doing and when she's coming back?"

Kris bit her lip. "Crenshaw asked me the same thing right before you stopped by. As I told him, I've only spoken with Beverly briefly. She called me last night and said she's still too upset to leave her house. She's not even sure if she'll make it to the visitation tomorrow night."

"Oh, wow. Poor Beverly. Let me know if there's anything I can do." Kris nodded, and I left her office.

It was disconcerting to imagine my tough, unflappable boss so fragile, but it was understandable. She was only human.

On the bright side, at least now I knew where Crenshaw got his news about Beverly.

Back at my desk, I pulled out the number Allison had given me and called the driver, Bob Franklin. After introducing myself, I asked if he could meet me later in the day. At first, he seemed confused as to why I wanted to meet in person, but when I couched the meeting in terms of an interview, he agreed.

I put in my full half-day's work, then headed out the door. It was close to 4:00 when I entered the Loose Rock, a casual bar and grill that doubled as a hip indie music venue. The Loose, as my friends and I affectionately called it, featured a small dance floor, a sizable drink selection, and a bighearted owner named Jimi Coral. It was Jimi who had introduced me to Wes. They had been college buddies, and then Jimi had helped Wes get back on his feet when Wes returned from New York broke and jobless.

In spite of the early hour, the place was moderately busy already. I spotted Jimi tending bar and waved at him. He flashed me a peace sign, then pointed toward a booth in the back. Following his gaze, I saw a man in business attire sitting by himself. It had to be Bob. *Evidently, he's punctual*, I thought. *That's a good sign.* I nodded my thanks to Jimi and walked over to the booth.

"Bob?" I asked.

He started to stand, but I waved him back down. "Don't get up. I'll sit." I slid into the booth, and we shook hands. As we exchanged pleasantries, I made a quick assessment of the chauffeur. He was on the heavy side and appeared to be in his mid- to late-forties, though his light brown hair had few strands of gray. His crinkly brown eyes were kind, with a tinge of sadness, and he spoke with the raspy voice of a smoker. I couldn't help but notice his iced drink looked a whole lot like Coca-Cola.

This should be interesting, I thought. Mila had

recommended I offer Bob a relaxing beverage, and here he was drinking caffeine and sugar.

A waitress stopped at our table, and I asked for a white wine. She returned in short order while I was explaining to Bob what I had in mind for the law firm. He seemed interested if not overly eager. He told me he had been a professional driver for fourteen years, and had worked exclusively for Edgar for the past five. He had been paid well, but he sometimes felt lonely and isolated living out at the ranch.

After a fortifying sip of wine, I proceeded to question him. "Did you ever drive for Gretta?" I asked.

"Nah. She used to drive herself or ride with friends, and now she can only travel in a mobility van. I told her I'd stay out at the ranch as long as she wants, but she said there's no need. She has plenty of help, between Ricardo and the other staff, plus all her friends. So, I've already started looking at apartments here in town."

"That's nice," I said. "Who's Ricardo?"

"Oh, he's Gretta's . . . gardener. And handyman. He lives out at the ranch, too."

"I see. How many people live at the ranch?"

"There are three cottages behind the main house: mine, Ricardo's, and Victor's. Victor's the chef, but he's out of town for the holidays. There's a cleaning staff, too, and a visiting nurse, but they don't live out there."

"What about Edgar's daughters? Doesn't the younger one still live at home?"

"Yeah, Annabelle lives at home. I've driven her a few times, but she never liked it. She always thought I was trying to be her babysitter." Bob chuckled. "Teenagers."

I smiled. "I suppose she's more of a young adult now, though. Isn't she eighteen?"

Bob grunted. "Eighteen going on fourteen. She's not the most mature kid I know. Like, just the other night, she wanted to leave the ball early and go to this slumber party on a houseboat. She about pitched a fit until Gretta gave in. I had to drive her all the way to Craneville and get myself back to the hotel before midnight." Bob shook his head in disapproval.

At the mention of the hotel, I felt my heart pitter-patter in my chest. Was this my opening? Bob was the one who had brought up the night of the ball. Maybe I wouldn't have to give him the truth serum after all. I took another sip of wine to calm my nerves, then forged ahead.

"So, Bob. When you took Edgar home Saturday night, did he talk about anything in particular? That you remember?"

Bob wrinkled his forehead in confusion, and I mentally kicked myself. *Come on, Milanni! You can do better than that.*

I swallowed. "I mean, uh, did Edgar mention any plans to come back to the hotel? Did he ask you to hang around and drive him back?"

Bob slowly shook his head and remained mute.

Ugh. What must he think? Even to myself, I sounded like a busybody fishing for gossip.

I finished off my wine and eyed Bob's glass. It wasn't quite empty, but it was close enough. I stood up. "Hey, I'm going to go get us another round. Would you like something besides Coke?"

"No, I'm good. I probably shouldn't stay much longer anyway."

"Oh, you can't leave yet! I mean, I'd still like to hear about your rates and availability. Besides, I'd really like to buy you a drink, you know, in appreciation for you meeting me on such short notice."

"I don't drink and drive."

"Of course not! I didn't mean to imply . . . What I meant was, have you tried Jimi's famous nonalcoholic vanilla Coke cocktail?"

Before he could answer, I bolted to the bar. *Good Goddess, what was I doing?*

Jimi saw me coming and met me at the end of the counter. "Everything okay, Keli?"

"Yeah, yeah. Do you have any vanilla syrup back there? Could I have two vanilla Cokes, please?"

"Sure. Want 'em with a shot of rum?"

"No. Just virgin, please. And add a long-stemmed cherry to make it special."

Jimi raised his eyebrows, but turned to make the drinks. While he did, I reached into my purse and pulled out the small glass vial Mila had given me. Cupping it in my palm, I whispered a spell under my breath:

To loosen tongue and open heart
Make strangers friends and play the part
Embolden words and truth to speak
Like water's pail with one big leak

When Jimi set the drinks in front of me, I scootched closer to the bar and hovered over the glasses. As discreetly as possible, I poured a couple of drops into one of them.

"Um, Keli?"

With a start, I looked up and met Jimi's curious eyes.

"Herbal supplement," I said, holding up the vial. "I feel a cold coming on."

"Ah." He seemed to relax. "I may have to borrow that from you. 'Tis the season, and I can't afford to get sick right now."

I laughed nervously. "Sure. Anytime." Then I looked back down at the drinks. *Oh, hell.* Overcome with guilt, I poured two drops in the other glass.

If one of us was going to open up tonight, then both of us would.

Chapter 10

When it came to real magic, I knew props and potions were often like placebos. Their effectiveness derived not so much from the objects themselves, as from the understanding and intent of the person using them. Belief itself was a powerful form of magic.

And I believed that Mila's truth serum would work. Maybe that's why I started talking a mile a minute right after I rejoined Bob and took my first swig of spiked vanilla Coke cocktail.

"Wow, this is sweet!" I said. "I don't usually drink soda, or, at least, not flavored soda, that is, unless it's cut with something hard like rum. I mean, this is tasty, but it's a little bit strong. Don't you think? Is it too strong? Do you like it?"

With a bewildered look, Bob took a sip. He made a sour face, then took another sip. "It's not bad, actually. Has an interesting spiciness to it."

"Yeah, spiciness. That's a good word. You know what they say. 'Variety is the spice of life.' It's good to try different things, don't you think? My friend Farrah is always trying to get me to try new things. Like, just the other day, she said she was going to book us a mud bath at this new spa over in Craneville. A mud bath! And I said, 'I'm not going to take off all my clothes and sit in a big goopy bath of mud.' And she said, 'What's the big deal? I thought witches—'" I choked on my words and forced myself to take a deep breath.

Good grief. I needed to get ahold of myself and focus on the mission at hand.

Fortunately, Bob seemed to be unfazed. He took a long draught through his straw, then sat back and loosened his tie. "I don't know if the interview is over, but this shirt is really itchy." He tugged at his collar, then he snickered. "Or maybe it's just too tight. I probably shouldn't mention this to a potential employer, but I have a bit of a doughnut addiction."

I pushed my glass away. "Bob, I think we can consider the interview over. If it were up to me, I'd hire you right now. You can be sure I'll put in a good word for you with my boss. But I have to be honest with you. The chauffeur job was not the only thing I wanted to talk to you about."

Bob nodded. "Somehow I got that impression."

"See, Edgar's death is really eating at me. I found him, you know, after the fall. He was a long-standing client of my firm and a close friend of my boss. And I just find it so odd that he went all the way home to his ranch after the party, then turned around and came all the way back. Plus, how did he get back if you didn't drive him? His car never left the hotel." I looked Bob in the eye. "Can you shed any light on this? Any at all?"

Bob looked away, and I could almost see the wrestling

match going on in his mind. It didn't last long. He finished off his vanilla Coke, then leaned forward.

"You didn't hear this from me. . . ." he said.

"Hear what?" I asked softly. I wasn't going to make any promises, but I did give him what I hoped was an encouraging look.

He propped his elbow on the table and cupped one hand to the side of his mouth. "Edgar never went home that night."

"He didn't? Where did he go?"

"No place. He never left the hotel."

Huh? My astonishment must have shown on my face, because Bob frowned. "Now, you have to keep this to yourself, you hear? I don't even know why I told you this in the first place."

Quickly I composed myself and dropped my voice to a whisper. "I don't understand. People saw him get in the car, and saw you drive him away."

"Yeah, and I drove around the block and came back through the parking lot behind the hotel. I dropped Edgar off at a back entrance."

"Oh!" That was unexpected. I had so many more questions, I wasn't sure where to begin. "So, was this prearranged? Did you know why he wanted to go back?"

Bob shrugged and avoided eye contact. I thought back to what I had overheard Gretta tell the police. Hadn't she implied that he had returned home after the party? As far as I was concerned, that was a lie by omission. But why? "Bob, do you know—"

He held up his hand, then stood up. "Look, there's one thing you need to know about me. I can keep a confidence. My word is my bond, and I gave my word to

Edgar. Now, if you'll excuse me, I really gotta take a leak. Good-bye, Ms. Milanni."

I watched Bob walk away and shook my head. I doubted if he would come back—he had taken his coat. I sighed. I probably wouldn't have gotten much more out of him anyway. I glanced at my half-finished, watered-down vanilla cocktail and curled my lip. It really was too sweet.

Reaching into my purse, I pulled out my phone to check my messages. Farrah was supposed to meet me here at 5:00 and it was a quarter past now. I sent her a quick text, then looked up and gasped. There was someone else sitting in the booth across from me.

"Zeke! I didn't hear you! Or see you. How did you do that?"

"I can be stealthy when I want to." He raised his eyebrows smugly. "Fancy meeting you here. Come to the Loose often?"

"Yes. I do. And I've never seen you here before."

"I saw you having a drink with that big dude," he said, deftly ignoring my unspoken question. "You sure have a lot of boyfriends."

"He's not my boyfriend, but thanks for noticing." I hoped my sarcasm wouldn't be lost on him.

"In that case," he said, "mind if I join you?"

"Actually, I'm meeting someone else here."

"Another boyfriend?"

Just then, Farrah walked over. "Boyfriend?" she asked. "Who has another boyfriend?"

"Hello," said Zeke, gazing at Farrah with interest.

Farrah sized him up, then looked at me. "Who's this?"

"Zeke Marshal. He works at Harrison Properties. He's an IT guy."

"Oh, then I should give him a business card." Farrah was good at her job as a legal software sales rep. She pulled out a card. "Here you go, young 'un. Now scoot. You're in my seat."

Grinning like an impish little kid, Zeke slid out of the booth and wandered over to the bar. *Thank Goddess.* I shuddered to imagine what I might have said to him under the influence of the truth serum. For a moment, I watched him chat with a waitress on the other side of the room. Had he come in here alone? *Never mind,* I thought. I had more important things to worry about—such as why Edgar had secretly snuck back into the hotel the night he fell over the balcony.

The waitress came by our table and took Farrah's order: a German lager and a grilled vegetable panini. I asked for a plain water. I needed to cleanse my palate. As soon as the waitress came back with our drinks, I told Farrah I had just met with Edgar's driver.

Farrah clapped her hands together and leaned in, her eyes glistening. "Well? Did you, you know, charm him?"

"You could say that," I said.

"Oh, wow, I wish I would've gotten here sooner. What did he say? Did he spill his guts?"

"Sort of. He told me the truth and nothing but the truth . . . but not the whole truth."

"*Qué?* What do you mean?"

I told Farrah everything. In spite of Bob's admonition not to repeat the secret, I had no qualms about telling Farrah. We were like an old married couple—telling one of us a secret was the same as telling both of us. I knew she'd keep it on the down low. Besides, she was the Sherlock to my Watson. Or vice versa.

Farrah sipped her beer thoughtfully. "I wonder why Edgar went back to the hotel immediately after leaving."

"Maybe he had an early-morning meeting the next day and just decided to stay the night in town," I speculated.

Farrah wrinkled her nose.

"Well, maybe he wanted to personally oversee the party cleanup, or check up on his staff."

Farrah shook her head. "Why go through the whole pretense of leaving and then return through the back entrance?"

The waitress returned with Farrah's panini. I snatched a French fry from her plate and blew on it to cool it off. Farrah poured some ketchup on her plate, then set the bottle down and looked at me. I could tell we had each come to the same conclusion.

"It can be only one thing," she said.

"He was meeting a woman."

"That's got to be it."

"Poor Gretta. I wonder if she knew. I mean, she had to know he never came back to the ranch, yet she lied to the police about that."

"Who knows?" said Farrah. "Maybe she thought she was protecting his reputation—and her own."

"Could be. If he really was meeting another woman, it would be embarrassing for his wife, even if she knew what was going on." I shook my head. "Can you imagine? I don't understand women who put up with philandering husbands."

Farrah shrugged. "They have their reasons." She sipped her beer and gazed around the bar. It was filling up and, along with the influx of people, came an increase in the noise level. "Who do you suppose he was having an affair with?" she asked.

I thought back to all the women I had seen at the ball. "It's hard to say. I'm gonna assume it wasn't one of the ladies who left with Cowboy Tuck."

"Hey," said Farrah. "You make us sound like groupies."

I grinned. "Sorry. I didn't mean it like that. Anyway, who all went with you to the nightclub?"

"Let's see. There was Sheana Starwalt."

"Wait. She left the party? Poor Crenshaw."

"Yeah, she was really miffed at him for some reason." Farrah took another bite of her sandwich, then wiped her mouth. "There were also a couple of women from Harrison Properties: a receptionist and a real estate broker. There was some other woman whose name I never caught, and . . . darn it. I guess Tucker was the only man. But it's not like we were his fangirls or anything. He and I snagged a table in the back as soon as we got there, and the others went up front to watch the band."

"And then you and he left together and walked back to his car . . . and he took you home?"

"Mm-hmm."

Was Farrah blushing? I sipped my water and held my tongue. Apparently, the truth serum was wearing off. Otherwise I might have pondered whether Cowboy Tuck was too old for her and advised her to give her old boyfriend, Jake, another chance.

Farrah slapped the table. "I know. Edgar's assistant. The one with the sleek hair and power makeup. She reminded me of an Amazon, all fierce and beautiful. What was her name?"

"Allison Mandrake. She made me think of a TV news

anchor more than a warrioress. Powerful nonetheless."
I recalled how Allison had appeared upset at Edgar in
one of the photos Wes had taken. Could it have been
jealousy? Or some kind of lovers' spat? "I suppose it's
possible," I said.

"It shouldn't be that hard to find out," said Farrah.
"People who have affairs think they're being sneaky,
but someone else almost always knows about it. The
hotel staff probably knew. Heck, maybe even his wife
knew."

"You're right. At the very least, a friend of one or
both of them probably knew." I thought for a moment,
then had an idea. "Hey, how well did Tucker know
Edgar? Weren't they golfing buddies? Is there any
chance he would know who Edgar was going to meet
that night?"

Farrah didn't hesitate. "I can find out. He invited me
to come out to his hunting lodge anytime. They have
cross-country skiing out there, as well as hiking, fishing, and horseback riding. You'd probably like it, other
than the hunting and fishing part."

"You really do have a thing for this guy, don't you?"

"What can I say?" she said, with a sly grin. "I guess
I'm a sucker for an old-school man's man. Strong, handsome, and chivalrous to a T. You know?"

"Of course," I said. "I know."

It was well past sunset when I left the Loose and
headed for home. Farrah had tried to persuade me to
stay and celebrate the winter Solstice with another round
of Jimi's homemade wassail, but I told her I needed to

get going. Wes was coming over later and I still had my own private ritual to conduct.

Two blocks from the Loose, I stopped for a red light at the intersection of North and Main. As I waited, I tapped on my steering wheel and whistled to the tune of "Let It Snow." Not that I wanted it to snow, but I was in a cheerful mood after hanging out with Farrah. Truth be told, I had started to second-guess my suspicions about Edgar's death. Maybe I had been reading too many detective novels. Just because I had found myself involved in more than one real-life mystery over the past year and a half didn't mean that *everything* was a mystery. For all we knew, Edgar might have sneaked back into the hotel to have another round of drinks. His death was probably just a tragic accident like the police had said.

At that moment, the streetlight above me burned out. *Hmm.* That was the second time in two days. When things like that happened, I paid attention. It was usually a sign. Like a finger snap from the Universe.

When the traffic light changed, I turned right instead of left and headed back downtown, away from home. I wasn't sure where I was going, but when I approached the Harrison Hotel I knew I had reached my destination. I parked in the lot and went inside.

I walked past the front desk and gave the clerk a pleasant smile without stopping. Maybe I'd just pop into the lounge for a minute, I decided. I pushed open the atrium door, half expecting it to be locked. It wasn't. I took a deep breath, mustered up my courage, and entered.

It wasn't entirely empty. A few people loitered by the fountain, while chattering voices drifted down from the second-floor bar. I noticed that the evergreen trees had been rearranged to block the area where I had found Edgar's body. For good measure, a velvet rope cordoned off the area as well. I wandered over to the trees and casually looked around. I hoped no one would think I was being morbidly curious. There didn't seem to be anything to see anyway. I backed away, then, almost against my will, I looked up.

How far had he fallen? My eyes scanned each floor from the top down. Something caught my eye. It was a piece of torn yellow tape, stuck to a railing directly above. I counted the floors from the bottom up. It was on the fourth floor.

Before I could change my mind, I trotted up the stairs to the second floor and took the glass elevator another two levels. The fourth floor appeared to be empty, and no wonder. Yellow caution tape blocked the entire east hallway. Apparently, anyone occupying the rooms in that section had to check out or relocate. The hotel was probably conducting its own investigation for insurance purposes. I ducked under the tape and wandered down the hallway to the point where Edgar had fallen, outside Room 428. From a safe distance, I examined the railing. It was approximately waist high and appeared to be intact. No clues there.

I took a few more steps to the end of the hall, opposite the emergency exit, and peeked around the corner. I expected to see an ice machine or vending machines, but was surprised to find the doorway to another room instead. A sign said it was the Guest Reading Room. The door was unlocked, so I went inside.

"How cute," I said to myself. It was a quaint little room with plush chairs and bookshelves on one side and computer tables on another. A small poster listed the Wi-Fi password and explained the rules for using the hotel computer and printer.

After a quick look around the room, I sighed and dropped into one of the chairs. What was I doing here? This might be the longest night of the year, but it wasn't like I had unlimited time. I fished into my overstuffed purse to find my phone, and in the process managed to tip my purse right off my lap. *Smooth.* As I leaned over to pick it up, something caught my eye on the floor. It was a crumpled slip of paper behind a table leg, out of sight from any vantage other than the one I happened to be sitting in. Curious, I reached for the paper and uncrumpled it. I gasped when I read it:

MEET ME AT 1 AM, 4TH FLOOR READING ROOM. E

"E" had to be Edgar. This confirmed it, at least in my mind. He *was* meeting someone the night he died! Was it a romantic rendezvous like Farrah and I had speculated? Or was it something else?

Chapter 11

I slipped the cryptic note into my purse and hurried back out to the hallway. I would take it to the police station first thing tomorrow. Surely this would prompt an investigation into Edgar's death. Wouldn't it? True, the note was somewhat obscure. It was undated, so there was no way of knowing how long it had lain on the floor, out of sight and beyond the reach of vacuum cleaners. And, of course, "E" was not necessarily Edgar. Still, the timing was all too coincidental.

Standing near the spot where Edgar had fallen over the balcony to his death, I pondered again what might have happened that night. So what if he had snuck back into the hotel to meet someone? He still could have accidentally fallen over the railing. He was drunk. It was dark. Maybe he was in a hurry so he wouldn't be seen, so he ran down the hall, bumped into the railing, and fell over. Perhaps he never made it to the reading room.

But what if he did make it? What if he had argued with whomever he was meeting? What if there was a scuffle? Wouldn't someone have heard? I turned and looked at the closed doors along the hallway. Rooms 422, 420, 418, and 416. Surely the police would have questioned everyone staying in those rooms.

Hang on. Room 418! How could I have forgotten? It was Mick's room. That was where I was headed when I stumbled upon Edgar's body. Maybe Mick had heard something that night.

I searched my recent calls for Mick's number and dialed. As it rang, I became aware of a faint ringing behind one of the closed doors. When Mick's voicemail picked up, I ended the call. I walked toward Room 418 and pressed REDIAL. Again, the moment Mick's line rang in my ear, a cell phone sounded behind the door to 418. *What in the world?*

I backed away and almost hung up, when I remembered Mick would see my number as a missed call. So I left a brief message: "Mick, it's Keli. Sorry I missed you the other night. Please give me a call when you have a chance."

I hung up and stared at the closed door to Room 418. Did Mick leave his cell phone behind when he checked out? Given the yellow caution tape, it was quite possible the rooms hadn't been cleaned yet. That would explain why the cleaning staff hadn't found and returned his phone. But wouldn't Mick have called the hotel as soon as he missed it? Maybe they were serious about not letting anyone down this hallway for any reason. Which meant I really shouldn't be up here myself.

Feeling suddenly nervous, I made a beeline for the exit.

* * *

A short time later, I was safe and sound inside my home. I still had an hour before Wes was due to arrive, just enough time for a solitary Yuletide ritual. As soon as I locked up, closed the curtains, and fed Drishti, I took a shower and dressed in my new white gown and cape. For fun, I accessorized with a large gold necklace, dangly earrings, and several gold bangles, then spritzed myself with a light frankincense perfume. Standing in front of the mirror, I struck a regal pose, then laughed at myself. *Add an Egyptian headdress, and I'm all set for a masquerade.*

Ever since I had dedicated myself to the Goddess back when I was a teenager, I had forged my own spiritual path. One of the things that most attracted me to Wicca was its lack of rules. As long as you vowed to "harm none," in accordance with the Wiccan Rede, you could pretty much practice your religion however you saw fit. For me, that meant honoring both the masculine and feminine aspects of divinity, though I connected most deeply with the Goddess. Whether maiden, mother, or crone, she went by many names and appeared in many guises. But, for me, her most significant aspect was as the creator. She was the first mother, as primordial as the fertility goddesses of yore. Perhaps that was why I always felt like she was looking after me.

I grabbed a few things from my bedroom and went downstairs to set up a temporary altar on the bricks in front of the living room fireplace. Front and center was a statuette of the Goddess Isis holding her son Horus on her lap. Around this, I placed offering bowls and candles. As I did, I spared a glance at Drishti, who was curled up on a blanket in my easy chair, her eyes half closed in a pose of relaxed indifference. I chuckled. As

Mila's familiar, Drishti was probably well accustomed to the magical workings of a dedicated Wiccan. Once everything was arranged, I lit the Yule log and settled back onto my meditation pillow.

Gazing at the fire, I took a deep breath and let it out. I continued to inhale and exhale through my nose until I felt myself transition into a calm, receptive state. As I relaxed my body and shed the day's pent-up tension, my mind flashed again to the question of Edgar's death. Why couldn't I let it go? Taking another deep breath, I resolved to stop obsessing over someone else's loss and worry about my own issues. Such as my relationship with Wes. In two days we would surpass the length of my relationship with Mick. If that was so significant to me, shouldn't I tell Wes? Wasn't it time we talked about our future together?

I shook my head to clear it. Back to the task at hand. *Trust the Goddess.*

I directed my attention to the figurine in front of the fire and bowed. Out loud, I recited my opening prayer:

> *Mother Isis, shining star, hold me in your power*
> *By your light, your endless grace, this is your blessed hour*
> *Year by year, you birth the sun, with hope my heart to fill*
> *I'm here for you, my mind wide open. Show me what you will*

I closed my eyes and surrendered to a deep, tranquil peace. In my mind's eye, I visualized a blank screen. In an instant, I saw a bright white light. I imagined myself walking toward it until it opened into a wide, sweeping expanse. Before me was a beautiful panoramic scene featuring snow-capped mountains and towering glitter-covered trees, like a postcard picture of the Swiss Alps. The whole experience was dreamlike—I felt I was really there, but I wasn't cold. As I admired the view, I zoomed in to ground level and found myself on a snow-covered path in the midst of an endless forest. At first, the trees appeared barren and gnarled, as if they were dead. Then I saw something shimmering in the air, fairy lights or will-o'-the-wisps. I followed them to a large clearing and beheld a circle of magnificent standing stones. It was an exact replica of Stonehenge.

In real life, I knew there would be a crowd of people at Stonehenge on the winter Solstice. Tourists and locals, Pagans and curiosity-seekers, would all gather to witness the sun's perfect alignment between the stones at both the sunrise and sunset. Yet, in my vision, I was alone.

Only, I wasn't quite alone. In the midst of the peace and quiet, I felt a presence. The will-o'-the-wisps appeared again, so I followed them back into the trees. In the glow of their effervescent green light, I saw the truth of things. I saw within and beneath and through everything. I saw the seeds of life within the trees and under the frozen earth. I had the sense I was receiving an important message. A powerful, reassuring message of hope and joy.

All at once, I felt it was time to leave. I headed back up the path, then I halted as a powerful feeling washed over me. It was a premonition, a visceral certainty that something was coming toward me, just around the bend. It would be a horse. I didn't know why, but I knew I would see a horse. Moments later, there it was: a gorgeous white mare. I patted the horse, then mounted it. We galloped off, so fast I felt I was flying. Then the earth fell away, and I floated effortlessly in space. The horse became a constellation, and I became a star.

After some time, I didn't know how long, my eyelids fluttered open and I found myself staring into the fireplace once more. Slowly, I pushed myself to kneeling, put my hands together, and bowed in gratitude for the vision. It had been a powerful mystical experience, filled with layers of meaning. I knew the Goddess had sent me a message, and I considered what it all meant. Perhaps she was telling me to be patient with my relationship with Wes. The seed had been planted. All I needed to do was nourish it and let it blossom in its own time.

But that wasn't all. There was more to the message. Before I could analyze the vision further, I heard a noise outside. And suddenly the peace was shattered by a raucous barking in the backyard, followed by a banging on the back door and a ringing at the front.

Then someone called my name.

"Keli! Open the door! Hurry!"

Chapter 12

The front door was nearest, so I ran over and peered through the peephole. It was Wes. I let him in, then dashed to the back door, where the pounding continued.

"Open up, Keli! It's freezing out here!"

It was Mrs. St. John. I opened the door, and she rushed in, cheeks flushed and hair flying. Chompy ran inside after her, yipping at her heels. If Drishti hadn't already darted from the room, she'd surely bolt for cover now.

"Mrs. St. John! Are you okay?"

"There was somebody out here in your yard! Chompy chased 'em off."

"Are you sure? Did you see somebody? Could it have been an animal?" Chompy had been known to go crazy over just about anything that crossed his path, from cats, squirrels and other dogs to plastic bags blowing in the wind.

"I didn't see him, but I heard a noise. Then Chompy flew out of his doggy door and came straight over here to chase away the trespasser. He's a good little watchdog."

She patted her thighs to call her dog. "Aren't you, baby? Aren't you a tough little watchdog?"

Wes flipped on the back-porch light and stepped outside. I grabbed a flashlight from the pantry and joined him. From my deck, we peered out at the backyard. The snow was trampled, all right. Besides Mrs. St. John's prints from her patio to mine, and the doggy tracks crisscrossing the yard, there were human footprints from the gate to the patio and back again.

I hurried down to the yard to examine the prints, while Wes ran to the back gate. He was back in no time. "Whoever it was, they're gone now."

"Look at this, Wes," I said, shining my flashlight on a footprint in the snow. "See the zigzags from the treads? Do you think we could figure out what kind of shoe made this pattern?"

Wes took a close look. "Actually, I've seen boot soles like that before. I used to have a pair of combat boots I picked up at an Army surplus store."

"Army boots, huh? How about the size?" I asked.

"Hard to say since the prints aren't perfect. Could be a man's nine or ten. I guess it could also be a woman's."

"Hmm. I guess combat boots are too common to prove anything." I looked up and noticed my snow shovel lying on the ground. I had propped it against the deck after shoveling my patio that morning. The intruder must have knocked it over. I shuddered at the thought of some creep standing in my backyard.

"Can I borrow your flashlight?" asked Wes. "I want to take another look and make sure the gate is latched tight."

I gave Wes the flashlight and went back inside to talk to Mrs. St. John. She stood in my kitchen holding a wet

Chompy in her arms. I handed her a towel and thanked her for coming over. That's when she noticed what I was wearing.

"Oh!" she said. "Don't you look lovely? Are you going to a costume party?"

I looked down at my dress. "Um."

Wes came back in, shaking his head. "I couldn't tell which way the person went."

"And what are you going as?" Mrs. St. John looked at Wes with questioning eyes. "Antony? Or—no, I know. Ramses? You would make a fine Egyptian pharaoh."

"Sorry?" Wes looked at me for help.

I thought fast. "That's right. We're going to a party. Wes is going to change there. We should probably be going so we won't be late. Are you sure you're okay, Mrs. St. John?"

"Who me? I'm fine. I won't keep you." Mrs. St. John backed out of the door. "You kids have fun. Take lots of pictures."

When she was gone, Wes gave me a bewildered look. Then he took in my outfit. "Ah," he said with a smile. "Costume party?"

"I had to say something."

"Of course."

"She'll be watching for us to leave now."

"What would you like to do?" asked Wes, stepping closer to me.

"Maybe we could go for a drive?"

He took both my hands in his. "As you wish, Your Majesty."

For a split second, I thought he was going to kneel down on one knee, and my heart skipped a beat. Instead, he lifted one of my hands to his lips. "You look gorgeous, by the way."

I exhaled. "I hadn't intended to keep this on."

"Too bad," said Wes, his lips twitching. "Looks like you're going to keep it on a while longer."

Wes retrieved my dress coat and helped me on with it. Feeling kind of silly, I slipped on my faux-fur boots and grabbed my purse. We left through the front door and headed to Wes's car along the curb. Without looking, I knew Mrs. St. John would be watching through her blinds.

"Your chariot awaits, my lady," Wes said. He held open the car door.

I sighed. "I wish you really did have a costume. I wouldn't mind seeing you in a toga. Or better yet, a loincloth."

Wes threw his head back and laughed. "It's a little cold for that," he said. He got in on the driver's side and started the car. "So, where to?"

"Wanna look at holiday lights? We can start at Fieldstone Park, then check out some of the neighborhoods."

"Sure," he said. He cranked the heat and tuned the radio to the twenty-four-hour holiday music station. When we reached the park, we coasted slowly through Candy Cane Lane, admiring the light displays sponsored by the Edindale Chamber of Commerce. The displays featured scenes from *The Nutcracker Suite*, *The Night Before Christmas*, *Charlie Brown's Christmas*, and other holiday classics. It warmed my heart every year. After giving our donation at the end of the lane, we cruised through town looking for homes with the biggest and brightest decorations.

As we drove, I thought about bringing up the subject

of our relationship. But when I opened my mouth, I spoke of Edgar instead.

"Don't you think the police were awfully quick to rule his death an accident?" I asked.

"I thought it was obvious," he said. "Sheana interviewed the police chief, and he told her no one heard or saw anything to suggest anyone was with Edgar when he fell. I guess the forensics unit hasn't formally issued its findings yet, but it seemed apparent to the responding officers that there was no evidence of a struggle."

"Yeah, I read the article. Still, the whole thing seems fishy to me."

Wes glanced over and gave me a suspicious look. "Is there something you're not telling me?"

My, he is perceptive. I was impressed. "Actually, yes. I spoke with Edgar's chauffeur earlier today." I told Wes what Bob had revealed about Edgar's returning to the hotel. Then I told him about the note I had found on the floor in the hotel. To me, this strongly suggested Edgar wasn't alone on the fourth floor.

Wes pulled over next to a front yard with a full-sized sleigh and eight LED-lit reindeer. He turned to look at me. "Should I be worried?"

"What do you mean?"

"You know what I mean. Last time you decided to play detective, you almost got yourself killed. Even if Edgar's death was an accident, you could still piss somebody off if you go poking around into other people's business. I don't want you getting hurt."

I reached for his hand and squeezed it. "Don't worry. I'd much rather leave the investigating to the police. I'll go see them tomorrow."

"Good."

We looked at each other for a long moment. I had the sense Wes wanted to say more, but I wasn't sure what. I glanced out the window as another car drove around us, and then I noticed where we were.

"Hey, this is Lerner Hill. Beverly lives in this neighborhood. Do you mind if we drive by her house?"

Lerner Hill was an upscale neighborhood with large front lawns and elegant brick and stone mansions. Most of the homes were well lit with tasteful, white icicle lights, but not Beverly's house. Her pillared colonial was completely dark.

"Wes, let's stop here. I want to check on Beverly." I didn't often see my boss outside of work, but I found it significant that we had ended up on her block. Besides, she could probably use a friend. She had divorced her husband years ago and didn't have children. I had heard her mention going on dates occasionally, and there was at least one special man with whom she sometimes vacationed. But she often joked that she was married to her job, which probably wasn't much of a stretch.

Wes parked near the curb in front of Beverly's house and turned off the car. I couldn't tell if her Audi was in the garage, but there did seem to be a light on in the house. It shone dimly from behind the closed curtains of a side window. Watching our step, we picked our way up the unshoveled sidewalk and rang the doorbell. After a few seconds, I rang it again.

"Maybe she isn't home," said Wes. "Lots of people leave a light on when they're not home."

"Maybe," I said. But my gut said otherwise. With a

twinge of worry, I rang the bell again, then banged on the door. "Beverly! Are you home?"

After a moment, I heard a shuffling sound on the other side of the door. "It's Keli!" I hollered, even though Beverly was probably peering through the peephole. Finally, the porch light came on and the door opened a crack.

"Keli? What's going on? Who's with you?"

"Hi, Beverly. Sorry to disturb you. This is my boyfriend, Wes. We were just out for a drive, and I realized we were in your neighborhood. I thought we'd drop by and see how you're doing."

She squinted in the porchlight and opened the door another inch. "I'm doing fine, but I'm not exactly dressed for company." She held a long, terrycloth bathrobe closed at the chest. Her silver-streaked auburn hair hung limply at her shoulders.

"Oh, we don't mind!" I said lightly. "And we won't stay long. But there is something important I need to talk to you about."

With obvious reluctance, Beverly stepped back and let us inside. We followed her through the dark foyer and into a well-appointed parlor. The only lights shone from a single Tiffany lamp and the flashing blue glow of a wide-screen TV. Beverly grabbed a remote to turn off the TV and waved us toward a sleek modern sofa. She dropped herself on the adjacent recliner, which was surrounded by dog-eared books, magazines, and crumpled tissues. A bottle of whiskey and a single glass tumbler sat on the end table next to her chair.

"Beverly," I began. "I am so sorry—"

She held up a hand to stop me. "Please. I can't take any more sympathy right now. Just tell me what's going on at the office. Is everything under control? Kris and Randall have been handling my clients, I believe."

I nodded. "Everything's fine. I met with a new client this week, and—" I stopped myself. I didn't come here to discuss work. At least, not our usual work. Switching gears, I opened the zipper on my purse. "I went by Edgar's office on Monday and found a piece of mail I wanted you to see. I thought it might be relevant to our assignment. That is, assuming we're still on the case."

Beverly narrowed her eyes, but sat up straighter. I withdrew the white envelope from my purse and handed it to her.

Wes leaned forward. "Where did you say you got that?"

"Edgar's office at Harrison Properties. I didn't open it, but—"

Before I could finish my sentence, Beverly grabbed a letter opener from a nearby desk and slit the envelope open in one swift motion.

"Wait!" I cried. Beverly and Wes both looked at me, startled. "There could be fingerprints," I said. "We should try to preserve them."

Beverly hesitated a moment, then set the envelope on the coffee table. "I'll be right back," she said.

As soon as she left the room, Wes turned to me. "Are you gonna tell me what this is all about?"

I touched his arm. "Edgar hired us to look into a personal matter for him shortly before he died. It's somewhat sensitive. I promise I'll tell you at some point, but could you just bear with me for now? Please?"

Wes's mouth twitched in a half smile and he squeezed my hand. "Of course." Then he looked up with wide eyes as Beverly reentered the room. She had pulled her hair into a bun at the back of her neck and put on kitten-heeled, feather-topped house slippers. On her hands were a pair of long, white satin opera gloves. Even in a bathrobe and without makeup, Beverly managed to look impressively regal. At least she didn't seem quite so depressed anymore.

"I couldn't find my Isotoners," she said. "And I don't have disposable gloves."

"That's okay," I said. I might've giggled, but for the seriousness of the situation. I was dying to know what was in the envelope.

Beverly sat down and reached for the envelope once more. This time, she moved carefully as she extracted the contents: a single sheet of folded white paper. She unfolded it and read to herself. From the way her jaw clenched, I knew I had been right to take the letter.

Without a word, Beverly held out the sheet of paper. Quickly I pulled my winter gloves from my coat pocket, slipped them on, and took the letter. With Wes reading over my shoulder, I read the typewritten words:

TIME'S UP. LEAVE 60K IN A STAPLED
BROWN BAG IN THE NW TRASH BIN
AT RYKER'S POND. 5 AM SHARP ON
12/21. ONE FALSE MOVE AND THE
WORLD WILL KNOW THE TRUTH
ABOUT CORNERSTONE.
P.S. DON'T BOTHER WATCHING
THE BIN. I'LL BE WATCHING YOU.

I blew out my breath and looked up at Beverly. I expected her to be waiting for my reaction, but she was staring at her unlit Christmas tree.

I scanned the note again, then folded it and returned it to the envelope. I handed it back to Beverly. "What's Cornerstone?" I asked.

"It was going to be a luxury housing development and golf course not far from here. Financing fell through with the crash of the real estate market a few years ago. The project was scrapped." Beverly met my eyes. "A lot of new construction halted back then. There was nothing unusual about Cornerstone. As I told you, this . . . blackmailer was trying to make something of nothing." She laughed without humor. "Their game's up now. I'm glad Edgar never paid them a penny."

Beverly stood up and walked over to her fireplace. She set the envelope on the mantel, then fussed with the logs and sticks in the fireplace. Wes and I watched as she struck a match and lit the kindling. The room was instantly cheerier when the flames leapt up and the logs crackled. Beverly stood again and grabbed the envelope. It took me a second to realize what was happening.

"Stop!" I cried, jumping up from my seat. "What are you doing?"

She turned and gave me a pained look. It was obvious what she was doing.

"Beverly," I said gently. "That letter is evidence of a crime. We have a duty to report it to the police."

"Do we? What's the point? It won't bring Edgar back. If anything, it will only tarnish his name."

Oh, boy. What could I say to make my boss see reason? "Beverly, listen to me. This could be connected to Edgar's death."

Beverly stared at me for a moment, then her expression changed as if a curtain had been lifted behind her eyes. "What are you saying? You don't think his death was an accident?"

I bit my lip. What *did* I think? Was I seriously about to suggest that Edgar had been murdered? I took a deep breath. "I don't know," I said honestly. "But I have a lot of questions. First off, how does a person just fall off a balcony, especially if that person is all by himself?"

"You think he was pushed?" Beverly had raised her voice, and I noticed Wes seemed to be biting his inner cheek.

"I—I think it's possible. And there's something else I wanted to tell you. I found out Edgar never went home after the ball. After pretending to leave, he returned to the hotel through a back entrance." I told Beverly about my conversation with Bob, the driver. For now, I decided not to mention the note I'd found on the floor of the hotel reading room. Given her reluctance to involve the police, I was afraid she might try to take the note from me. "I suspect Edgar was going to meet someone," I continued. "If we can find out who he was meeting, we'll be one step closer in figuring out what really happened that night."

Beverly turned pale and reached for her glass on the side table. Seeing that it was empty, she fumbled for the bottle and dropped her glass. It bounced on the carpeted floor. Wes picked it up and poured her a drink.

"Are you okay?" I asked.

"Yes, sorry." She took the drink and downed it. "It's just . . . that hadn't even occurred to me. I didn't hear—" She shook her head and looked at me, her old stern expression back. "I didn't hear anything about foul play being suspected. Now that you mention it, I can think of a few people who would have liked Edgar out of the picture."

"That's what I was thinking! Maybe someone who didn't want him to become mayor?"

Beverly narrowed her eyes. "One person in particular. And she's so crazy, I wouldn't put murder past her."

She? Was Beverly referring to Allison Mandrake? Perhaps Allison didn't really want Edgar to become mayor after she found out his daughter would take over the family business. Maybe that's why she had asked Wes to take pictures of Edgar at the end of the night when he didn't look his best. Was she trying to sabotage the election? Could Edgar have caught on and confronted her about it?

Or was I just being ridiculous?

"She's always hated Edgar," Beverly continued. "And she could have easily entered the hotel that night. She used to work there."

"Wait, what? Who are you talking about?"

"You know. That crazy eco-nut who lives 'off the grid' outside of town. Fern Lopez."

The name clicked in my memory. Fern Lopez was the woman who had known my aunt Josephine, back when they lived at the Happy Hills commune decades ago. Fern was nice enough when I reached out to her, but I remembered thinking there was something a little bit off about her. I wondered if perhaps she wasn't being entirely truthful when she told me she didn't know what had happened to Josie.

"What did Fern have against Edgar?" I asked.

"She opposes all land development on principle," said Beverly, with a flippant wave. "She used to appear at every zoning hearing to speak out against Harrison projects. She even filed a lawsuit against Edgar personally, but it was dismissed. After that she became even more aggressive, trying to dig up dirt on Edgar. She got a job as a hotel maid and was caught trying to plant a bug in Edgar's office. She was fired, of course."

"Wow. A bug? That does sound extreme."

Wes, who had been following our exchange in silence, finally spoke up. "Fern Lopez is an artist, isn't she? I've seen her at arts festivals selling crafts and jewelry."

Beverly nodded. "I believe so."

Jewelry. Fern designed handmade beaded jewelry. I had seen some of her work when I had visited her last spring. She used lots of natural materials, such as hemp, shells, and turquoise—just like the pieces I had found in the hotel cloakroom and in the conference room at Edgar's office. No wonder they had seemed familiar.

Maybe it was time I pay Fern Lopez another visit.

By the time we finally left Beverly's place, clouds had rolled in again, blotting out the moon and stars. Wes took the back way out of Lerner Hill, following a two-lane highway around the outskirts of Edindale. Houses were fewer and farther between out there, making the road seem long, dark, and mysterious— kind of like this Solstice night was turning out to be.

I was glad Beverly had perked up before we left. She had even made coffee and brought out a tray of snacks. At one point, she noticed I was still in my coat and invited me to take it off. I assured her I was comfortable and changed the subject. I might have seen my boss in her bathrobe, but there was no way I was going to let her see me in my ceremonial garb.

Yet, as relieved as I was that Beverly had returned to her old, aggressive self, I was more confused than ever about what had been going on with Edgar. We seemed to have come up with a lot more questions than answers. As I thought about it, I realized any number of people might have had it out for Edgar. Perhaps someone held an old grudge, such as Fern Lopez or anyone who was disappointed in the failed Cornerstone project. Or perhaps someone didn't want him to become mayor, such as his political opponents or people who disagreed with his policy positions—again, like Fern Lopez. At least Tucker had an alibi, since he was with Farrah at the time of the death.

Of course, there could also be people with personal motives, such as Allison, who seemed to be upset with Edgar, or Zeke, who had behaved strangely ever since I met him. And if Edgar was secretly meeting a woman at the hotel, I might as well add jealousy and revenge to the mix of possible motives.

For some reason, Beverly's rather intense state of bereavement popped into my mind. Was it possible she and Edgar had been more than friends? I dismissed the thought. If I lost a close friend, I knew I'd be a mess, too.

I looked over at Wes and took in his strong, beautiful profile. Smiling in the dark, I felt immensely lucky to have him by my side. What other boyfriend would have so generously given up a date night to spend the evening with his girlfriend's depressed boss?

I was about to reach over and squeeze Wes's hand

when I became aware of headlights coming up behind us at a worrisome clip.

"Jeez!" said Wes, as he tilted his rearview mirror. "Don't people know they're supposed to turn off their brights when they approach another car?"

The vehicle sped around us so fast I couldn't get a good look at it. I was still seeing spots from the bright lights.

"That was scary," I said. "What could possibly—wait. Where'd he go?" We were on a straight stretch of road, yet the crazy driver's taillights had disappeared. I strained to see down the highway.

"That's weird," said Wes. "He was just there. It's almost like he just turned his lights off. But that doesn't—"

"Oh, my God! Watch out!"

Wes swerved, and I screamed. Before I knew what was happening, we veered off the road, bounced through the ditch, and landed with a thud in a bank of snow. Wes's car lights illuminated a white barren field.

"Are you okay?" Wes asked breathlessly. His eyes, filled with concern, roved over my body, top to bottom.

I swallowed the bile in my throat. "Yeah. I think so."

"I can't believe the airbags didn't deploy," he said. "Are you sure you're okay?"

I nodded. "How about you? Are you hurt?"

"No, I'm fine. Just thoroughly pissed. What in the *hell* was that guy thinking? He almost got us all killed."

"It's a miracle we didn't slam into him." I reached over and touched Wes's face. "Good thing you have quick reflexes. You saved us."

Wes inhaled raggedly and then blew out air with a huff. "Let's get out of the car, okay? Then I'll call for a tow."

Wes opened his car door, while I searched for my purse on the floor. Good thing it was zipped up, I thought, as I put my hand on the bag. Otherwise the contents would be scattered all over Wes's car.

I glanced back toward the road and caught my breath. Someone was standing at the top of the ditch.

Chapter 13

"Where did he come from?" I asked, eyeing the shadowy figure at the top of the ditch. Actually, I couldn't be sure it was a man. The person wore a puffer coat with the hood pulled up.

"There's a truck up there," said Wes. He got back into the car and shut his door. "I'm not sure, but that might be the psycho who ran us off the road."

Chills coursed through my blood as I stared at the person looking down at us. I had a very bad feeling about the whole situation. Just what kind of game was this crazy driver playing? What did he want with us?

Suddenly the stranger turned to look up the road. Then he—or she—took off running, jumped into the truck, and peeled out.

Just then another car pulled up, its high beams lighting up the entire area. A few seconds later, two men appeared, side by side, and peered down at us. This time, my instincts told me we were safe. Wes and I pushed our doors open at the same time and clambered out. We waved at the two men.

"Are you okay?" they shouted.

"We are now," I said. *Thank Goddess.*

It was quite a struggle to get out of bed the next morning. The long night had gotten even longer when we had to wait for a tow truck and then try to file a police report with absolutely no information to give the police. Luckily, our rescuers, a nice couple on their way home from a holiday party, stuck around and gave us a ride back to town. Wes stayed the night with me, partly since his car was in the shop—but mostly because we both felt a little too freaked out to be alone.

Once we had settled down in front of my fireplace with mugs of cocoa and a midnight snack, Wes found the perfect way to take my mind off the evening's troubling events. He pulled a small foil-wrapped box from his coat pocket.

"What's this?" I asked, my eyes growing wide.

"Just a little Yuletide gift. I figured I should bring you your present today, since this is the holiday you really celebrate. Right?"

"That's right. You remembered." I touched the tiny satin bow, so moved at his thoughtfulness that it almost didn't matter what the box contained.

Wes nudged my knee. "The gift is actually inside the box."

Smiling, I opened the package. Inside was a delicate crescent moon necklace made of yellow gold with a tiny diamond accent. "It's beautiful," I breathed. "I love it."

"It reminded me of you," he said.

I put the necklace on, then surprised Wes by bringing out the present I had bought for him: a glossy photography book I knew he had been eyeing. Of course, then he wanted to look through the whole thing. I didn't mind. I snuggled up next to him and fell asleep in the crook of his arm.

In the morning, after a quick breakfast together, I dropped Wes off at the newspaper office on my way in to work. I was a little sore from being jostled around when we careened off the road, but my anxiety had all but evaporated. The more Wes and I had gone over the events of the night before, the less scary they had seemed. We realized we had no proof the strange person had meant us harm. There were lots of possible reasons to explain the person's behavior: he or she could have been sick, drunk, stoned, or mentally ill. The driver probably stopped to see if we were okay, and then fled out of fear. Maybe they didn't have car insurance.

As soon as I arrived at my office, my thoughts turned to Beverly. I went straight to her office—only to find out she hadn't come in to work. Again. She had promised me she would make it to Edgar's memorial service the next evening. I hoped she would remain true to her word.

After checking messages and reviewing some files, I told Julie I would be out the rest of the morning. I had an appointment with a homebound client who wanted to update her will, and I wasn't sure how long it would take. As it happened, the update was simple and I was finished by 10:00 a.m. *Perfect*, I thought. Now I would have time to stop by the police station to discuss Edgar

Harrison. I was about to start up my car, when my cell phone rang. It was Farrah.

"Hey, you," she said. "Any chance you can meet me for an early lunch? I spoke with Tucker, and I have some info for you."

"You saw him already?"

"After you left me at the Loose last night, I may have had a few more drinks. I got a little bold and called him."

"Oh, geez. Tell me you didn't—"

"Relax, girlfriend. We had a little chat, that's all."

"So, what did he say?"

Farrah hesitated. "I'd rather tell you in person. Can you get away from the office?"

Now I was thoroughly intrigued. "Where are you now? Want to go for a drive with me?"

"I'm at home. Swing by now, if you want."

A few minutes later, I pulled up in front of Farrah's apartment complex. She was waiting outside, bundled up in a fleece-lined coat and rainbow-striped pom-pom hat. She hopped into the front seat, and I drove off, heading for the edge of town. I was going to make the most of my free time this morning.

"Where we goin', Jeeves?" she asked.

"You first," I said.

She sighed. "You might not like it."

"What? Just tell me."

"Okay. So, I told Tucker I had heard a rumor that Edgar was having an affair."

"Good thinking. Keep your sources vague."

"Exactly. Well, he didn't even act surprised."

"So we were right?" I asked. "Edgar was seeing someone on the side?"

"It would seem so."

"Did you ask Tucker if he knew anything about it?"

"I did. And he wasn't positive, but he suspected who Edgar might have been seeing."

"And?"

"And . . . he said he believed Edgar could have been romantically involved with his lawyer. Beverly."

"No." I shook my head. "They were just friends." Beverly would never be someone's mistress. Would she?

"I knew you wouldn't want to hear this," said Farrah.

I waved away her concern. "I'm fine. I guess it's not a farfetched idea. Still, he didn't know for sure, right?"

"Right. It was just a guess."

I drove in silence, taking River Road out of town and following the winding country roads for several miles. I considered what Farrah had said. Was it naïve of me to dismiss the idea of Beverly having an affair with Edgar? The problem was, assuming for the sake of argument that it was true, something was still off. I couldn't put my finger on it, but the whole idea of Beverly and Edgar just didn't make sense.

"Hey, dreamy," said Farrah. "Do you have a destination in mind, or are you just burning fuel for no reason?"

"Oh, God no. I have a destination. There's someone I want to see." I told Farrah what I had learned about Fern's grudge against Edgar and about the beads I had found. "I've been meaning to visit her again anyway," I said. "I was hoping she might tell me more about my aunt Josephine."

"Sounds good to me. Maybe I'll buy some jewelry from her."

After a couple wrong turns, I finally found the lane leading to Fern's homestead. It was well off the main road and partially hidden by overgrown shrubs and trees. Somehow I had the impression this was not by chance. When we reached a gate blocking the lane, it was even more apparent that Fern didn't welcome guests to her property.

I pulled my car to the side of the road and parked.

"What now?" asked Farrah.

"Now we walk."

The barrier gate was a single bar to prevent vehicle traffic from entering the property, but it was easy enough to circumvent on foot. A sign on the gate said NO HUNTING—PRIVATE PROPERTY.

"You sure about this?" asked Farrah. "She doesn't seem to be open for business. Or visitors."

"It's fine," I said. "We're not here to hunt. And this is where I met her before."

Of course, last time she had been expecting me. On the plus side, at least the lane had been plowed. We trudged along until we finally came to a circular driveway leading up to the main house and several outbuildings. The house was a low-slung prairie-style ranch, which reminded me of a modest Frank Lloyd Wright design. As with the first time I had seen it, I couldn't help thinking half the house must be hidden underground. The blinds were all drawn, and there were no cars in sight.

"Looks like nobody's home," said Farrah.

"Let's not give up just yet," I said, ringing the doorbell. As we waited, I noticed a small camera wedged discreetly under the eaves. I rang the bell again and this time put on a friendly smile and called out, "Hello! Anyone home?"

An intercom crackled, causing Farrah to jump. "Come to the workshop around back," said a harsh female voice.

Farrah and I looked at each other and shrugged. We made our way to the back of the house where we found a two-car garage painted teal, with pink trim. The navy blue door opened and Fern Lopez stepped out.

"What can I do for you?" she asked. With her long dark, gray-tinged hair and her baggy pants and turtleneck, Fern looked very much the part of the aging boho artist. Her demeanor was reserved, but at least she didn't kick us out.

"Hello, Fern," I said. "I'm not sure if you remember me. I'm Keli Milanni. We met several months ago when—"

"I remember," she said. "You're Josie's niece."

"That's right. This is my friend Farrah Anderson. I was just telling her about your jewelry, and we wondered if you have any shows coming up. I also thought of another question about Josephine."

Fern narrowed her eyes, as if she didn't quite believe me. But she let us in anyway.

"I don't get a lot of visitors out this way," she said. She picked up a glue gun and returned to the project she had been working on. "Thought the gate was down."

"How do you get mail?" asked Farrah.

"Post office box in town," Fern answered.

"Ah."

Farrah and I stood in the middle of the workshop and looked around. The side walls were adorned with macramé hangings and abstract metal sculptures. On the back wall a pegboard held loops of string, wire, and various tools. A large worktable occupied the center of the room, while cabinets and smaller tables took up much of the rest of the space. There was no place to sit down.

"So," I began. "I think I told you that my aunt sends postcards to some of our family on a sporadic basis. I was wondering if you've received any, or if you've heard from her lately."

Fern didn't answer right away. She regarded me closely, then looked back down at her work. "No. Sorry."

"Oh. I know it was a long time ago, but do you remember what was going on at the commune when she left? I mean, did anyone else leave with her?"

"Happy Hills broke up right around the time she left. We lost our land, so everyone had to find another place to live. Some people left for greener pastures. Others, like me, found new land in the area."

"What's this?" asked Farrah. She pointed under one of the tables at a stack of picket signs. I tilted my head to read them. The two on top said: SAY NO TO FAT CAT EDDIE and SLOW GROWTH NOT FAST EDDIE. They each featured a caricature of Edgar Harrison in a circle with a diagonal line.

"I was planning a rally," said Fern. "Obviously, there's no need now."

"A rally already?" said Farrah. "He just announced his candidacy a few days ago."

"It doesn't take long to mobilize," said Fern. "Especially for an important cause."

I eyed the number of signs. "Was it going to be a big rally?"

"If you want to know how many others were with me, it was a lot. Plenty. I'm not alone in my opposition to Fast Eddie and all that he stands for." She pursed her lips. "Stood for."

"Really?" I asked. "I thought he was generally well regarded."

"Well feared is more like it. He had a number of enemies, I'm certain of it. And I'll bet ya his death was no accident, either."

Farrah's eyes got big, while I tried to keep a poker face. Here I had wanted to speak to Fern about Edgar's death, and she was the first to bring it up.

"You know," I said carefully. "I had wondered about that myself. What makes you think it wasn't an accident?"

"Men like Edgar Harrison don't just fall off balconies. No. That's just a cover-up. Mark my words."

"A cover-up?" asked Farrah. "By whom? Who do you think was responsible?"

"I don't think. I *know*."

"If you know," I said, "shouldn't you go to the police?"

Fern appeared stricken. "You can't trust the police! Some are all right, but some are in on it. I can't take any chances."

In on it? I was beginning to notice Fern's tendency to speak in the language of conspiracy theories. Still, I wanted to hear more.

"So, who were his enemies?" I asked.

"Who were his enemies?" she echoed. "How about the people he defrauded? The people he stole from?"

"What do you mean?" I asked.

"Do you have proof of this?" asked Farrah in a skeptical tone.

Fern scowled. "He was shifty. Hard to pin down. Fast Eddie. That's who he was."

"Is that what you were doing when you worked at the Harrison Hotel?" asked Farrah. "Looking for proof?"

Fern flared her nostrils and didn't answer, so I quickly changed the subject. "Speaking of the hotel, I found something there the other night that made me think of you." I dug into my purse for the broken buckle. "Did you happen to drop this?"

Fern looked sharply at the piece in my hand, then shook her head. "I do sell my handiwork, you know. It's nice to know someone was wearing it. Too bad they dropped it. Looks like it was stepped on. It wouldn't have broken on its own that easily."

"It's beautiful," said Farrah. "Do you have more like it that I can see today?"

Fern gave Farrah an appraising look, then apparently decided she was being sincere. Fern went to a cabinet and withdrew a tray of bracelets and necklaces. While Farrah tried on jewelry, I tried to steer the conversation back to Edgar's death.

"Fern, I think you raised a good point before, about how unlikely it is for a person like Edgar to simply fall off a balcony. But, isn't the alternative just as unlikely? I mean, wouldn't it be awful tough for someone to get away with murder out in the open like that? In a hotel full of people?"

Fern appeared thoughtful. "I haven't been there in years, not since my employment was terminated. Edgar took out a restraining order against me." She rolled her eyes. "From what I recall, it wouldn't be that difficult. Since the hallways curve around the atrium, you could be three feet from a person and not see them. Plus, there are those wide posts every couple yards. What time did the murder take place?"

"Well, we don't know for sure that it was murder," I said. "But it must have happened sometime between one and one-thirty a.m."

"Between shifts, then," said Fern. "It would have been pretty dead around there at that time. Pardon the pun."

"What were you doing Saturday night?" asked Farrah. She said it so innocently that Fern didn't bat an eye.

"At one a.m. I was in a chat room discussing wind energy projects with my sisters in Denmark. It was eight a.m. Central European time."

"You have sisters in Denmark?" I asked.

"Friends," said Fern. "'Sisters' is just a figure of speech."

"Do you use wind energy on your farm?" asked Farrah.

"Not yet. We have geothermal and solar. I'm planning on installing a wind turbine as soon as I can get the necessary approvals."

"That's so cool," I said. "So, you're completely self-sufficient out here?"

"Pretty much," said Fern proudly. "We grow all our food and raise cows, sheep, and chickens. We also have beehives. I have honey for sale, if you're interested."

"Not right now, but I'll take these bangles," said Farrah.

As Farrah paid for the jewelry and Fern wrapped it up, I glanced at the protest signs again. "So, will you be voting for Tucker Brinkley next spring? He seems to be pro-environment."

Fern snorted. "He's pro-himself. They all are."

Farrah frowned and I raised my eyebrows.

Fern shook her head. "Keep your eyes open, missy. You'll see. They're all in bed together, the corporate fat cats and the politicians. You're a smart girl. You'll figure it out."

Chapter 14

After leaving Fern's countryside compound, Farrah and I talked the whole way back to town. Farrah was mostly amused by Fern's manner. She called the older woman "a riddle wrapped in an enigma wrapped in a hemp leaf." I laughed, but I couldn't help thinking Fern might be onto something. There was definitely something up with Edgar's dealings. Nevertheless, I didn't share Fern's distrust of the police. As soon as I dropped Farrah off at home, I drove straight to the Edindale police station.

I planned to see the one police officer I knew personally. He was a friend of Farrah's ex-boyfriend, and we had all hung out in the past. But when I approached the counter, I thought better of it. Instead, I asked for Detective Adrian Rhinehardt. He was the cop I'd met the last time I had found a dead body. I shuddered. *And may this one truly be the last.*

After a short wait, the detective came out and escorted me to his office. Dressed in plain clothes rather than a uniform, he was a burly man of few words. From what

I recalled, he was usually hard to read, but he seemed smart and was polite enough.

"How have you been, Ms. Milanni?" he asked, gesturing toward a chair next to his desk.

"Fine, thanks. And please call me Keli. How have you been?"

"Fine," he said, with the tiniest hint of amusement. "What can I do for you?"

I cleared my throat. "I wanted to talk to you about Edgar Harrison. I'm the one who found him at the hotel the other night."

"I know. I read your statement. Did you want to add to it or amend it?"

"Not exactly. I've learned a couple things since that night. And . . . I have reason to believe Edgar was planning to meet someone on the fourth floor of the hotel. Or, perhaps, he had already met with someone."

"So?"

"So, perhaps he wasn't alone when he fell."

Detective Rhinehardt gave me that inscrutable look I remembered so well. "Do you have information to suggest he wasn't?"

I handed him the note signed by "E." "I found this on the floor in the hotel reading room yesterday evening," I said, omitting the part about crawling under the caution tape. "I realize it might not have been written by Edgar, and I don't know when it was dropped. But it's awfully suggestive. Maybe you can compare the handwriting to Edgar's?"

Rhinehardt studied the note, scratching his chin. "This also doesn't tell us who the note was meant for."

"Right. But there is someone who might know. Edgar's driver, Bob Franklin."

"Mr. Franklin said he didn't bring Edgar back to the hotel Saturday night."

"You might want to ask him again," I said.

"Hmm." Rhinehardt grunted noncommittally. "Is there anything else?"

"No. Except . . ." I trailed off. Was now the time to mention the blackmail scheme? If I did, I'd be going against Beverly's wishes, not to mention treading on thin ice when it came to protecting our client's confidentiality. I sighed. If the police would just open up an investigation, maybe I wouldn't have to say anything after all.

"Except what?" prompted the detective.

"Well, I understand Edgar had a few enemies." I cringed when I said the word. I was starting to sound like Fern Lopez. Rhinehardt just stared at me, waiting for me to elaborate.

"Doesn't his family want you to investigate his death?" I asked.

"I'm not sure there *is* anything to investigate," he said. "The autopsy showed he had a high blood alcohol level. From all appearances at the scene, he fell over by accident."

"There was an autopsy?"

Rhinehardt tilted his head ever so slightly and gave me the barest flicker of a smile. "Trust me, Ms. Milanni. I know how to do my job."

"Of course. So . . . you'll talk to the driver again?"

"I'll talk to the driver."

I left the police station satisfied that the cops would take another look at the so-called accident at the Harrison

Hotel. Now I needed to get back to the office and clock some billable hours. I had definitely fallen behind over the past few days. Another thing I was falling behind in was my workout schedule. In order to get in at least a little bit of cardio exertion, I decided to leave my car near the police station and walk briskly to the office.

I was only a block down the sidewalk when it happened again. I had the overwhelming sensation that I was being watched. I slowed my steps and looked around. Nothing unusual stood out. There was a moderate amount of traffic on Main Street. A few other pedestrians scurried to and from the courthouse or the shops across the street. Still, I was unnerved by the feeling. Maybe it was because of being run off the road after leaving Beverly's house the night before. Work could wait for a few more minutes. I decided to pop into Moonstone Treasures and see Mila.

When I entered the shop, it wasn't Mila behind the counter. It was her employee, Catrina. Catrina was an interesting young woman. I often thought she was like a tough cookie with a soft candy heart center. The hard impression she gave, with her spiked black hair, dog collar choker, and several piercings, was softened by the smile that lit up her face when she saw me.

"Hey, Keli! Happy Yule! You should have come to our celebration yesterday. We had a blast."

"Thanks, Catrina. Maybe next time."

"What's that?" said Mila, coming in through the curtains from her back room. "Did I just hear Keli say she might join us at our next sabbat celebration?"

I had to laugh. "We'll see. I did have an interesting night of my own, though." I shared a little bit of my vision, and also told them about the excitement with Mrs. St. John and the close call later that night.

"Have you pissed someone off?" asked Catrina. "This reminds me of those creeps that were harassing Mila earlier this year."

"Oh, it's not nearly that bad. I'm probably just being paranoid." I snickered lightly. "I even thought someone might be following me outside a minute ago, but there was no one there. I've just got the jitters."

Mila looked at me with concern. "I would say there's definitely more to your vision than the obvious symbolism. You should let me give you a reading."

"Thanks, but I really don't have time now."

"What about tomorrow morning when I stop at your house to pick up Drishti? Catrina will be watching the shop. How is Drishti, by the way? Is she behaving herself?"

"She's the perfect houseguest: quiet, clean, and independent. I'm going to miss having her around. But, as for the reading, I don't think tomorrow will work either. I have to put in another day's work before I take off for Nebraska on the twenty-fourth. How about if I call you when I get back?"

Catrina put her hands on her hips. "Delving into the astral plane is all well and good, but you need protection now. You should carry an amulet."

"Catrina's right," said Mila. "You should also cast a shielding spell."

"I agree," I said. "That's why I'm here."

While Mila and Catrina bustled about gathering supplies and ingredients, I browsed the greeting cards and calendars. Flipping through the pages of a glossy wall calendar, I paused when one of the pictures jumped out at me. It featured a beautiful witch with long flowing silver hair. She was a mature woman, at the "crone" stage of life, but she appeared radiant. She stood in a grassy meadow at sunset, surrounded by fireflies that glowed like fairy lights. Standing next to her was a magnificent white horse.

"What is it?" asked Mila, coming up behind me. "You look moonstruck."

"This picture," I said, feeling somewhat dazed. "It features some images from my Solstice vision. And the woman . . . she looks exactly how I imagine my aunt Josephine would look."

Mila looked at the picture, then touched my arm. "Everything is connected, dear. Perhaps this is a reminder."

"Perhaps," I agreed. I didn't know why or how, but I had a strong sense of Josephine's presence. Even stranger, I had a feeling that she *was* connected to the other things going on in my life—including the mystery of Edgar Harrison.

After lunch, I concentrated on work, finishing up several client matters. As my last task of the day, I called an opposing counsel to iron out the terms of a settlement agreement. Once we reached a tentative agreement, I had to wait around for him to get his client's approval and call me back. I knew my client was anxious, so I didn't want to leave until I had confirmed the deal was final. At last, the attorney called me back, and we made arrangements to sign the final document after the holidays. I sent a quick message to my client, happy that I was able to negotiate favorable terms for her. On the downside, all of my colleagues had already left for Edgar's visitation.

I gathered my things and headed over to Willison Funeral Home by myself. Wes would have come with me, but he had to see about his car. On top of that, Jimi had called begging Wes to help him out at the Loose. His regular bartender had come down with the flu, so Wes agreed to fill in.

By the time I arrived at the funeral home, the receiving line was already so long it snaked through three rooms of the Victorian mansion. I made my way through the crowd, nodding to acquaintances and murmuring quiet hellos, until I spotted Pammy and Crenshaw.

"Hi, guys," I said softly. "Have you seen—"

"The line begins over there, near the kitchen," said Crenshaw.

"Oh. Okay. I wasn't going to cut."

"Mm-hmm."

Pammy gave me an apologetic smile and rolled her eyes. "Don't mind Crenshaw. He's always cranky when he's hungry."

Crenshaw looked affronted. "I'm never cranky. I have no idea what you're talking about."

I shook my head. "I'll see you later."

I continued through the mansion and took my place at the tail end of the line behind an elderly woman with a cane. With a rueful smile, she nodded at me and sighed. "I guess I should have gotten here earlier," she said. "These old knees of mine don't appreciate standing for long stretches. I'm not sure if I can make it."

"Why don't you go sit on one of the couches?" I

suggested, pointing toward the viewing room. "I'll hold your place and call you up when we get close."

"Oh, would you? That would be wonderful."

When the woman left, I moved ahead one step and found myself standing behind Lonnie Treat. He bounced on his heels, surveying the crowd as if he was looking for someone.

"Quite a turnout," I said.

He looked at me in some surprise. "Yes. Such a tragic loss. I still can't believe he's gone."

"Were you very close?" I asked.

He nodded. "Quite. We were business partners." He puffed up his chest in an oddly smug manner, until a lanky man walked up and punched Lonnie on the shoulder.

"Well, if it isn't Lonnie Treat! How's the mattress business these days, old buddy? Do people really buy new mattresses that often? I've probably had mine for twenty years."

"Then it's time for you to replace it," said Lonnie, with a tight smile. He handed the man a business card. "Come and see me tomorrow. I'll give you a good deal."

The man clapped him on the arm and headed for the exit. The line inched forward, and I decided to try to make another attempt at conversation. "So, you're in both mattress sales and real estate?"

"What?" Lonnie looked at me as if I'd sprouted wings.

"You said you were Edgar's business partner, so I just assumed . . ."

"Oh, right," he said. "I've got many irons in the fire.

A real estate project was one of them." The line moved ahead into the next room, and Lonnie scanned the clusters of people milling about. "There he is," he said, almost under his breath.

I followed his gaze and spied Tucker Brinkley speaking with Allison. Tucker struck a handsome figure in his black suit and gray shirt. It amazed me how tan he still was for the end of December. *He sure must spend a lot of time outside.* Once again, I had a hard time picturing him behind a desk.

Lonnie must have read my mind. "There's our next mayor," he said.

"You think so?" I said. "The election is still a few months off."

"He's the clear frontrunner, now that Edgar's gone."

At that moment, Tucker turned and looked directly at Lonnie. Something flickered in his eyes. Recognition, maybe? Then someone passed between us, and when I looked again, Tucker was gone.

A few minutes later, the line picked up the pace and we finally had a view of the flower-shrouded casket. I turned to beckon to the woman with the cane, but she was already on her way up. She took her place between Lonnie and me, and I turned my attention to Edgar's family.

There was Gretta in her wheelchair, dressed in black and appearing tired but composed. By her side was her elder daughter Diana, the surgeon, standing next to her husband and children. On Gretta's other side was her younger daughter, Annabelle. I felt a pang of sympathy for them all. When it was my turn to express my condolences, I shook their hands, told them how I was acquainted with Edgar, and offered my deepest sympathies. If they realized I was the one who had found his body under the hotel Christmas tree, they didn't let on.

From the viewing area, I wandered among the other guests looking for any sign of my colleagues. I wondered if Beverly had made it out as she said she would. In the front parlor, I stood in the doorway and scanned the crowd. On the other side of the room I caught sight of someone else who was also people watching: Tucker Brinkley. He seemed to be studying each face. Eventually, his gaze fell upon me, and his expression brightened. I gave him a pleasant nod and was rewarded with his languid cowboy grin. He ambled toward me, and I met him halfway.

"Miss Keli, if I remember right?"

"Hello, Mr. Brinkley. I'm so sorry for your loss. I know Edgar was a friend of yours."

He took my hand between his large palms and gave it a gentle squeeze. "He was a friend to many, as evidenced by all the folks who turned out today. But, yes. Ed 'n I, we went way back. I knew him before he became the bigwig he turned out to be." He chuckled softly.

"Did you go to school together?"

"We did. Edindale High, class of . . . well, I best not say. You might start looking at me like I'm your grand-dad or somethin'."

I smiled. "I doubt that."

"So, where's your girlfriend this evening?" he asked, looking around.

"Farrah? She had a sales call upstate this afternoon. She's probably on her way back to town now."

"She's a real sweet girl. You tell her I said that." Tucker's eyes twinkled like the charmer he was.

"I will, Mr. Brinkley," I promised.

"Say," he said, as if an idea had just occurred to him. "I s'pose I'm obliged to you for helping me become reacquainted with Miss Farrah. She told me you received tickets to Edgar's ball just last Friday. I believe you were doing legal work in the real estate office?"

"That's right," I said. "It was really kind of Edgar to invite my colleague and me." Actually, it had been Allison who invited us, but that didn't seem important now.

For a moment, Tucker regarded me from beneath his bushy eyebrows. Then he dropped his eyes. "Such a damn shame," he said, almost under his breath. "I still can't believe he's gone, the old blowhard."

"Yeah," I said, sympathetically. There wasn't much more to say. Death was tricky like that. Always hard to believe, regardless of the circumstances.

Of course, in this case, the circumstances weren't exactly clear. And that fact weighed on my mind like a sack full of coal: heavy, dirty, and downright unpleasant.

After saying good-bye to Tucker, I continued through the funeral home. I figured I must have missed Beverly. As soon as the thought crossed my mind, she rounded the corner in front of me. She was with Crenshaw and they were carrying their coats. I hurried over.

"Oh, hello, Keli," said Beverly. "It was nice of you to come."

"How are you doing, Beverly? Are you taking off?"

"Yes. I've already been here quite a while. Crenshaw and I are going to grab a bite to eat. Care to join us?"

"I'd love to."

I was eager to speak to the only two people besides me who knew Edgar was being blackmailed. That is, the only people other than the blackmailer him- or herself.

Chapter 15

Crenshaw and Beverly voted for Gigi's Bar and Grill, a classy but low-key restaurant known for its steaks. With its wood-paneled walls and tea candles on every table, it had a warm, romantic atmosphere. We settled into a booth in the back and placed our orders. I opted for salad and a glass of wine.

Crenshaw steepled his fingers at his lips as he tended to do when he wanted to wax poetic. "The true measure of a man is in the number of lives he touched. Edgar was clearly a great man."

Beverly smiled sadly. "He was incredibly generous. Whenever any of his friends would ask for a favor, he'd always say yes. And if you ever found yourself at a restaurant or bar with him, you'd know he always insisted on buying, no matter who he was with or what the occasion."

Crenshaw nodded. "Someone told a story tonight about Edgar's bottomless wallet. Evidently, if anyone needed a loan, Edgar would open his wallet and produce the cash on the spot, no questions asked."

Beverly chuckled. "He was never without cash, that's for sure."

"That's another way he was old-school," I remarked. "He must have preferred paper money just like he preferred paper records."

"That's true," said Beverly. "He even had a safe in his office to make sure he'd always have cash on hand."

"Really?" I said. "How fascinating. Was it behind a painting?" I thought of the blackmail letter, demanding $60,000 in cash. I wondered if the blackmailer knew about the safe.

"As a matter of fact, it *was* behind a painting." said Beverly. "Someone even tried to break into it a couple years ago."

"Oh? I don't remember hearing about that." I glanced at Crenshaw, and he shook his head. He hadn't heard of it either.

"Edgar didn't want the publicity. Besides, the burglar wasn't successful," said Beverly. "They broke the lock on Edgar's office door, then apparently tried to pick the lock on the safe. When that didn't work, they made a mess of Edgar's desk searching for the combination. Ultimately, they gave up and left. Still, the building hired a twenty-four-hour security guard after the incident. Nothing like that ever happened again."

"So, about Edgar's will," I began.

"I already filed it with the clerk," said Crenshaw. "I did it as a favor for Beverly on Monday."

"How thoughtful," I said, trying not to make a face. *Brownnoser.* "But I was curious about Edgar's businesses. Is it true that Annabelle will take over the real estate company?"

"Annabelle? Heavens no," said Beverly. "She's only eighteen. Where did you hear that?"

"From Zeke, the IT guy."

Crenshaw scoffed. "Not a very reliable source."

We ate in silence for a few minutes, each absorbed in our own thoughts. I was still wondering about Allison. She was definitely upset about something. If it wasn't over who would take over the business as Zeke had said, then what?

The waiter came to refill our drinks. After he left I decided to try to steer the conversation back to the blackmail letters. Beverly had promised me she wouldn't destroy the letter I'd lifted from the mailroom, but she wouldn't let me take it, either. I looked around to make sure no one was close enough to hear, then lowered my voice and leaned in.

"Beverly, did you tell Crenshaw about the letter we opened last night?"

She put her fork down and gave me a warning look.

"What letter?" asked Crenshaw. "What do you mean 'last night'? Did I miss something?"

"I found another blackmail letter at Edgar's office," I explained. I told Crenshaw what the letter had said, then turned to Beverly. "Can you tell us more about the Cornerstone project? What is it that the blackmailer claimed to have over Edgar?"

Beverly sighed. "I honestly don't know. Edgar never told me the details. All I know is that it was going to be a self-financing development, which of course is valid and legal. The down payments from the first buyers would pay for the initial construction costs. There was also another source of funds, an investment company called American Castle Fund. That funder was going to cover the costs of getting the land ready, as well as some of the other initial outlays."

"American Castle Fund?" said Crenshaw. "I've never heard of it."

"I wasn't Edgar's financial advisor," Beverly said, somewhat defensively. "Perhaps Edgar didn't make the wisest choice in selecting it. The fund went belly-up when the market crashed. Around the same time, a lot of the real estate buyers backed out, and that was that."

"Any idea who the buyers were?" I asked. "Any local folks?"

Beverly thought for a minute. "I do remember when Edgar was courting investors. He held a lot of luncheon meetings around that time. There were definitely a few locals, including the chief of police—he was one of the first to back out. There were also a few local business owners."

"Was Lonnie Treat one of them? Of Treat Mattresses?"

Beverly nodded. "Now that you mention it, I do recall Edgar mentioning he had lunch with the mattress fellow."

"I saw him at the visitation," I said. "He told me he was business partners with Edgar. He must have been referring to Cornerstone. I wonder if he backed out, too, or if he ended up losing money on the deal."

Beverly gave me a stern look. "Now, don't go inventing motives. I'm telling you, if anyone held a grudge against Edgar, it was Fern Lopez."

"I know," I said. "I went to see her this morning."

"Who?" asked Crenshaw. "What are you talking about?" He clearly didn't like being left out. Beverly repeated to him what she had told me about Edgar's history with Fern.

"I can confirm the fact that Fern didn't like Edgar," I said. "She made no secret of that. But she also mentioned she was under a restraining order. So, I don't see how she could have been privy to any information that might be used to blackmail Edgar."

"As I said before, there was no information. It was all fabricated."

Crenshaw looked from Beverly to me and back again. "What do you propose we do?" he asked. I could tell he was torn between a desire to please the boss and his belief that this was all a wild goose chase.

"We do nothing," said Beverly.

"What?" I looked at Beverly in surprise. "I thought you agreed with me that Edgar's death is suspicious."

"I don't know what to think anymore," said Beverly. "Perhaps I was just trying to find someone to blame. I was trying to make sense of the senseless."

"Perfectly understandable," Crenshaw murmured.

"I think," Beverly continued, "the best thing now is simply to move on. Gretta is the executor of Edgar's estate. I'll see if she needs assistance. Perhaps she'll want to commission a memorial or have a building named after Edgar. I can help with that."

"I think that's a fine idea," said Crenshaw. I wanted to kick him under the table. Instead, I turned to Beverly once more.

"Beverly, extortion is still a crime. I think we should—"

"The point is moot," Beverly interrupted. "What we should do is let sleeping dogs lie." And she said it with a finality that left no room for argument.

* * *

After dinner, I left the restaurant and headed for home. It had been a frustrating evening. I had really hoped to get Beverly's blessing to share the blackmail note with the police. It seemed unlikely that would ever happen. Now I could only hope the police would be able to get more out of Bob than I had—such as the name of the person Edgar had been planning to meet.

I was so absorbed in my own thoughts and disappointment, I didn't notice anything wrong when I unlocked my front door. I flicked on the light and kicked off my boots in the foyer. It wasn't until I stepped into the living room and became aware of my surroundings that I froze in my tracks. My place was a wreck.

Someone had broken into my home and torn it apart.

Chapter 16

With my heart thudding in my chest, I backed out of my house and ran over to the St. Johns'. I pressed their doorbell, then punched 9-1-1 in my cell phone. Through chattering teeth, I gave my name and address and explained why I needed the police. I had just hung up when Mrs. St. John came to her door.

"Why, Keli! What are you doing over here without shoes?"

I looked down at my stocking feet. No wonder I was so cold. "Someone broke into my house, Mrs. St. John. Did you hear anything? See anything unusual?"

"Oh, my! Oh, dear. It must have happened while we were out. Otherwise, Chompy surely would have raised the roof. We took him for a drive and only just got back a little bit ago."

I glanced over at my front door. Whoever did this probably came and left through the back. Surely they were long gone by now. I was itching to get back in there and assess the damage.

"Come inside and have some cocoa," urged Mrs. St. John.

"Thanks, but I need to wait for the police."

"Well, at least let me get you some shoes."

While Mrs. St. John went in to find some shoes, I called Farrah and told her what had happened. She said she'd be right over. I was just slipping into Mrs. St. John's yellow rubber boots, when a police car pulled up. Two officers, a man and a woman, stepped out and met me on the sidewalk.

"You had a burglary?" asked the male officer.

I nodded. "Someone trashed my place. I don't know if they stole anything. I haven't looked yet."

"Wait here," said the female officer.

I fiddled with my purse strap and bit my lip as I waited for the officers to search my house. I wasn't worried the burglar might still be in there. I was sure he or she must have left before the St. Johns had returned home. I wasn't too worried about Drishti, either, expert hider that she was. No, I was worried about the state of my altar. I was queasy at the thought of some crook pawing through my magical tools and sacred objects. Or even *seeing* my Wiccan things. *God, what will the police think when they catch sight of my cauldron and witch's broom? My wand and chalice? My Book of Shadows?*

Finally, the female officer poked her head out and called me over. I tried to remain calm as she told me what they'd found. "The back door is busted in," she said. "It would've made quite a lot of noise, so I'm guessing the perp knew your neighbors weren't home."

The other officer came downstairs. "Could you do us a favor and check to see if any valuables are missing?

Your TV and computer are still here, and your silver candlesticks and decorations. If you could just check on any jewelry or money you might have had hidden away, we'll go ahead and write up the report. We'll need you to sign it."

I did as I was asked. Thankfully, nothing appeared to be missing, though I couldn't be one hundred percent sure. My house looked as if it had been shaken like a snow globe. It would take hours to sift through the debris.

Farrah arrived as the police officers were leaving. She had an overnight bag on one arm and a hunky guy on the other. "This is Trey," she said. "He's the handyman in my building. He agreed to take a look at your back door."

"Aw, thank you. That's awesome." It paid to have such a charming friend.

"Also, I'm staying the night," she said. "I knew you wouldn't want to leave with your place a mess, and it could be late by the time we get everything cleaned up. Plus, you said Wes is bartending tonight, right?"

"Yeah, I haven't even called him yet. He'll be too busy to take a phone call, and I don't want him to worry."

While Trey worked on my door, Farrah and I began to restore order, picking things up and putting them away. We started in my home office, which seemed to be the worst.

Farrah reached for a book splayed open on the floor, then hesitated. "Did the cops dust for prints?"

"No. They shone their flashlights at the back door and various surfaces to see if there might be any prints to lift. They said it looked to them like the intruder wore gloves. Figures, huh?"

"Hmm. Too bad." She slid the book in my bookcase, then snapped her fingers. "Ooh, we should watch out for clues while we clean. Like . . . pieces of cloth that might have ripped from the burglar's clothing, or footprints, or some piece of identification the crook might have dropped."

"Like his driver's license, maybe? That would be helpful."

Farrah made a face, and I smiled. The truth was, I hoped for a clue, too. I kept a sharp lookout as I retrieved items from the floor, one by one, like in a game of pickup sticks.

Working methodically, one room at a time, Farrah and I refiled papers, stacked magazines, and returned cushions, pillows, and blankets to their rightful places. When we reached my bedroom, Farrah froze at the sight of my altar. There, in the midst of the candles, bottles, and Solstice charms, sat Drishti, still as a statue.

"Who's this? Your guard cat?"

I walked over and gently stroked the top of Drishti's head. "Didn't I tell you? I'm a pet sitter now. This is Mila's cat."

"If only she could talk," said Farrah, as she looked around. "Hey, did you cast a protection spell in here? Is there, like, a force field around your altar?" Farrah's voice held a tinge of awe.

I laughed. "No, but I think I will now." I was grateful the police had made no comment about my Wiccan things. Some of my supplies were locked away in the cedar chest at the foot of my bed, and luckily the vandal hadn't broken into it. As for my craft tools out in the open, the police must have assumed they were just decorations. Either that, or they were professional enough not to care. I did find it interesting, though, that the vandal hadn't messed with my altar or knocked over my Yule tree. In fact, it didn't appear as if anything was broken or torn. Perhaps destruction wasn't the goal. The person just wanted to make a mess. *Or send a warning?*

By the time Farrah's handyman friend left and we had finished with the cleanup, it was almost 10:00. I told Farrah she could go to bed if she wanted, but I still needed to make cookies for my office holiday party.

"I'm not tired," she said. "Got enough ingredients to make a double batch? Then I can take some to Trey tomorrow."

"Great idea. In fact, we can make two kinds: date-nut and oatmeal chocolate chip. They're both vegan, gluten-free, and delicious."

While I set out the ingredients, Farrah wandered into the dining room to check out the tulips on the shelf. The vase of flowers was another item untouched by the burglar. "Want me to refresh the water in this vase?" asked Farrah. "It's looking a little cloudy."

"Sure, thanks."

"Wes really is a sweetheart, isn't he," said Farrah. "You guys are so cute together."

"He is," I agreed. "Those flowers weren't from him, though. Didn't I tell you?"

"Tell me what?"

I told Farrah about running into Mick at Edgar's holiday ball and the fact that he had admitted sending me the chocolates and tulips. "Mick also told me he had something that belonged to me. That's why I was going to see him that night when I, you know, found Edgar's body."

"What? You said you were at the hotel to pick something up. I thought it was something you'd forgotten at the party."

"No. Mick had called me later and asked me to come back to the hotel. I guess I forgot to mention it, because it didn't seem important anymore. Mick is ancient history. He was just in town to vet Edgar for his PAC. Now that Edgar is gone, I doubt I'll see Mick again anytime soon. Although . . ." I trailed off as I realized I didn't really believe what I was saying. My intuition told me I probably *would* see Mick again.

"What is it?" asked Farrah.

I shook my head. "I've been so preoccupied between work and worrying about Beverly. And thinking about Edgar's death. I told you I stopped at the hotel again yesterday, right?"

"Yeah. You found that note which you gave to the police. Was there something else?"

"Um, maybe." I told Farrah about calling Mick and then hearing a phone ring behind his hotel door.

"Are you kidding me?" said Farrah. "I can't believe I'm just now hearing about this! What if he didn't actually check out?"

"What do you mean? That wouldn't make sense. He said he was leaving the morning after the party. And there was caution tape blocking off the whole hallway."

"So? Maybe he lied. Maybe he's crazy . . . like a crazy, jealous stalker. He could be the one who ran you off the road! And broke into your house!" Farrah grabbed her phone. "How do you spell his last name?"

I told her, and she looked him up. "That was easy,"

she said. "He's all over social media. Looks pretty normal, actually. Not bad-looking, either."

"Well, that settles it," I said. "If you're cute, you can't be bad."

"Ha-ha," said Farrah. "I'm calling the hotel."

I went back to my cookie-making, while Farrah made the phone call. Unfortunately, her charm didn't work this time. The manager insisted it was against hotel policy to give out guest information. He wouldn't even confirm whether or not Mick had checked out.

Farrah joined me in the kitchen and washed her hands. "The hotel is probably being more discreet than usual because of the accident. They must be getting a lot of questions."

"No doubt," I said.

"Have you tried calling him again?"

I set down my mixing spoon and found my cell phone. I pulled up Mick's number and made the call. Again, there was no answer.

"You could send him a message online," Farrah suggested.

"Yeah, I don't really want to do that," I said, taking up my spoon again. "I have no interest in maintaining any connections with Mick MacIntyre, virtual or otherwise."

Lying in bed later that night, I tossed, turned, kicked off my covers, and then pulled them back on. I couldn't relax. It wasn't that I felt unsafe. I knew my doors and windows were secured, and Farrah was in the guest room. Plus, I had cast a protection spell around the whole house. Still, I couldn't seem to fall asleep.

I knew what it was. It was all the unanswered questions nagging at me like so much unfinished business. Why had someone broken into my house and not taken anything? For that matter, they hadn't left anything, either—no warning notes, no clues. No turquoise beads like I'd come across in other places. What was the point of breaking in?

I thought about the things that had been disturbed and the things that hadn't. Statues, lamps, and other items out in the open had been left alone, while anything with contents had been turned upside down. Drawers had been pulled out, boxes emptied, baskets overturned. Even my gym bag and spare purses had been rifled through. It was as if the person had been looking for something.

I sat up in bed as it hit me. The burglar thought I had something. Something small enough to fit into a purse. Or inside a book. Like something made of paper.

Perhaps something of Edgar's? It was no secret I had found Edgar's body. And several people knew about the paperwork audit I was doing at Edgar's office. Well, that Crenshaw and I were doing.

Crenshaw. I needed to warn him. If someone thought we'd found something during our audit, they'd want to search his place as well.

I fumbled for my phone on the nightstand and found Crenshaw's number in my list of contacts. He picked up on the first ring.

"You're working late, too, Milanni?"

I squinted at my alarm clock. It was after midnight. If Crenshaw was still on the clock at this late hour, there was no way I was making partner before him.

"Not exactly," I said. "I need to tell you something. Someone broke into my house tonight."

"Good Lord. Were you home? Are you all right?"

"I wasn't home. I think it happened while we were at Gigi's, after the visitation. My neighbors happened to be out at the same time."

"So, what was stolen? Did you have any client files at home?"

"That's just it. Nothing was stolen. I think the burglar was looking for something." I explained my theory and cautioned him to be alert.

"While I appreciate your concern for me," he said, "I'm not sure I agree with your conclusion."

"But it makes perfect sense."

"On the contrary," he said, "I think it's quite a leap. Now, don't take this the wrong way, but you do tend to have an active imagination."

Active imagination? He probably didn't mean it as an insult, but I couldn't help taking it that way.

"Very well," I said stiffly. "Don't say I didn't warn you."

Chapter 17

I arrived at the firm extra early on Thursday morning. Farrah had agreed to stick around at my house until Mila came by to pick up Drishti. I wanted to get in a couple hours of work before the office closed early for our annual holiday potluck.

I managed to make a few phone calls and draft a handful of letters, but then my mind wandered back to Edgar. Was his death related to the blackmail threat? My gut told me it was, but I had no way to prove it. If only I could figure out who Edgar had planned to meet in the hotel reading room.

Beverly wanted me to let the whole thing go. Crenshaw wanted me to let it go. At this point, even Wes wanted me to drop it—especially after I'd called him this morning and told him about the break-in at my place. But I couldn't help wondering: Did someone else want me to give it up, too?

I fingered my new crescent moon necklace, which took a place of prominence above my hidden pentagram, and silently asked the Goddess for guidance. *Should I let it go? What more can I even do?*

At that moment, I heard music coming from the lobby. I went out to investigate and found Julie hooking up speakers to her computer.

"Starting the party early?" I asked.

"I'm just creating a playlist," she said. "And I wanted to try out these speakers. I figured most people will be in either Beverly's lounge or the conference room, since that's where the food will be. I want to make sure we can hear the music everywhere."

"Ah. Good thinking." I turned to go back to my office, when the music started up again. It was Mariah Carey singing "All I Want for Christmas Is You." I'd always thought the song had a faintly sad undertone. It made me think of broken hearts and love lost. Of course, that was probably my own slanted interpretation based on how I was feeling at the time. That was worlds away from how I felt now.

For some reason, Edgar popped into my mind again. If he had really gone to see a lover the night he died, I could only imagine how that woman must be feeling now. I didn't condone cheating, but I felt sorry for her. She couldn't exactly be open about the depth of her grief.

Back in my office, I gazed out the window as another thought rose to the surface. Who was the most likely candidate for the role of "other woman"? The obvious choice was someone Edgar worked with. When Farrah and I were speculating at the Loose, she had immediately thought of Allison. It did make a lot of sense, now that I thought about it. Edgar and Allison certainly worked close together. And all the other women from

Edgar's office had left the ball with Tucker and Farrah. But not Allison. Then there was my impression that she had been upset with Edgar.

That's it, I decided. I would just have to go see Allison. I wanted to talk to her and find out what I could learn.

I grabbed my coat and purse and headed out the door. Then I stopped in my tracks. I needed a pretext for returning to Harrison Properties. I no longer had any involvement in the records audit. And I'd already conveyed my condolences and asked for Bob's phone number. What other reason could I possibly have for going to see Allison?

Then I had another idea. I didn't have to go there specifically to see Allison. I could go to see Zeke. He had been so friendly—he and I were practically best friends. I'd pop in and say hello to him. Maybe I'd even share some of the cookies I'd made for my own office holiday party.

With my excuse at the ready, I hurried down the block. A short time later, I stood before the front desk at Harrison Properties. I smiled at the receptionist and asked for Zeke.

"Sorry, Ms. Milanni, but he doesn't work here anymore."

My mouth fell open and I promptly shut it. I guessed he wasn't kidding about moving on. I just hadn't expected him to quit right before the holidays. *So much for us being buddy-buddy.*

"Is Allison available?" I asked.

"I'll check."

While the receptionist called Allison, I looked at the paintings in the lobby. I couldn't look at any painting now without thinking of the safe hidden in Edgar's private office. I had never seen a safe behind a painting in real life.

Allison entered the lobby. "What can I do for you, Keli?" *No hello? No invitation to come in and have coffee?*

Thinking fast, I circled back to my original excuse. "I was wondering if I could speak to you for a minute about Zeke."

Two tiny lines formed on Allison's smooth forehead. "What about him?"

"Um . . . could I take just a minute of your time? It's somewhat delicate."

Allison checked her watch. "I have five minutes," she said. Which really meant *I* could have five minutes.

I followed her to her office and took a seat in a comfortable wingback chair across from her large, mahogany desk. Who knew executive assistants made out so well? Or could the plush surroundings be indications of Edgar's fondness for her?

"Zeke quit yesterday," said Allison. "He said he didn't want to work here without Edgar. He felt there would be too much uncertainty. I can't say that I blame him—though, he had better not count on me to give him any glowing recommendations. It's unprofessional to quit without providing at least two weeks' notice."

"True," I said. "That wasn't very smart of him. Anyway, the thing I wanted to tell you . . . is that Edgar had some concerns about Zeke."

"Oh?"

I chose my words carefully. I wanted to be honest without divulging more than I should. As I well knew, the attorney-client privilege didn't die with the client. "When Edgar hired us for the audit, he expressed some qualms about going digital—as you mentioned the other day. He seemed to be afraid his records wouldn't be secure. And he thought that Zeke might have the ability to access information he wasn't authorized to access."

"Is that so?"

"Yes. So, with Edgar gone, I thought you should be aware. That is, I assumed you would be in charge of the company now?"

Allison nodded. "That's correct. At least for now. Gretta will inherit the business. Once the estate is settled, she can decide whether to keep it or sell it. And, if she does keep it, whether to make any changes. As for Zeke, I appreciate you telling me this. This might explain one of the last things Edgar said to me."

I raised my eyebrows. *Edgar's last words?*

Allison looked away. "It was at the ball, in the lounge. He was having yet another drink, and I tried to slow him down. He told me to relax, said he was celebrating. And I said, 'You haven't won yet. The campaign has barely begun.' He grinned at me and said that wasn't it. He said, 'I've figured something out. I figured out who's been messing with me, and now I can put an end to it.'" Allison looked at me again. "He must have meant Zeke."

It took me a moment to find my voice. "Could be," I said.

Allison stood up. "Well, thank you for informing me about Zeke. Edgar might or might not have been right to be suspicious. Now that Zeke is gone, it doesn't really matter. I've already changed all the passwords he knew."

It was obvious Allison was trying to end our meeting,

but I remained seated. "How is the new attorney working out?" I asked. "The other day you mentioned something about things not being in order for much longer."

"I just meant the records are in a state of disarray because of the transition from paper to digital. Sometimes you have to make a bigger mess in the process of cleaning one up."

I slowly stood up. "If you need any help cleaning out Edgar's office, or—"

"That's kind of you to offer," said Allison, as she opened the door wide. "But I have it under control. Edgar may have had an old-fashioned filing system, but I was well acquainted with his methods."

With that, she guided me out of the office much like she had given Lonnie the heave-ho the week before. I would have been miffed, but I knew I had no right. My time was up.

Back at the office, the mood was festive. Julie had put on her music and my colleagues milled about, evidently done working for the day. I brought out my cookies and arranged them on pretty plates in the private lounge outside Beverly's office. The lounge was more like a formal sitting room than anything else, complete with a fireplace, sofas, and an elegant wooden liquor cabinet. It was a nice space for small meetings and informal gatherings.

I was happy to see Beverly back in the office and in good spirits. She poured champagne, then called us all over for a toast.

"I have good news, everyone," she said. "Kris, Randall, and I had our year-end partner meeting this morning.

I'm pleased to report that we turned another tidy profit. Everyone will receive a nice bonus in their next paycheck."

"Here here!" said Pammy. "I already know what I'm going to spend it on."

Everyone laughed, applauded, and raised their glasses. Then the noise level rose, as people chatted over the music and loosened up with a few drinks. At one point, Crenshaw decided to sing along with the Christmas carols. When "White Christmas" came on, I swear he thought he was channeling Bing Crosby. He hit every note just right with his rich baritone. I almost wished I could hear him by himself, to get the full effect.

Just then, the music cut off. *Did I do that with my mind?* Crenshaw sang another bar on his own before he realized the room had fallen silent and all eyes were on the door.

Julie stood in the doorway. A police officer stood close behind her. And next to the officer was Detective Rhinehardt.

"Uh, Beverly?" said Julie.

"Yes," said Beverly, stepping forward.

"These men would like to see you."

"What's this all about?" Beverly demanded.

Julie moved aside to let the men in. The police officer removed his hat and Detective Rhinehardt flashed his badge. "Sorry to interrupt your party, ma'am. Do you mind if we ask you a few questions?"

"What kind of questions?"

"Questions about the death of Edgar Harrison."

Chapter 18

The color drained from Beverly's face as she confronted the officer and the detective. Still, she stood tall and kept her voice steady. "Now?" she hissed. "Does it have to be now?"

"Now would be best," said Rhinehardt, in his quiet, polite manner. "We could do it here, if you'd like. Or you can come down to the station with us."

Randall rushed to Beverly's side. "She doesn't have to go with you," he said.

Beverly put her hand on Randall's arm. "It's all right," she said. "I don't want to break up the party. I'll be back later."

"Beverly, that's not—"

"It's fine," said Beverly, raising her voice. "Really. I'll just get my coat and purse."

We all watched in stunned disbelief as Beverly retrieved her things from her inner office, then followed the cops out of the lounge. On her way out, I heard her say, "Julie, turn the music back on." A few seconds later, "White Christmas" resumed where it had left off.

At first, we all just looked at one another. Then everyone started talking at once. I jumped when someone grabbed my arm.

"May I have a word?" said Crenshaw sternly.

I followed him to his office. He closed the door behind us, then turned on me. "Well?" he said.

"Well, what?"

"You know what," he said. "Tell me. Why did the police take Beverly in for questioning? Why would they think she might have any information related to Edgar's death?"

"I have no idea. I mean, I did go see the police yesterday. All I said was that they should talk to Edgar's chauffeur, because he might know who Edgar had planned to meet that night."

Ohh. The lightbulb flashed in my mind. I dropped into Crenshaw's desk chair.

Tucker was right. Edgar and Beverly *were* having an affair. That had to be it. I suddenly recalled how rumpled she had looked when I saw her in the hotel lobby after the accident. And with no coat. *Of course.* She didn't come in from outside. She had come down from one of the hotel rooms upstairs. Bob must have known she was the one Edgar had planned to meet up with. That's why the police wanted to talk with her.

And it was all my fault.

I looked up at Crenshaw and winced. *Should I tell him?*

No. I had done enough blabbing lately. This was Beverly's secret. It was not mine to tell.

I stood up and brushed past Crenshaw.

"Keli?"

"Sorry, Crenshaw. There's something I have to do."

Back in my own office, I shut the door and took a deep breath. I did have to do something. The problem was, I didn't know *what* to do. I was certain Beverly didn't have anything to do with Edgar's death. She might have been in a hotel room waiting for him, but there was no way she had been with him when he fell. I had seen how shocked and heartbroken she was that night when she found out he was dead. If anything, she was a victim here, not a criminal.

Still, she had withheld information from the police. And if they were to determine that Edgar's death was not an accident after all, as I kept insisting . . . well, that didn't exactly bode very well for Beverly.

I wiped my hands over my face, then paced to the window. Gazing outside, I was almost surprised to see it was dark out. The rising moon's bright round form hung in the inky sky like a promise of things to come.

"What should I do?" I whispered to the sky.

I turned and looked around my small office. I took in my computer and desk, the small round conference table, the locked door. *I know what I need. I need guidance from the Goddess.* I needed her to speak to me. And the surest way of hearing the voice of the Goddess was to draw her down and let her speak through me.

But, here? I argued with myself. I had never performed a ritual in my office before. All my colleagues were just yards away, eating and drinking, singing and laughing. And Crenshaw? Who knew where he was now? But he had seen me enter my office. What if he knocked on my door to try to get me to talk to him again?

That was a chance I would just have to take.

With my decision made, I moved quickly. I cleared off the round table and dragged it away from the wall.

Then I cast about the small room for items I could use in my ritual. I needed something to represent each of the four elements. I looked at my desk and eyed my purple amethyst, a gift from Mila. Near that was a peppermint-scented soy candle I kept around for aromatherapy. Crystals came from the earth, and candles produced fire. Two down, two to go.

I placed the amethyst and candle on the table, then looked around for something to represent air. I had no feathers in here, nor any pictures of birds, butterflies, or fairies. I glanced at my computer. I could print out a picture, I thought, but that seemed like too much trouble. Instead, I grabbed a piece of paper and a pencil and sketched a picture of a dove in flight. *Not bad*, I thought, placing the drawing on the table.

Now, for water. I often had a bottle of water on my desk, or at least a mug of tea. Today there was nothing. *Why don't I have any water in here?* I thought, feeling suddenly parched. I might have drawn a picture of a raindrop, but my thirst only intensified. *Jeez, I can't believe this.*

With fingers crossed, I opened my door a crack and peeked out. The coast was clear. I ran out to the lobby and ducked behind Julie's desk. She always had a cooler full of water bottles for clients. As much as I hated to use plastic, desperate times called for desperate measures. I grabbed a bottle and dashed back to my office. Safely ensconced once again, I promptly drank three-quarters of the bottle, then poured the rest in my empty mug. I set it on the table with the other objects, then arranged them in their proper place: The bird, for air, sat in the east. The candle, which I lit for fire, sat in the south. The water sat in the west, and the crystal sat in the north. Finally, I removed my pentagram necklace and placed it in the center of the table.

I needed only one more thing. I opened the bottom drawer of my desk, pushed aside a box of teabags and a set of bamboo utensils until I found what I was looking for: two small packets of salt. I tore open the corner of one packet and poured the salt into my cupped palm. Then I rubbed my palms together and mimicked the act of washing my hands and face with the salt. Thus purified, I was ready to cast the circle.

I tore open the second salt packet. Beginning in the east, I walked around the table, sprinkling salt on the floor. *I draw this circle for protection and security. May no dark forces enter herein.*

I walked the circle a second time, this time using my hand as a wand. *I visualize the circle rising, as a ring of fire, to contain my magic herein.*

Lastly, I walked the circle a third time slowly, Zen-like, allowing myself to surrender to a calm, meditative state. *Calling on the spirits of air, fire, water, and earth . . . I open myself to receive the power that grows herein.*

I stood at the table where I could see the moon out the window and crossed my arms over my chest. I took three deep breaths, then began my invocation:

> Goddess of a thousand names,
> White as snow, with hair like flames
> You shine your light and lead the way
> You move us with your glorious ray
> Artemis, Diana, Luna, Selena
> Hecate, Psyche, Phoebe, Athena
> Come to me, join me, enter me now
> That we may be one, as you will allow.

I stepped my feet apart to shoulder width and raised my arms up and out. I stared at the moon, took a deep breath, then closed my eyes. My fingertips tingled as I felt a rush of energy flow through my fingers and arms, then down through my torso and on down to my legs and feet. My body hummed. I wouldn't have been surprised if I appeared to be glowing. The Goddess was inside me.

With a fullness of presence and utter self-confidence, I spoke the words I heard in my mind. They were beautiful, eloquent words, showering me like gentle raindrops on a summer's day, crystal clear, earthy, and strong. *I am one . . . I am the vessel, the spark, the breeze . . . You are one . . . You are the mountain, the lion, the trees . . . We are one . . . We are the answer, the hope, the key.*

As I repeated the words, I felt my energy rise, until the words ended with a familiar refrain: *That which you seek, you shall find within.* "If it harm none, do what you will."

I opened my eyes and lowered my arms. With an outpouring of gratitude, I closed the circle and returned my office to its former appearance. Now that I had worked magic here, I was sure it would never feel quite the same again.

Still buzzing with energy, I sat at my desk and performed a quick Internet search. A few minutes later, I put on my coat and grabbed my purse. I was invigorated and alert, my senses heightened like a comic book superhero's. I felt that I would be processing the experience for the next several days.

Quietly I opened my office door and headed down the hall. As I passed Crenshaw's office, his door flew open and he stepped out, obstructing my path. He must have been listening for me to come out, I realized.

"What were you doing in your office?" he demanded.

I smiled at him, unfazed. "Nothing."

He narrowed his eyes and peered closely at my face. "Were you doing *drugs* in there?"

"No. Don't be silly. I was just thinking." I patted Crenshaw's arm. "Now, if you'll excuse me, I have to see a man about a mattress."

Thanks to the Goddess Luna, I felt more clearheaded than I had in a long time. Colors seemed brighter, sounds were sharper, smells were more pungent. As I passed through the lobby, I caught a strong whiff of fried chicken. Someone must have brought a bucket to the party. I wrinkled my nose as I dashed to the exit. I was sorry to miss the office shindig, but not sorry to escape the building. The cold, crisp air felt refreshing on my still-flushed face.

As I walked to my car, I went over the insights I had received after performing the ritual. With perfect clarity, I had immediately realized my block when it came to Beverly. I saw why I had so stubbornly resisted accepting her as Edgar's mistress. For one thing, Beverly was an upstanding person. She wasn't the type to cheat with another woman's husband. Based on my respect and regard for my boss, I decided not to jump to any more conclusions or form any more opinions about the affair until I heard her side of the story.

But that wasn't all. The other thing that had been bothering me was the note I'd found. *Meet me in the reading room at 1 a.m.* Why would Edgar meet his paramour in the public reading room when he had a whole hotel full of bedrooms at his disposal?

He wouldn't. Beverly had to have been waiting for him in a private room.

Not only that but, from what Allison had told me, it sure sounded as if Edgar had figured out who was blackmailing him. That could mean only one thing. The person Edgar had intended to meet in the reading room was the blackmailer.

So, if he gave the blackmailer the note . . . and the blackmailer dropped the note in the reading room, then that meant Edgar actually *did* meet with the blackmailer.

And then he wound up dead.

I couldn't be certain, but it sure seemed as if my instincts were correct. Edgar's death was related to the blackmail attempt. Find the blackmailer, find the killer. It was the surest way to exonerate Beverly.

As the first order of business, I needed to know more about the basis of the blackmail threats. What information did the blackmailer have? All I knew was that it concerned Cornerstone. Before I'd left my office, I searched the Internet for anything I could find out about the failed development project. There wasn't much out there. I did find the location, however, as well as a permit application and storm water management plan on the city's website. One interesting tidbit I noticed was that part of the property encroached upon a protected wetland. Getting permission to build in that area would have been quite a feat, even if the financing hadn't fallen through.

Once I had exhausted all online avenues, I tapped my fingers on my desk. What I needed was the inside scoop. Who could tell me more about the project? The investors, that's who. Beverly had mentioned two buyers in particular. I wasn't exactly keen on questioning the chief of police at this point, so I decided to track down the other person she had mentioned by name: Lonnie Treat.

Treat Mattresses was located in a shopping plaza on a busy thoroughfare lined with strip malls and fast-food places. Although it was after dark, there were bright lights everywhere I looked as last-minute shoppers crowded the streets and filled the parking lots. I had to park a few doors down from the mattress place, in front of a coin laundromat and a tanning salon.

The moment I climbed out of my car, I heard someone call my name. I jerked my head around and quickly spied none other than the boy wonder himself, Zeke Marshal. He was standing by the open door of a tiny black-and-white Smart car.

"I thought that was you," he called, slamming his door shut. He walked up to me, wearing his usual sly grin.

"Are you following me?" I demanded.

"I know, right? We've got to stop meeting like this."

I stared at him, trying to get a read on his sincerity or lack thereof. After a second, he raised his eyebrows. "Are you serious? You think I'm following you? I got here first. In fact, I was just leaving. If anyone's following anyone, you're following me."

I narrowed my eyes, then relaxed my stance and forced a laugh. "I'm just kidding. Duh. So, what's new? Finishing up your holiday shopping?"

"Actually, I'm fundraising." He lifted his hand to show me the clipboard he was holding. "I work for

Tucker Brinkley now, and all his staffers have to pound the pavement. Would you like to make a donation?"

"You work for Tucker?" I said, ignoring his request for money. "Doing IT work?"

"Of course," he said. "That's what I do."

"So, if Tucker becomes mayor, will you join his team at City Hall? Or will you stay and work at his lodge, or hunting business, or whatever it is he does?"

Zeke laughed. "I'll go wherever I'm needed."

"I see." *How altruistic*, I thought, *especially for a guy who doesn't seem to have a loyal bone in his body.*

"Well, I gotta run. I've got two more strips to hit before calling it a day. Let me know if you change your mind about donating." He winked at me and turned to go.

"Hey, Zeke."

He turned back. "Yes, darlin'?"

"Did Lonnie Treat contribute to Tucker's campaign?"

A strange look came over Zeke's face. "You know Lonnie Treat?"

"Doesn't everyone? He's practically famous. He's on TV."

"Right. He's a real character. He said Tucker's a shoe-in and shouldn't need to raise any funds. But then he said to come back in a couple months, when it's closer to the election. If it seems like Tucker could use some help, Lonnie said he'd be more than happy to pitch in."

I shrugged. "Oh, well. Good luck."

Zeke took off and I proceeded to Treat's Mattresses. The minute I pushed open the glass door and entered the large, open store, I felt like I'd walked into a bright and shiny carnival of mattresses. Balloon bouquets and multicolor plastic pennant banners gave the place a festive air—but also added to the whole used-car-lot vibe. Everywhere I looked, there were mattresses, mattresses, and more mattresses, as well as signs advertising mattresses: BLOWOUT SALE! REDUCED PRICES! ZERO PERCENT DOWN! In the back of the room, a thirty-six-inch TV played Lonnie's homespun commercial on a loop: *"What a treat is a good night's sleep!"*

Oh, great. Now that jingle will be playing in my head all night.

I wandered down the center aisle until I spotted Lonnie emerge from a back room. He was wearing the same shabby brown suit he had on the first time I saw him. I walked up to him and stuck out my hand. "Hello, Mr. Treat. Keli Milanni. We met yesterday at the visitation for Edgar Harrison."

"Oh, yes," he said, pumping my hand. "I remember. You're one of the lawyers."

"That's right," I said agreeably. But inside, I felt a sudden twinge of doubt. I didn't recall telling him I was a lawyer. Then I mentally shook myself. *Stop being so paranoid.* I put on a sweet smile. "I just ran into a friend outside collecting donations for Tucker Brinkley's campaign. I remember you saying you predict he'll be our next mayor."

"No competition," he said. "No one even knows who the other candidates are. Let's see, there's a dentist, I think. And a schoolteacher. What else? A butcher, a baker, a candlestick maker?" He snorted at his own joke.

"Good point," I said. "I'm kind of curious about their platforms, though. I mean, Edgar was pretty different from Tucker, if you think about it. He was pro-development, while Tucker is pro-conservation. Take Cornerstone, for example. A project like that would have never seen the light of day under a Tucker Brinkley administration. Even if the financing were there."

I watched Lonnie carefully and was surprised when his expression turned smug. "You don't think so?" he asked. "Why not? Tucker is a smart businessman. He's not as opposed to progress as people might think."

"Oh. Well, in that case, do you think Cornerstone might get off the ground yet? Edgar's widow could pick up where he left off. Or she could sell the property."

Lonnie's eyes took on a wistful cast. "I doubt it. There's not enough wealth in this town. Too many buyers backed out the first time." He cocked his head then, and looked into my eyes. "So, what brings you here today?"

"Well . . . I was in the neighborhood and thought I'd pop in and see what these sales are all about."

"We have some great deals going on. To thin out the end-of-year surplus, you know. Make room for new inventory."

"I see. I thought the best sales usually happened after Christmas."

Lonnie stuck out his lower lip. "Mattresses are different. You're not usually gonna see a mattress with a great big red bow underneath a Christmas tree." He snorted again, then proceeded to rattle off all the features a person could ever possibly want in a new mattress. He talked about coils and springs, firmness and fabric and foam. I listened politely until he stopped at last and invited me to lie down on one of the display beds.

"Um, okay." I perched on the edge of the bed and

bounced a little. "Nice," I said, feeling like Goldilocks. "Not too hard, not too soft."

"Go ahead and lie down. Don't be shy. Take off your shoes and curl up like you would at home. Make yourself comfortable. I'll be right back."

He walked away, leaving me to stare after him. *Ugh.* Why hadn't I called Farrah before coming over here? I was going to have to see this ruse through. I slipped off my ankle boots and crawled up onto the king-size mattress. Feeling completely silly—and strangely vulnerable—I rested my head on the display pillow. Just as I settled in, I heard the click of a heavy lock from the front of the store. Then the lights flicked off, cloaking the store in darkness.

Chapter 19

I bolted upright. "Lonnie!" I called. "What's going on?"

For a split second, the only sound was the rapid pounding of my heart. Then a clinking of keys, and the lights flashed back on.

"Sorry about that," yelled Lonnie. "I was just putting up the 'closed' sign. Accidentally hit the light switch."

I scrambled off the bed, pulled on my boots, and grabbed my phone from my purse. I glanced at the time and saw that it was 6:50. It was still ten minutes till closing time. Why was he so eager to lock up?

He appeared before me again, jingling his keys as he walked. "You don't have to rush," he said. "Do you have any more questions for me?"

"I beg your pardon?"

"About the mattress. What did you think?"

"Oh. It was nice." I backed away from him and bumped into another display bed. "I need to think it over, though."

"You can't beat these prices." He drew closer to me, even as I backed away. "And it's a limited time only. You better decide fast before we sell out." He showed his teeth in an oily smile that didn't quite reach his eyes. We both knew these mattresses weren't going anywhere.

"I'll keep that in mind," I said. "I actually have to go now, though. My boyfriend is waiting for me." I turned and ran for the door. I tried to yank it open, but of course it was locked. I fumbled with the latch, my fingers refusing to cooperate. Lonnie came up behind me and grabbed my arm with his bony fingers. I yelped as I jumped back.

"Let me help you with that," he said, using his key to unlock the door. "I didn't realize you were in such a hurry."

"Yeah, sorry. Thanks for everything." I slipped past him and tossed off a quick, backward wave. I was sure he thought I was crazy. I didn't care. I just wanted out of there.

That's the last time I question a possible murder suspect by myself.

Once I was safely in my car, with the doors locked and the key in the ignition, I took three deep breaths. *What was that all about?* Had I overreacted? I didn't think so. Something about Lonnie Treat set off my warning bells. The guy gave me the creeps.

I kept my eyes on the front of the mattress store as I tried to get my nerves under control. I must have stared into the harshly lit windows for several seconds until my phone buzzed. It was a text from Farrah:

Want me to stay the night again? I have a date but can come over after.

I typed in my reply: No, I'm cool. Then I paused. Was I cool? The truth was, I felt pretty freaked out. Between the break-in the night before and Lonnie's weirdness, I didn't exactly feel like being alone.

My phone buzzed again. This time it was Wes: Office party over yet? I'm home for the night.

Smiling, I finished my message to Farrah: Heading to chez Wes. I pressed SEND, then texted Wes that I'd be there soon. Before I left the parking lot, there was one more person I wanted to hear from. I dialed Beverly's cell phone. She didn't pick up, so I tried her office number. Still no answer.

When I arrived at Wes's apartment ten minutes later, I tried Beverly again with no luck. After a glass of wine and a bite to eat, I tried yet again.

"That's it," I said, hanging my head. "She's avoiding me."

"Why would she do that?" asked Wes, as he cleared off the table.

"Oh, I don't know. Maybe because I sold her up the river?" Then I had a worse thought. *What if the police have arrested her?*

"I'm sure she doesn't think that," said Wes. He held the wine bottle in front of me and gave it a little shake. "Want any more?"

I waved away the bottle, then changed my mind. "Yeah. Just a little more. I'm going to call Crenshaw."

It was hard to say where Crenshaw would be at eight p.m. on the evening before Christmas Eve. Probably working. I tried his cell phone first.

"Ms. Milanni," he said, by way of greeting.

"Always so formal," I muttered. "Hey. So, is the party over? I was wondering if Beverly ever made it back."

Crenshaw hesitated. "Yes, and yes."

I breathed a sigh of relief. "How was she? Is everything okay?"

Another pause. Then I detected another voice in the background. A female voice.

"I'm sorry," I said. "Am I interrupting something?"

The background voice got louder. "Is that her? Is that Jessica Fletcher? Always poking her nose into other people's business. Well, you tell *Miss Marple* she can stick—"

I recognized the voice. It was Beverly, and she sounded three sheets to the wind.

"Keli," said Crenshaw, his deep voice cutting into my thoughts. "Now is not a good time."

"Why didn't you tell me you're with her?" I demanded. "Where are you?"

"We're at the office. Everyone else just left." He dropped his voice. "At the moment, Beverly is in the ladies' room. I've been trying to sober her up a bit before taking her home."

Yikes. "Did it go that badly at the police station?"

"I'm not really sure. From what I gather, Beverly harbors more worry about gossip and innuendo than any concern over being arrested."

"Did she say anything about Edgar? Or about her . . . relationship with him?"

"Wait a minute. Are you telling me you already knew? Did Beverly entrust you with a secret that you failed to keep? Is that why she's so upset with you?"

"No! She didn't tell me anything. I just put two and two together."

"Of course you did."

"Does everyone know now?"

"I don't think so. But the more she drank, the more she talked. I encouraged everyone to leave when she started using rather intimate terms of endearment for Edgar."

"Poor Beverly," I said. "She must have really loved Edgar. No wonder his death hit her so hard."

"Evidently so. Even now, she's more concerned about protecting his posthumous reputation than her own."

"Really? What exactly did she say?"

Crenshaw scoffed. "She said a great many things. I couldn't begin to repeat it all."

"Come on."

"Well . . . you know I don't normally deign to partake in petty gossip."

"Yes, yes, I know."

"But she did make one surprising revelation."

"She did?"

"Now, I'm sure she wouldn't want this repeated. She probably didn't even realize what she was saying."

"Crenshaw! Just tell me."

"Fine. She said that Edgar's marriage was a sham. She said Edgar and Gretta considered divorcing years ago, but decided to stay together for their children. As the children grew up, they found it was important to keep up appearances for political reasons. They were a powerhouse couple with a carefully crafted public image. Behind closed doors it was another story."

"Oh." I couldn't help thinking those sounded like typical words for "the other woman" to say.

"According to Beverly," Crenshaw went on, "Edgar and his wife led separate private lives. And Edgar wasn't the only one to indulge in extramarital relations. It would seem that Gretta had someone else, too."

I suddenly recalled my conversation with Bob the driver. He had mentioned Gretta's gardener and handyman, Ricardo. Bob had made it clear that Gretta wouldn't be alone at the ranch. Now it seemed that was even truer than I'd understood at the time.

"So, does this mean Gretta knew about Beverly?" I asked.

"I don't know," said Crenshaw. "It's possible."

"Hmm." I was still a little thrown by the thought of my boss having an affair with a married man. But if Edgar's was an open marriage, I supposed that made it somewhat better. I wondered if any part of this soap opera could have anything to do with Edgar's death. If Gretta had her own secret lover, she could hardly be a jealous wife, could she? Besides, considering she was confined to a wheelchair, there was no way she could have pushed Edgar over the balcony.

These thoughts brought me back to my overriding question: What really happened that night?

"Crenshaw, I'd like to talk to Beverly. Could you put her on the phone?"

"You're kidding, right?"

"No. I need to ask her something. Please."

"Keli, I'm afraid you're not her favorite person right now."

"I know. I just . . . Oh, never mind. I'll call her tomorrow."

"Good night, Keli."

"Crenshaw?"

"Yes?"

"Thank you for being there for Beverly. You're a good friend."

"Right. Good-bye."

I hung up and rubbed my forehead. *What a mess.*

"Everything okay, babe?" Wes called from his living room couch. "Come and sit with me. *It's a Wonderful Life* is about to come on."

I flopped down next to him. "I can't believe this is happening."

Wes muted the TV and looked at me with concern. "What is it?"

I shook my head. "I don't know. My boss is falling apart, and I seem to have made it worse."

"No way," said Wes. "You didn't do anything. You've only been trying to help her."

"I told the police Edgar was meeting someone at the hotel the night he died. They looked into it and found out he was meeting Beverly."

"Do you think she knows something about the accident?"

"No. We saw her that night, remember? She was as stunned and broken up as everyone else." I shook my head again. "Edgar met someone else that night. I'm sure of it."

Wes squeezed my hand and spoke gently. "Kel, why don't you leave the investigating to the police this time? This is not your problem to solve."

I looked into his worried eyes and softened my tense muscles. I leaned over and kissed him. "You're right. Let's watch the movie."

I pushed unmute on the remote and snuggled up next to Wes on the couch. Almost immediately, I started playing with my crescent moon necklace. As I did, my mind traveled back to my moon goddess ritual. As the memory returned, so did my earlier feeling of perfect clarity.

This is all tied to the blackmail scheme. And the blackmailer had mentioned the Cornerstone development. But what about Cornerstone could lead to extortion? The project had failed. It never happened. It wasn't like Edgar got away with anything. He couldn't have cut any corners with the siting or construction or anything. What secret about the project could be worth $60,000? That was *a lot* of money.

Money. That was the key. People lost money on the deal. *Follow the money.*

The movie went to a commercial, and Wes stood up to close his window shades.

"Hey, can I borrow your laptop?" I asked. "I want to look up something."

"Have at it," he said.

With Wes's laptop on my knees, I spent the rest of the movie scouring the Internet. I reread everything I had already found out about Cornerstone. Then I remembered the investment company Beverly had mentioned the other night at dinner. It was a firm neither Crenshaw nor I had ever heard of: American Castle Fund. I searched all publicly available information about the fund—which, as it turned out, wasn't much.

As I learned, American Castle Fund, LLC, was a subsidiary of another company called AC Investmore, LLC. And AC Investmore was registered in Delaware as an anonymous corporation. The only contact information was a third-party registered agent service company.

Even stranger was the absence of any information about either company's past activities. It appeared that the only function of AC Investmore was to serve as the parent company for American Castle Fund. But what about the child company? Although American Castle Fund was now dissolved, it had been around for a number of years before its involvement with Cornerstone. However, when I tried to find information about the fund's past performance, I kept coming up empty-handed.

This is odd, I thought. The company had a long history of corporate filings, but no actual business activity. I also couldn't find any information about the company's officers, personnel, or investment portfolio. I kept digging, determined to get some answers. At last, my persistence paid off.

"Aha," I said.

Wes muted the TV again. "Found what you were looking for?"

"Sort of. I found the precursor to American Castle Fund. Its name was changed from ABC Value Co., which I found on an old list of aged shelf corporations for sale."

Wes stared at me. "Am I supposed to understand what that means?"

"Sorry. A shelf company is a preestablished corporate entity that's set up as a sort of holding place. It's a company 'on the shelf,' so to speak. A person who wants to start a business can buy a ready-made, pre-filed corporation so it looks like they've been in business for a long time."

"Is that legal?"

"Yeah. It sounds a little shady, but it's not illegal. It saves time for new business owners and supposedly enhances their credibility. They can change the name of the shelf company to suit their new business, and it will still look like they've had years of filing history."

"Is this related to Edgar somehow?"

"In a way. Part of the financing for the Cornerstone project was supposed to come from this fund that went belly-up. It seems really strange to me that a smart businessman like Edgar would have relied on an unproven investor like this." I yawned. "I don't know what it all means. Maybe nothing. I'll look into it more tomorrow."

We turned back to the TV in time to see the final bell ring, indicating that the angel got his wings. I had to laugh. "I really do love this movie, in spite of being on the computer through the whole thing. That was really rude of me. I'm sorry."

Wes made a face. "Please. No apologies necessary. I've seen this movie a million times. I'm just happy being with you." He pushed up from the couch and went into the kitchen. I set the laptop aside and followed him. I leaned against the counter and watched as he unloaded the dishwasher.

"I know what I'll do," I said. "I'll ask Crenshaw to speak with his contact who specializes in business law. Maybe he can help me 'pierce the corporate veil' and find out who was responsible for American Castle Fund."

Wes dried his hands on a towel and looked at me in the dim light of the kitchen. "You never cease to amaze me," he said.

"In a good way?"

He grinned and took me in his arms.

"In a very good way. I still don't know how I managed to land such a smart, beautiful woman. You're way out of my league, you know."

I could tell he was teasing by the glint in his eyes, but I still felt a warm flush. The truth was, I always felt like I was the lucky one. Biting back a smile, I matched his light tone. "'Landed,' huh? That has such a ring of finality to it."

"You know what I mean. 'Landed,' 'caught,' 'scored.'" He grimaced. "Ooh, those all sound bad."

I laughed, and he pulled me in closer.

"Actually, it's really the other way around," he said. "You're the one who captured my heart."

Aww. I pecked him on the lips and felt my heart speed up. *This is it.* It was the perfect time to bring up our future together.

A loud buzzing from the dining room interrupted the moment. It was coming from my phone, which I had left on the table.

Wes smirked good-naturedly. "Smart, beautiful, and popular. I shouldn't be surprised."

"It's probably just Farrah," I said. "But I should probably—"

"Go ahead," he said, releasing me from his hold.

"Don't go away," I said, heading for the table. "This will just take a second."

I opened the text message, and then dropped into the nearest chair when I read it. It was from Mick:

Hey Princess. Are you gonna be home soon?
I'm at your house waiting for you.

Chapter 20

"What's wrong, Keli?"

Wes joined me in the dining room and put his hand on my shoulder. I just shook my head. There was so much wrong, I didn't know where to begin. I handed him my cell phone.

"'Princess'? Are your parents in town? Whose number is this?"

I swallowed hard. "It's from Mick. I have no idea why he thinks it's okay to call me that. I didn't like it when we dated in college, and I certainly don't like it now."

"Mick? That guy from the hotel bar? He's at your house?" Wes's voice escalated with every word.

"This is so weird. I didn't even know he was in town." It had been two days since I'd called Mick and heard his phone ring behind the door of his hotel room. Maybe he had just come back to town to retrieve his phone. That had to be it.

"Why would he just show up at your house? Especially at this hour? It's after ten o'clock."

"He's kind of an impulsive guy. At least, he used to be. I really don't know him anymore."

"Let me call him. I'll tell him to bug off and leave you alone."

"No, don't do that. I mean, I do want him to leave me alone. Just not yet. I have a couple questions for him." I stared at my phone, my fingers hovering over the keypad. The problem was, I didn't know how to answer *his* question. I wasn't going home tonight, but I wasn't sure I wanted him to know that. My home had already been broken into once. Not that I thought that Mick was the housebreaker. Not really.

"Why do you want to talk to him?" asked Wes. "He might get the wrong idea. False hope, you know?"

I mustered up a reassuring smile. "Don't worry. I'll make sure he doesn't get the wrong idea. I'll keep it brief."

I decided a short text was the way to go, so I dashed off my reply: Tonight isn't good. Tomorrow?

Two seconds later, my phone rang.

"Oh, come on!" said Wes. "Let me talk to him."

I stood up and moved toward the small foyer. "It's okay," I said to Wes. "Trust me."

"Hello, Mick," I said into the phone. "This is unexpected. When did you get back to town?"

"Surprise!" he said. "It's a long story. I'm staying out at Stag Creek Lodge. If I can't see you tonight, you'll have to go out there to see me tomorrow."

"The other day you mentioned you have something of mine. Did you happen to bring it?"

"Maybe I did and maybe I didn't."

I took a deep breath. *He's just trying to be cute*, I told

myself. *He has no idea he's grating on my last nerve.* "Come on, Mick. At least tell me what it is."

"All right. That's fair. It's a book. Now, will you come by tomorrow evening? And wear something pretty. Tucker Brinkley is throwing a holiday bash for all his guests."

A book. Aunt Josephine's book.

"How about tomorrow morning?" I said.

"No can do. I have meetings all morning. Wanna do lunch?"

"I can meet you after lunch. One o'clock?"

"Fine. It's a date."

I closed my eyes. *It's not a date, you nincompoop.* Out loud, I simply said, "See you tomorrow, Mick."

"Looking forward to it, princess."

I hung up and turned around to find Wes standing in the doorway to the living room. His fists were clenched. "You're really going to meet this turkey?" he asked. "I don't have a good feeling about this."

"Wes, I think he has my aunt Josephine's book. It would mean so much for me to have it back."

"I know. I just wish I could go with you. I have to cover the Christmas parade and Santa house tomorrow."

"I'll get Farrah to go with me. Don't worry. It will be fine."

As I dialed Farrah's number, I sincerely hoped my words would prove true.

The next morning, I kissed Wes good-bye and returned to my house. It was going to be a busy day. I had to pack for my trip to Nebraska, make a dish to bring to Wes's parents' house, and meet up with Farrah for our trek out to Stag Creek Lodge. As I walked up the sidewalk to my front porch, I glanced at the overcast sky and felt a twinge of apprehension. The gray clouds appeared awfully heavy. I hoped my flight wouldn't be delayed that night. The last thing I wanted to do was spend the night before Christmas at the airport.

Up in my bedroom, I pulled out my suitcase and took a quick inventory of my closet. It didn't take long to discover that my favorite jeans were at the bottom of the dirty clothes pile. *It figures*. I filled a basket and started a load of laundry, then went to the kitchen and cleared off a work space. For the next twenty minutes, I washed, peeled, and chopped. Finally, I tossed the colorful medley in a big bowl with a drizzle of olive oil and dried herbs, and stuck it in the fridge. I would roast the veggies in Darlene's oven later.

Now to take care of myself. I hopped in the shower, idly wondering what I should wear for my non-date with Mick. *Oh, it so doesn't matter*, I told myself as I rinsed and shut off the water. As I reached for a towel, I became aware of a ringing sound. I froze and listened carefully. There it was again. My doorbell. *Crap*.

With one towel around my body and one around my hair, I slipped into my bedroom to check my phone. No missed messages. I was supposed to pick up Farrah at her house, so it wouldn't be her on my doorstep. And Wes was at work. Who else would just drop by without calling first?

Mrs. St. John. Mick MacIntyre. A burglar/blackmailer/ murderer.

I had half a mind to ignore the uninvited caller when the bell rang again—rapidly, three times in a row.

Ugh. I pulled on a robe and hurried downstairs.

"Who is it?" I yelled.

"Crenshaw," came the loud, booming answer.

I threw my door open and gaped at him. "Why didn't you call before coming over?"

He stared right back at me, as if he'd forgotten where he was, before sputtering, "Why—what—because I was already here!"

"Well, come on in. You're letting in the cold air."

Crenshaw stood awkwardly in my front hall as I closed the door behind him. When I faced him, his eyes roved everywhere but at me. I tightened my robe. "What's the emergency, Crenshaw? I assume it's important. You've never come to my house before."

"It *is* important," he said, finally looking at me. "But, it can wait while you get dressed."

I sighed. "Okay. Have a seat." I ran upstairs and returned three minutes later with my wet hair brushed back and my robe replaced by a long gray sweater over black leggings.

"Break it to me gently," I said, sitting on the couch next to him. "Is it Beverly? What's happened?"

He cleared his throat and twisted to look at me. "Um," he began, "it would seem that I owe you an apology."

"Oh?" This was a first.

"I take it you haven't seen the news recently?"

"No, not in the past hour or two. Why?"

"Well, you see, the Edindale Police Department made an interesting announcement this morning. They are now treating Edgar's death as a murder investigation."

I fell back against the couch cushions. *I knew it*. I knew it in my bones, knew it all along. But to hear it now was still jarring.

"If you want to say 'I told you so . . .'" Crenshaw trailed off.

I gave him an arch look. "Please. That's not my style. So, what else did they say? Was there a press conference?"

"There was a brief interview with the police chief. He said forensic evidence suggests there was a struggle before Edgar fell. Also, incredibly, someone has come forward to say they overheard yelling in the hall outside their hotel room. This was shortly after one a.m."

"Yelling?"

"As in an argument, though the witness couldn't identify the speakers. Apparently, only one of the voices—a man's voice—was loud." Crenshaw pursed his lips. "Lord only knows why this person didn't come forward sooner."

"Yeah," I said, as the news sank in. "This witness, was it Beverly? Was she the one who heard the argument?"

Crenshaw shook his head. "I highly doubt it. In fact, she's afraid it's only a matter of time before a warrant is issued for her arrest."

"Oh, no," I groaned. "Did she say that last night when she was drunk?"

"No. This morning. I called her after I heard the news. She informed me that the detective on the case has tried to reach her several times today. She plans to 'lie low,' as it were, for the time being."

"Hang on." I jumped up to retrieve my phone. "If she spoke to you, maybe she'll speak to me." I dialed her number. Just when I thought it would go to voicemail, she picked up.

"Keli," she said.

I spoke quickly. "Beverly, first of all, I am so sorry for what you're going through. Secondly, I did not tell the police *anything* about you or Edgar or our assignment. I never intended—"

"Keli," she interrupted, "what's done is done. Is there anything else you have to say?"

I cringed. "Just that I want to help. And I might be onto something. But I have to ask you one question. Did you see Edgar that night after the ball? Did he say anything revealing? Do you know who else he planned to meet besides you?"

"That's three questions," said Beverly.

"I know." I crossed my fingers and waited for her to make up her mind about how to answer. After a few seconds, I heard her sigh.

"I am seriously considering pleading the Fifth on this," she said. "However, I—I could really use some help. I can trust you, right?"

"Of course!"

"Fine. Yes, I saw Edgar. It was around twelve-thirty, I think. He came to my hotel room, Room 408, on the opposite side of the floor from where he . . . fell. We had a drink, and we talked. And Edgar told me he needed to tell me something very important."

"He did? Was it about the blackmailer?"

Beverly laughed without humor. "No. It was of a more personal nature. He told me he wanted to end our relationship. After seven years, he had decided to try to win his wife back."

"Oh, Beverly," I whispered. "I'm sorry."

"We talked for a little while. At first, I didn't believe he was serious. But he was adamant. Then he said he had to take care of something and would come back. When he left, I had another drink, or two, and then . . . I blacked out. I didn't wake up until I heard people screaming and running outside my door. By that time he was gone."

For a moment, I didn't know what to say. Beverly's position was even worse than I had thought. "I'm sorry," I murmured for the second time.

"So am I. On top of everything else, it would seem that I'm the only suspect the police have."

"Beverly, about our duty of confidentiality to Edgar, don't you think this situation fits an exception? If only the police knew about the blackmail threats."

"Not yet," she said. "Didn't you say you were onto something?"

"Possibly," I hedged. "But, I'm missing some key pieces of the puzzle."

"Well, see what you can do. I'm hoping Rhinehardt will leave me be until after Christmas."

"You mean the day after tomorrow?"

"Right. Well, if anyone can uncover the truth in that amount of time, I'm sure you can."

With that note of confidence, Beverly told me good-bye and good luck. I turned to Crenshaw and relayed all she had said. When I told him that Beverly had been jilted, and then blacked out, right before Edgar was found dead, Crenshaw's eyes bulged.

"Good Lord! You don't think she actually—?"

"No! Absolutely not," I said. "There was someone else. Edgar confronted the blackmailer that night. I'm sure of it."

Straightening to his full height, Crenshaw set his jaw. "What can I do to help?"

After Crenshaw left, I paced my living room like a caged tiger. Someone had gotten away with murder, and now it seemed that Beverly, already brokenhearted and miserable, would face the blame. It was so unfair. I wanted to help her—had led her to believe I could help. But what could I do? All I had by way of leads were a couple of shifty-acting people who might have had something against Edgar. Oh, and some unknown stalker who might have something against *me*.

I had asked Crenshaw to explore the investment side of the Cornerstone project and see what he could dig up on American Castle Fund. He vowed to leave no stone unturned. I believed him, though I didn't know how much luck he'd have getting people to talk to him the day before Christmas.

And what about me? I had told Crenshaw I had an appointment at Stag Creek Lodge this afternoon, which is not far from Edgar's ranch. If I had time, I would stop by to see Edgar's widow. I had avoided bothering her the past few days, because I didn't want to seem insensitive to her grief. Besides, I really didn't think she had anything to do with the blackmail scheme. However, the stakes were higher now. Plus, I was out of ideas and running out of time. I would be leaving town in less than twelve hours.

I looked out my living room window at the gloomy sky. I hated the thought of being away during Beverly's arrest. That is, *if* she was going to be arrested. I still found it hard to believe Rhinehardt would actually do that. I wished I knew what he was planning. If only I could see into the future.

Wait. What was I saying? I *could* see into the future. Or at least see a hint of what was to come. I had dozens of divination tools at my disposal: tarot cards, runes, I Ching coins, tea leaves. As I had mentioned to Mila, I communicated with the Divine best through visual means. Of course, one of the clearest methods of seeing the future was to gaze into a crystal ball. I didn't have one of those, but I did have something close. I could use my scrying bowl.

I ran up to my room and opened the chest at the foot of my bed. I shifted aside my spell books and seasonal altar cloths and pulled out a black metal bowl. After closing my curtains to darken the room, I filled the bowl halfway with water from the bathroom tap, then set it in the center of my altar. Next, I added three drops of sandalwood oil and placed a quartz rock crystal in the bottom of the bowl. I stood before the bowl taking slow, purposeful breaths to ground and center my being. Finally, waving my hands above the bowl like a magician—because the motion helped put me in a magical frame of mind and was also fun—I uttered a spontaneous spell:

> Mother Goddess, by your grace,
> Show the truth that I might face
> Grant to me the gift of sight
> So I can help to make things right

I stared into the bowl of water and waited. And waited some more. I saw nothing but water.

Taking a deep breath, I lifted my hands and tried again. This time, I said:

> Oh Great Goddess, Divine oracle,
> I beseech you for a miracle.
> To serve justice and do what's right
> Guide me to the path of light

Once again, I peered deeply into my scrying bowl . . . and saw nothing but water. I kept at it, as patiently as possible, until finally the edges began to blur. I still saw water, but it was different. I seemed to be seeing it from a distance. Now the water appeared to be frozen. And it was surrounded by land: a snowy field, trees, and . . . a parking lot.

What is this place?

As soon as I thought the question, the answer popped into my head: Ryker's Pond. The drop-off location mentioned in the blackmail note.

I blinked and the image disappeared. Bowing before the bowl, I thanked the Goddess and promised to follow her lead.

I wasn't sure what it meant, but I intended to find out.

Chapter 21

Ryker's Pond was one of several natural water bodies in Pine Bluffs State Park, about fifteen miles outside Edindale. Easily accessible by car, it was a popular spot for fishing and picnicking in the spring and summer months. Now, as I drove slowly along the one-lane road that bordered the pond, I was struck by how peaceful it was. There wasn't a soul in sight.

Using the compass on my phone, I made my way to the northwest side of the pond and pulled into the empty parking lot. I sat in my car for a minute and looked around. The scene was remarkably similar to the vision in my scrying bowl. And just as stark. Between the gray of the pavement, the gray of the sky, and the bare trees set against the snow-packed ground, I felt like I had dropped into the middle of a black-and-white movie. Maybe an early Hitchcock film, I thought, as I stepped out of my car and walked over to the lone trash bin at the edge of the picnic area.

The extortion letter I'd lifted from the mailroom at Harrison Properties had directed Edgar to leave the money here. I couldn't imagine how coming here now was going to do any good, but I trusted the Goddess. It was pure curiosity that made me lift the lid on the trash bin.

As I expected, it was pretty much empty. There had been no campers, hikers, or fishermen out this way all season. The only thing in the can was a folded-up newspaper at the bottom. To confirm my hunch that the place hadn't seen visitors in months, I grabbed the paper to check the date. The moment I moved the paper, I saw what was hidden underneath: a fat brown envelope.

No way.

I stared into the bottom of the trash bin trying to make sense of what I was seeing. I glanced at the top of the newspaper and honed in on the date: December twenty-third. Someone had been here yesterday. Or earlier today.

With a quick look over my shoulder, I reached inside and grabbed the envelope. It was sealed shut with clear packing tape. Based on its shape and bulk, I was pretty sure I knew what the envelope contained. Still, I had to see it for myself. I tore off the tape and looked inside. *Yep.* Just as I thought. Cash. In one hundred dollar bills, it was easily several thousand dollars' worth.

Holding the package in my hands, I suddenly began to shake. What did this mean? Who left the money here? Edgar couldn't have done it. The letter I saw demanded the money to be left by 5 a.m. on December twenty-first. Edgar was killed in the wee hours of December nineteenth. Surely the money wasn't sitting in the bin all that time. Impossible. Besides, Edgar never received the letter. It was unopened in the mail room.

Of course, there had been other letters before the one

I found. Beverly had said Edgar destroyed them. I wondered if any of those letters had mentioned the drop-off location. Could someone else have found one of those letters and decided to proceed with the payoff?

That didn't make sense. Based on the date of the newspaper, this money was left a couple of days after the deadline in the letter. So, that must mean . . . someone else was being blackmailed?

I stared down the quiet road and fretted over what to do. My instinct was to take the money directly to the police station. Let Rhinehardt figure it all out. He could send some cops out here to watch the bin.

But then I thought about the possible consequences of this move. What if the blackmailer came to retrieve the money and it wasn't there? The blackmailer would think the person who had left this money didn't pay up. Wouldn't that expose the person to having their secret revealed? Or, worse, would they end up like Edgar?

I was jarred from my paralysis by the rumble of an engine. There was a car on the other side of the pond, heading my way. I tossed the package back in the bin and dropped the newspaper on top. Then I ran to my car and peeled out.

By the time I arrived at Farrah's house, I was so frazzled I could hardly put two words together. She took one look at me and put her hands her hips. "Spill it."

I proceeded directly to her living room and sprawled out on her sofa as if it were a psychiatrist's couch. "Give me a minute," I said.

She sat down on the coffee table and looked at me with concern.

"Okay," I said finally. "Here's the deal. You're an attorney. In that capacity, I am officially bringing you on as a researcher for a client matter my firm is working on. Got it?"

"Uh, no. What are you talking about?"

I sat up and looked her in the eye. "I'm bringing you into the fold, so I can share some confidential information with you. You'll be bound by the attorney-client privilege."

"Ah. Now I get it. And Edgar is the client?"

"Exactly."

For the next several minutes I brought Farrah up to speed about the secret reason Edgar had hired us for the legal audit. I felt immensely better afterward.

Farrah clasped her hands together. "So, if we can figure out who the blackmailer is, we'll have solved Edgar's murder." She was a quick study.

"That's my assumption," I said. "And I might have just blown my opportunity to meet the blackmailer face-to-face." I told her about my experience at Ryker's Pond.

"Jeez, are you a *magnet*, or what? Your timing these days is uncanny."

"Well, I may have been led there by a little magical tip-off."

Farrah shook her head in wonder. "Crazy," she murmured. "And scary. I think you did the right thing by fleeing the scene."

"Yeah, but what do I do now? I'm not sure how going to the pond helped me."

"Are you kidding? It looks to me like you're about to

crack this case wide open. I think you also learned something about the blackmailer."

"What did I learn?"

"The creep isn't very smart. I mean, who tells somebody to leave sixty thousand dollars in a trash can? Edgar could've staked out that park and caught the blackmailer red-handed."

"True. But then the blackmailer might've spilled his secret. Maybe anonymity wasn't as important to the blackmailer as getting the money."

"Hmm, maybe." Farrah rubbed her palms together and stared into space. "I wonder who the blackmailer is. How about that IT kid? He could have hacked into Edgar's private computer files."

"He probably could have," I agreed. "But it could just as easily have been Edgar's assistant, Allison Mandrake. She also had access to Edgar's files."

"Oh! How about that Fern Lopez woman? She was snooping around, trying to bug his office at the hotel, right? She might have found some incriminating information. I guess that was a few years ago, but she could have been saving the info for the most opportune moment—such as Edgar's candidacy for mayor."

"Yeah, possibly. But remember, we're also looking for someone strong enough to push Edgar over the fourth-floor railing."

Farrah grimaced. "Ugh. What a horrible thought. But you're right. I'm not sure if Fern could've done it. However, if Edgar was as drunk as all that, and she caught him off guard . . . that might be a different story."

I stood up and checked the time. "I need to think about this some more. Now, though, we need to head out to the lodge. I've got to carry out this non-date with my ex-boyfriend."

Stag Creek Lodge was a year-round destination for outdoor enthusiasts of all stripes. Day-trippers could enjoy the scenery and the trails, while overnight guests had the benefit of a nice restaurant and comfortable amenities in the rustic inn. One of the most photographed indoor locations at the lodge was the large central common area. It was decorated like the living room of a luxury log cabin, complete with massive stone fireplace and all the obligatory stuffed animal heads.

When Farrah and I arrived, she took off to go find Tucker. I entered the common room and spotted Mick waiting for me on a love seat next to the fireplace. As I walked up to him, I did my best to avoid the glassy stare of the boar's head mounted on the wall behind him. I must have flinched, because Mick let out a hearty laugh.

"You always did hate hunting, didn't you? Are you still a vegetarian?"

"Yep. Still a vegan. So, do you have my book?"

Mick's face fell. "What's your hurry? I thought we could catch up a bit. I mean, c'mon, we were so close back in the day. I have no idea how we lost touch like we did. I feel bad about that. I—I've missed you." He clasped his hands on his knees and flexed his fingers in a nervous gesture. I had the sense that he'd just blurted something he hadn't intended to reveal so early in the conversation. I couldn't help feeling a teensy little tug on my heartstrings.

"I'm sorry," I said. "It's just that I don't have a lot of

time. I'm having dinner with my boyfriend's family tonight, and then I have a late-night flight to Omaha."

"Tonight? It's only one o'clock now. You have plenty of time. Can't you spare a few minutes for your old Micky Bear?" He peered at me from beneath his long eyelashes and gave me a small, hopeful smile.

Oh, God. What was he up to? In spite of my reservations, I returned his smile. "Of course," I said. "I can spare a few minutes." I dragged a chair over and sat down across from him. "So . . . you're back in town. Is your PAC vetting Tucker now?"

"Mm-hmm."

"I'm surprised Edindale was even on your radar. Wouldn't the mayor of a bigger city be more influential?"

"This is a progressive college town, a county seat, and a popular vacation spot. The current Edindale mayor was tapped for a position in the governor's cabinet, so this position could be seen as a stepping-stone." Mick shrugged. "Besides, I'm the boss. I get to decide who we consider. The committee will make the final vote."

"So, it wasn't so much Edgar Harrison personally, as it was the position itself?" I was still confused about why a national PAC would be so interested in Edindale's political scene.

Mick hesitated. "No. It was Edgar more than anything. But after Edgar's untimely death, I decided to check out Tucker Brinkley. Also . . . I like this town. I was glad for an excuse to come back."

"I see." I had a feeling he wasn't being entirely truthful. And what about his cell phone? If he'd forgotten it, why didn't he just say so? I decided to press him.

"Wasn't that kind of a hassle to go all the way back to DC, then turn around and fly back here a few days later?"

"I fly all the time. It's not a big deal." He raised his hand as if to halt my interrogation. "Hey, I have a question for you. Do you remember that time we went for a walk on campus and snuck inside the old gymnasium? We made a game of trying out every single piece of equipment."

"Uh, yeah. I guess so."

"We were both so sore the next day we couldn't move." Mick laughed. "I still think about that every time I work out."

Every time he works out? For the past ten years?

"So, Mick, just out of curiosity, are you seeing anyone, or—"

"Nope," he interrupted. "I'm completely available."

"What I mean is, since college, hasn't there been anyone special in your life? Anyone you considered a serious girlfriend?"

"Oh, sure. I've had plenty of girlfriends. But none have been as sweet and special as you."

That does it. I couldn't let this go any further.

"I'm sure you'll find someone," I said, "that is, if you're looking. I know I feel really lucky that I found Wes. I'm in love with him, and we're really happy. I wish that for you, too."

Mick closed his eyes and sat back in his seat. I waited for him to say something. Finally, he opened his eyes and spoke softly. "I'm glad you're happy. I was just wondering . . . do you ever think about me? Wait. Don't answer that. I—" His voice hitched.

Good grief, were those tears in his eyes?

He took a breath and seemed to pull himself together. "I'm sorry. I've just been doing so much thinking lately, you know? I realized I made a huge mistake in letting you go. Probably the biggest mistake of my life."

"Oh, don't say that! We went our separate ways, that's all. Don't romanticize the past." Looking into Mick's sad eyes, it finally hit me. All that business about supporting local politicians was just an excuse. "Did you really come to Edindale just to see me?"

"Maybe. Sort of," he said, looking down at his hands. "It's true I was considering Edgar for my PAC. But you being here might have factored into my decision. Then, when I saw you at the ball, that sealed the deal. It opened up all these feelings."

I looked away, as a group of people strolled into the common room. They admired the pictures on the walls and laughed at the holiday balls someone had hung from the antlers of a deer head. All I could think was, *poor Rudolph*.

Then I noticed a woman walk by outside the room, and I started as I recognized her. It was Allison Mandrake. I wondered if Tucker had invited her to his holiday party. They did seem to be acquainted with each other, so I shouldn't have been surprised. All of a sudden, I remembered the question I had been most eager to ask Mick.

"Hey, so what happened to you the night Edgar died? You asked me to come to the hotel, so I did. Then I never saw you or heard from you after that."

Mick mumbled a reply about how hectic it was that night with all the people and the commotion. But I didn't buy it. His face was turning red.

"Edgar fell right outside your room. Did you hear

anything? The police said one of the guests overheard Edgar arguing with someone."

Mick smoothed his hair and refused to meet my eyes. I leaned forward. "Mick? What aren't you telling me?"

His Adam's apple bobbed up and down, and I was reminded of my attempt to wheedle information out of Bob the driver. Come to think of it, I still had some of Mila's truth serum in a vial in my purse. I would totally use it on Mick if I had to. I was about to suggest we go have a drink, when he finally spoke.

"It was me," he said in a small voice.

"I beg your pardon?"

"I'm the one who overheard the yelling. It was shortly after I got off the phone with you. I heard raised voices outside my room."

"You did? Why didn't you say anything before?"

"Because . . . I was ashamed. I heard the yelling and thought about opening my door or calling the front desk, but I didn't. I wanted to take a shower and fix myself up before you arrived."

"Oh." I was beginning to understand.

"So, I ignored the yelling. The fan in the bathroom was so loud, I didn't hear anything else until I got out of the shower. Then I heard all this screaming. When I found out what had happened, it really freaked me out. I realized I could have prevented the accident."

"You don't know that," I said.

"I still feel guilty. I felt so terrible that night, I just checked out and left. That's when I came out here to the lodge."

"You never went back to DC?"

He shook his head. "I still wanted to reconnect with you. But I couldn't call you, because I accidentally left my phone at the hotel, I had left so fast. Your number was in my phone. I actually saw you walking downtown one evening and almost flagged you down, but I chickened out."

"Was that Tuesday night, near the health club?" I remembered the noise I'd heard behind me, scaring me half to death.

"Yeah, that sounds right."

"What about Wednesday? Did you see me that day? Did you follow me?"

"What? No. I never followed you." He appeared genuinely perplexed, but I wasn't sure I believed him considering all his other stalky behavior. I wondered what the police made of his confession. He must have lied to them that night before he checked out. Who was to say he wasn't lying now?

I glanced over at the crackling flames in the stone fireplace. For a moment, I allowed myself to take a slow breath in and out as I consciously honed my intuition. I recalled the clarity I had received from the Goddess following my moon ritual. With this sharpened awareness, I turned to Mick again. I regarded him closely with an intensity that made him squirm.

"I promise you, Keli," he said, "I'm telling you the truth. I admit I hid my real motive for coming here. But I'm through being childish. And I feel terrible about what happened to Edgar."

About what happened to Edgar. My inner voice nudged me to ask one more question.

"Mick, about that argument you overheard. Can you remember any details at all? Any words you might have overheard? Think really hard."

He shook his head. "Like I told the police, I didn't

make out any specific . . ." He trailed off, as a look of astonishment washed over his face. "Hold on. I just re-membered something. I did hear some actual words amidst the muffled arguing."

I leaned forward. "What did you hear?"

"A man's voice, maybe Edgar's. I can't believe I forgot this. I distinctly heard him say, 'You were never my partner!'"

Chapter 22

I stood in the foyer of the Stag Creek Lodge waiting for Farrah to either show up or reply to my text. I was eager to tell her about the revelation from Mick. I wasn't sure what to make of the exclamation he had overheard. There were a few different angles I could think of, but I wanted to go over them with Farrah.

I checked my phone again, then roamed back and forth through the carpeted lobby. I clutched my newly recovered book to my chest. As soon as I had been satisfied that Mick had told me everything he knew about the night Edgar died—and made him promise he would tell the police what he had remembered—I let him know I needed to go. I shook his hand and wished him well. Fortunately, he seemed to understand there was never going to be the "us" he had hoped for. To his credit, he remembered the book he had promised me, and he handed it over before I left.

Now I rubbed my finger along the spine of the book and read its title once more: *Johnny Appleseed Was a*

Friend of Mine. It was a whimsical, colorfully illustrated children's book, with historical facts about the real Johnny Appleseed. Mick had borrowed it for a class he had taken on American folklore. He hadn't kept the book on purpose, but when he found it among his college things he'd held on to it as a memento of our time together.

I opened the book and reread the girlish handwriting on the inside of the front cover: *Property of Josephine O'Malley.* I was so happy to have the book back. I looked forward to reading it cover to cover when I had more time.

I tucked the book in my purse and tried calling Farrah again. Still no answer. Where was she? If we didn't leave in the next few minutes, I wouldn't be ready when Wes came to pick me up for dinner. I decided I had better go find her. First I checked the dining room, which was starting to fill up already. The hostess said she hadn't seen Farrah or Tucker. Neither had the guy at the check-in desk or the valet. I wandered farther into the lodge, peeking into every room I passed, including the game room, the small exercise room, and the sauna. Not knowing what else to do, I climbed the stairs to the second floor and strolled down the hall past the private rooms.

This is ridiculous, I thought, checking the time again. When I reached the end of the hall, I looked out the window. It provided a nice view of the grounds behind the lodge. In the foreground were the ski rental shed, outpost building, and indoor firing range. Beyond that, white rolling hills led to the edge of the forest, where little wooden signs marked half a dozen trailheads.

But the thing that really caught my attention was the weather. Snow flurries whirled in the wind like mini-tornadoes. *Farrah, where are you?*

I took the back stairs down to the first floor. Toward the bottom, I glanced down and caught sight of a tiny blue bead. On the next step was a tiny green bead. *What is it with all the beads I keep finding?* I picked them up and held them in my palm up to the light. They were the same type of beads as in the broken buckle I'd found. Fern had confirmed the buckle was one of her creations, but she hadn't taken it back. It was probably still buried in the bottom of my purse. I wasn't going to dig it out now.

I looked at the floor again. At the foot of the stairs was a tiny red bead and a few feet ahead was a yellow one. I picked them up as I went, following the trail of beads down the narrow corridor until I came to a door marked EMPLOYEES ONLY. I paused. What would I find on the other side? Was Fern skulking around the lodge? For that matter, had she been in the hotel cloakroom the night of the ball, or in Edgar's conference room at some point during our short audit? If so, why?

Beverly was convinced Fern had it out for Edgar. And Fern was definitely an unusual woman.

My gut told me Fern wasn't dangerous. Maybe I was biased because of her connection to Aunt Josephine, but I had no qualms about running into Fern Lopez. More than anything, I just wondered what she was up to.

I turned the knob and slowly pushed open the door. The room was dark, so I felt along the wall for a switch and turned it on. Inside were vending machines, a kitchenette, a couple of tables, and a vinyl sofa. On the floor were the trusty little beads showing me the way. I continued to pick them up until at last I reached the final bead and the source of the whole mess. On the floor next to the sofa was a blue backpack. Attached to one of the straps was a tasseled key chain missing half of its beads.

I glanced back at the door, which I had left ajar. *Well, I've come this far.* As quick as a cat, I shut and locked the door, then unzipped the backpack. Trying to touch as little as possible, I took a peek inside and saw bunches of pamphlets. I pulled one out and read the boldfaced words: VOTE FOR TUCKER. The backpack contained campaign materials?

This isn't Fern's backpack. I unzipped another pocket and found a library card issued to one Zeke Marshal. *Huh.* Zeke had been the one dropping all the beads.

The doorknob rattled, causing me to jump. *Crap.* I reclosed the backpack and moved toward the door. When the lock clicked, I planted my feet and prepared to face the music. The door swung open, and I found myself looking at none other than Zeke himself.

His eyebrows shot up when he saw me, and he took a step back. "Whoa! You scared me."

I decided to go on the offensive. "Hello, Zeke. What are you doing here?"

"Me? I told you. I work for Tucker now. What are you doing here?"

So much for my offensive strike. "I'm looking for my friend Farrah. Have you seen her?"

He gave me a suspicious look, then nodded. "Yeah, actually. I saw her with Tucker a while ago. They were headed for the firing range."

"I need to go find her," I said. "But first, can I ask you a question?"

"Sure, why not?"

"I suppose you heard the police are treating Edgar's death as a murder investigation now."

"Yeah. Heavy, huh?"

"Do you have any theories? Who would do such a thing?"

Zeke hesitated a second, then shrugged. "He was a public figure. Rich and powerful. I imagine he probably made a few enemies on his road to success. Not that I think he deserved to die or anything, but, you know. When you make your bed, you gotta lie in it."

Hmm. What an odd thing for him to say. He moved past me and flopped down on the sofa. "Are you staying for the holiday party?" he asked. "Maybe this time I can finally have that dance you promised me."

"I never promised you a dance. Anyway, I'm not staying. I need to get home." I looked at the beads in my hand and gave them a squeeze. "But, first, I do have one more question."

Actually, I had many questions. Why did Zeke have handcrafts made by Fern? Did he know her? And why had he been sneaking around Edgar's office? Did he set off the fire alarm?

"Shoot," he said. "I'm all yours."

"Okay. What I want to know is . . . why did you think Edgar's daughter would be taking over his real estate business? I found out that's not true. His wife inherited the business."

For a brief moment, Zeke furrowed his brow. Then his face became impassive again, and he shrugged.

"I guess I heard wrong. We don't always get accurate information."

"'We'? What do you mean 'we'?"

Zeke looked down at his cell phone, a small smile tugging at his lips. "Stick around tonight, and maybe I'll tell you."

Ugh. I'd had enough of Zeke's boyish games. I was out of there.

After leaving Zeke, I proceeded down the hall and around the corner where I found myself in the foyer again. A small crowd milled about the front desk, including Farrah and Tucker. Farrah rushed over when she saw me.

"There you are! I've been looking all over for you."

"I was looking for you, too! Why didn't you pick up your phone?"

"I wasn't allowed to bring my phone into the firing range. Tucker was showing me how to shoot a hunting rifle. I'm so sorry I missed your calls."

"That's okay. I had my own little diversion. I'll tell you all about it on the ride home. We gotta get going."

"Uh, Keli. Have you looked outside lately?"

"What do you mean?"

Just then, the front door burst open and Lonnie Treat blew in with a gust of wind and snow. "Jiminy Christmas! It's a blizzard out there!"

Farrah squeezed my arm. "That's what I was trying to tell you. I don't think we're going anywhere, anytime soon."

Tucker walked over, holding a walkie-talkie. "Just heard from my guy down the way. Roads are impassable.

County sheriff is closing Rural Route Three. They already have at least a dozen stranded motorists between here and Edindale."

"Oh, no." I groaned. There went my holiday travel plans.

Tucker flung his arm over Farrah's shoulder and gave me an encouraging grin. "Now, don't you worry. I'll put you up for the night. We have nice rooms, hot food, and a full bar. Might as well enjoy the party."

"Yeah," said Farrah, her eyes twinkling. "We might as well make the best of it. It could be fun!"

Yeah, right, I thought. Being trapped in a hunting lodge, surrounded by the stuffed carcasses of so many wild animals, was not high on my list of fun. Of course, Farrah would find it exciting. She got to hang out with her romance-hero of a cowboy. Besides that, Farrah's mom didn't live far from Edindale, so Farrah could see her anytime. I saw my parents only a couple of times a year.

I headed to a quiet corner of the common room to make my phone calls. Mick was nowhere in sight, thank goodness. First I called Wes to tell him the bad news. He was just relieved I was okay. He had been afraid I'd been caught in the storm. He told me his mom promised we'd have our Christmas Eve dinner another time.

When I called my parents, they said they had been expecting to hear from me. They'd been watching the weather reports and knew that flights had been canceled all across the Midwest. Like Wes's folks, they said they would celebrate with me any day of the year. They were also just glad I was safe.

I had just ended the call with my parents when my

phone rang in my hand. The display informed me it was Crenshaw.

"Hey, what's up?" I said.

All I heard was the sound of muffled static.

"Crenshaw?"

"Drat it all," he said. "Keli, is that you?"

"Yes. You called me. What's going on?"

"I don't have much time. I need to conserve my battery. But I had to warn you."

"What are you talking about? Why does it sound like you're in a wind tunnel?"

"I seem to have slid off the road. I'm currently hunkered down in my car somewhere along Rural Route Three."

"Oh, my gosh! Are you okay?"

"Yes, yes. I've already contacted the authorities. They assured me I'll be rescued in due time, though it could be a while. Fortunately, I always carry an emergency kit in my trunk."

"Well, that's good. Where were you going anyway?"

"I was going to find you. Are you at the Stag Creek Lodge?"

"Yes. Looks like I'll be staying the night here. But why—"

"You *must* be careful, Keli. I'm afraid you could be in grave danger."

The phone filled with static again.

"Crenshaw? Are you still there? Crenshaw?"

There was the sound of rushing wind, then his voice cut in, apparently in the middle of a sentence. ". . . information I uncovered. I have reason to believe Edgar's killer . . ."

"What? Can you speak up? I can barely hear you."

"I'm going to have to hang up," he said. "The connection isn't good. Please promise me . . ." Again, his voice was drowned out by the background noise.

"Crenshaw! What did you say?"

"I don't have proof, but I believe the killer is there, at the lodge. You must—"

An abrupt silence filled my ears as the line was disconnected.

Chapter 23

I stared at my phone in disbelief. As Crenshaw's words echoed in my mind, a prickle of fear crawled up my skin. I tried calling him back, but he didn't pick up.

What had he learned? And why would I be in danger? Whatever it was, he said he couldn't prove it. Yet, he did sound awfully certain.

"Was it Marley?"

I jumped at the sound of Farrah's voice. She stood next to me with an amused expression. "You look like you've seen a ghost. Was it Jacob Marley? Or the Ghost of Christmas Future?"

I bit my lip and looked over her shoulder as a few other guests entered the room.

"What is it, hon?" Farrah touched my arm.

"Well, for one thing, Crenshaw is in a ditch. He's one of those poor stranded motorists Tucker was telling us about."

Farrah clapped her hand over her mouth.

"He'll be okay," I said. "Hey, can we get out of here? Is our room ready yet?"

"I have our keys," Farrah said, handing me a key card. "But let's grab dinner first. I'm famished."

"Yeah, okay."

The dining room was bustling. Between the planned guests and the unexpected guests, like us, there was hardly an empty seat in the house. Farrah and I placed our orders. Then I dropped my voice and told her what Crenshaw had said to me.

"Holy crap! The murderer is *here*? I guess that narrows down the suspects. Should we start a list?" Farrah gazed around the room with narrowed eyes. "It could be him, or him, or her, or—oh, there's your stalker boyfriend. Maybe it was him!"

"Who, Mick?" I followed her gaze. Mick was signing his bill, then he stood up to leave the restaurant. Part of me wanted to hide under the tablecloth. We had already said our good-byes. Any further encounter would be too awkward. "I don't think so," I said.

"How about *him*?" said Farrah, cocking her head to the side. I looked over and spotted Zeke walking across the room. When he noticed me, he raised his eyebrows and pointed at me and then himself, then did it again. The clearly implied question was *"You and me?"* I assumed he was referring to a dance again. I looked away.

"He's definitely up to something," I said. "I just haven't figured out what it is. Yet."

Our food arrived, and we fell silent as we ate. Before long, Tucker entered the restaurant and made the rounds, stopping at each table to chat. Farrah kept one eye on him the whole time.

"Has he said much to you about the mayoral race?" I asked.

She nodded and took a sip of water. "Yeah. He's thinking of dropping out."

"Really? Why?"

"In the beginning, it was sort of a friendly rivalry between him and Edgar. Now that Edgar is gone, he said he wouldn't feel right taking the job. He said it's like winning a contest just because the other side didn't show up. Winning by default doesn't seem fair to him."

"Hmm." Something about Tucker's reasoning didn't sit right with me. Maybe it was because of all the fundraising and campaigning Zeke had been doing on Tucker's behalf. Why print up pamphlets and ask for money if you're planning on dropping out? Before I could mention it to Farrah, Tucker walked up to our table. He put a hand on Farrah's shoulder.

"Ladies, good to see you're making the best of an unexpected situation."

I smiled and Farrah raised her glass. "Compliments to the chef," she said. "The food here is fabulous."

Tucker dipped his chin in gratitude. "Indeed. If you'd like to have your dessert in the common room, cookie's got a spread of Christmas goodies in there."

Farrah nudged me. "Isn't it cute how he uses cowboy terms?"

Tucker grinned. "Anyway, it's real cheerful in there. Ricardo, our handyman, is doubling as the deejay tonight."

"Ricardo?" I asked. The name rang a bell from my conversation with Bob. "Is he also the handyman at the Harrisons' ranch?"

"Yep. Their ranch is just over the ridge, not far from here. He lives over there and does odd jobs for folks all over the area."

"He must be extra handy," said Farrah, "if he can deejay, too."

"Well, I reckon we'll see about that," said Tucker. "This is his first gig. I need to head over there now and see what all he's picked out to play." Tucker squeezed Farrah's shoulder. "Hope I'll see you in there real soon."

Farrah dabbed her lips with her napkin. "Actually, I'm finished with my dinner now." She gave me her *pretty please* look.

"Go ahead," I said. "I'll take care of the check and find you later."

Farrah took off with Tucker, and I pulled out my wallet. After paying the bill, I took out my cell phone and shot off a few texts, including one to Wes and one to Crenshaw. Crenshaw didn't reply, but I still hoped he'd see my message and feel less alone. I felt bad to think he was spending Christmas Eve in his car on the side of the road. I'd have to be nicer to him from now on, I decided.

I was just putting my phone away when I noticed Allison sitting by herself at a table for two in the corner. She sipped from a coffee mug and gazed vacantly in front of her.

Tucker had said to make the most of our unexpected situation. Maybe I should do just that. As long as we were here, I might as well try to get some answers. I walked over to her table.

"Mind if I join you?" I asked.

She gestured toward the empty chair. "Help yourself."

A waitress stopped by to see if I wanted coffee. I accepted, if only so I'd have something to hold on to.

"Allison, there's something I've been wondering

about," I began. "Do you remember that day the fire alarm went off at Harrison Properties?"

"Yes, of course."

"I happened to be outside your office at the time, because I was just coming to see you."

"Oh?"

"Yes. I didn't mean to eavesdrop, but I couldn't help overhearing you on the telephone. You were speaking rather loudly. It sounded as if you were upset."

She blinked rapidly, then shook her head. "I have no idea what you're talking about. I don't remember being upset. I don't even remember a phone call. I'm sure it was nothing."

So much for information gathering, I thought. I blew on my coffee and looked around the room. Lonnie Treat stood at the entrance speaking with the hostess. He sported a new haircut and an elegant fitted tuxedo. I couldn't help thinking his attire would have fit in better at Edgar's ball than here. He was a bit overdressed for a hunting lodge.

Allison observed him, too. "I'm glad to see he's doing better for himself," she said. If I wasn't mistaken, there seemed to be a note of bitterness in her voice.

"That *is* quite a change from his usual brown suit," I said lightly. I smiled at Allison, but she didn't return it. "Maybe the mattress business has picked up," I suggested. Allison only scowled.

I considered Lonnie's new look and wondered what it could mean. Could he have recently found himself with a large influx of cash? Possibly money he had retrieved from a garbage can as payoff for his silence? With his shifty behavior, it wasn't difficult to picture Lonnie as a blackmailer. But I didn't know how he could have been privy to any sensitive information about Edgar.

I glanced at Allison and tried to get a read on her. She was staring into her coffee mug again. As far as I knew, Allison didn't know Edgar was being black-mailed. Edgar hadn't told anyone but Beverly. That is, assuming Allison, herself, wasn't the blackmailer. But she could be the blackmailer's second victim.

"Allison, how long did you work for Edgar?"

"It would have been thirteen years next month."

"So, you were around when the Cornerstone project was proposed?"

She looked up sharply. "Yes. Why do you ask?"

"No reason. It's just that . . . I seem to recall hearing that Lonnie Treat was one of the early investors. I be-lieve he lost money when the deal fell through." I watched her carefully to see how she'd react to my bluff.

"He did," she affirmed. "If I remember correctly, he lost more than anyone else. But it was his own fault. He should have pulled out while there was still time."

"Interesting," I murmured. "I wonder if he held a grudge against Edgar because of it."

Allison seemed to consider the possibility. "If he did, he never showed it. If anything, he doubled down on his efforts to join Edgar's inner circle. Lonnie has always been little more than a wannabe social climber."

"Oh?"

"I have to hand it to him. He may not be the brightest bulb on the tree, but he is persistent. I bet he'd stop at nothing to get what he wants."

* * *

After leaving Allison at the restaurant, I walked over to the common room and peered through the wide, open doorway. I was trying to decide if I wanted to pop in and be social, or skip the soirée and go on upstairs. Several people milled about, laughing and drinking, while a few danced in place to the upbeat rhythm of "Feliz Navidad." It was hard to fathom that one of them could be a murderer.

Now that I thought about it, it was even harder to believe that I was trying to sniff one out. Who did I think I was anyway, V. I. Warshawski? What did I know about murder? Not much, that's what. I tried to recall what I had learned in law school about the percentage of murders that were premeditated versus crimes of passion. In Edgar's case, he was the one who set up the meeting on the fourth floor. That would seem to rule out premeditation. Perhaps that's what the police thought, too. If they were viewing Edgar's death as a crime of passion, that wasn't going to help Beverly's position.

Under normal circumstances, one would think the wife of a cheater would be a more likely suspect than the mistress. But Gretta apparently already knew about Edgar's extramarital affair and accepted it. Anyway, there was no way she could have pushed Edgar over the railing, not from her wheelchair. And she wasn't even at the hotel when he died. She had gone home in a mobility van, then returned the same way when the police notified her of her husband's death.

I thought about the secret Beverly had told me about her final moments with Edgar. Evidently, he was breaking up with her because he wanted to reconcile with his wife. That certainly didn't help Beverly's defense. But she wasn't the only one who might not be thrilled at this turn of events. There was someone else who might not want Edgar to get back together with his wife: Gretta's companion, Ricardo.

My eyes swept the room until I spotted the source of the music. A modest sound system was set up on a table against the far wall. Behind the table was a short, wiry man with a shiny bald spot surrounded by trim dark hair on the sides of his head. He appeared to be in his late fifties, and, if his big smile was any indication, he seemed to be enjoying himself.

As the song ended and the next one, "Rockin' Around the Christmas Tree," filled the air, Ricardo adjusted the volume. Then he came out from behind the CD player and walked over to the refreshments table where he helped himself to a glass of punch. I decided to make my move.

"Hello," I said. "Nice music choices."

"Thanks," he said affably. "It's hard to go wrong with country Christmas tunes."

He started to walk away, so I held up a hand to stop him. "Can I talk to you for a minute?"

"Uh, okay. The next few songs are all queued up, so I have a couple minutes. What can I do for you?"

I looked around the room. "Can we go over there?" I pointed to a small reading nook in an alcove off the main room.

Once we were seated, I introduced myself and got right to the point. "How is Gretta holding up?"

"She's doing all right," said Ricardo. "She's a strong lady."

"She's lucky she has you by her side." I gave him a

small, knowing smile. He squinted his eyes ever so slightly, as if trying to figure out what I meant.

I leaned forward conspiratorially. "It's okay. Beverly told me everything. I know all about Edgar and Gretta's . . . arrangement. Your secret's safe with me."

Ricardo relaxed his shoulders, but still appeared wary. "Not many people know," he said.

"She told me something else," I said, watching him closely.

"Oh, she did, did she?"

I nodded. "She told me Edgar planned to win his wife back."

Ricardo stared at me a moment, then burst out laughing. I sat back, perplexed. What was so funny?

"I'm sorry," he said, still chuckling. "It's just the way you said it, like you thought you were breaking the news story of the year. Bless your heart."

I frowned. "What do you mean? You already knew?" *And if he knew, then that proves he had a motive for Edgar's murder. Hardly a reason to laugh.*

"Knew Edgar was full of s-h-i-t? Absolutely. He probably asked Gretta to take him back a hundred times over the years—especially when he'd had too much to drink, and most especially around the holidays. In fact, after the ball that night, she predicted he'd come home and do it again. It was a—what do you call it? A pattern of his."

"Beverly sure didn't act like she'd heard it before," I said.

Ricardo shrugged. "Maybe it was the first time he said it to her. But, believe me, he'd said it to Gretta plenty of times. The first few times, years ago, she gave him the benefit of the doubt. She'd remain faithful to him, then he'd go off and cheat on her again. She finally wised up."

Ricardo looked me in the eye. "Not to speak ill of the dead, but Edgar was not the most honest person. He lied all the time. Don't get me wrong, he had his good points, too. Gretta cared for him and agreed to keep up appearances. But she learned long ago that he couldn't be trusted.

"I see. Well, that doesn't sound like the Edgar Beverly knew." *And loved.*

"What can I say? Love is blind. Maybe she didn't see his flaws because she didn't want to. Or maybe she wasn't around him often enough, or with him long enough." Ricardo shook his head. "I'll tell you one thing, though. I wasn't too surprised when I heard the police say Edgar was murdered. With his . . . shall I say, 'lack of scruples,' it's more surprising somebody didn't try to bump him off long before now."

Chapter 24

The room Tucker assigned to Farrah and me was a charming double at the end of the second-floor hallway. With Southwestern-style quilts, lamps made from bleached driftwood, and knotty pine dressers, it was easy to imagine I was in a cabin in the woods. Which, come to think of it, wasn't too far from the truth.

After leaving the holiday party downstairs, I'd come upstairs to kick off my shoes and get some rest. It had been a long, eventful day. Now I flipped on the TV in time to catch the weather report at the tail end of the local news. Snow was predicted to continue throughout the night. Rural Route 3 wouldn't open until sometime tomorrow morning.

There was a tap at the door and the lock clicked open. For a brief moment, my heart jumped to my throat. I hadn't forgotten about Crenshaw's warning that I could be in danger. Farrah stuck her head in, and I breathed a sigh of relief.

"Is it safe to come in? Are you decent?"

"Why wouldn't I be decent?" I asked, flopping down on the bed nearest the window.

"You never know," said Farrah, as she came into the room. "You could be in here doing some naked witchy ritual. Or you could have a guy in here, like your old 'Micky Bear.'"

I rolled my eyes. "I knew I was gonna regret telling you about that nickname."

Farrah laughed. "Actually, forget old Mick. You'd more likely decide to rob the cradle and hook up with that cute young IT guy."

"Hey," I protested. "Have you forgotten about Wes? I'm a one-man woman now."

"You know I'm only teasing." She waved away the idea. "Here, I brought you a present." She tossed me a plastic shopping bag. I dumped it out on the bed to find two large T-shirts and an assortment of complimentary toiletries.

"Take your pick of the shirts. I'll take the other. For sleepwear," Farrah explained.

I held up first one T-shirt, then the other. One was all green camouflage, while the other was black with a large bullet-ridden shooting target. They both said STAG CREEK HUNTING LODGE across the front.

"I gotta say, this is one article of clothing I never thought I'd wear," I said, handing Farrah the shirt with the target.

"You'll look fabulous," she said, as she disappeared into the bathroom. A few minutes later, she came out in a white terrycloth robe. "I'm heading down to the laundry room," she said. "Here's another robe. Want me to wash your clothes and T-shirt, too?"

"Sure, thanks. And while you're gone, can I borrow your iPad? There's a Wi-Fi connection in here, right?"

"Yep. Have at it," she said, removing the tablet from her purse.

After Farrah left, I took a hot shower, then wrapped myself in a robe and settled on top of my bed to browse the Internet. My mind kept going back to what Ricardo had said to me about Edgar's dishonesty. It seemed to corroborate Fern's claims, as wild as they had seemed at the time. What had she called Edgar? Fast Eddie.

As I recalled, Beverly had mentioned that Fern had sued Edgar a few years ago. I was curious to know what the lawsuit was about, so I opened up a legal research website. Since I was using Farrah's device, and legal research was her business, I was pretty sure I'd be able to access the site. I soon found I was right. Her login ID and password were saved in the computer. Once I was signed in, it didn't take long to find the case titled "Fern Lopez vs. Edgar Harrison."

It was a defamation case. The circuit court had dismissed the claim for being filed after the statute of limitations had run. Fern had appealed, arguing that she had only learned about Edgar's slanderous statements about her years after the harm was done. The appellate court was not persuaded, and she lost the appeal.

After reading the procedural summary, I skimmed the short recitation of facts at the beginning of the court's written decision. Fern claimed that Edgar had falsely accused her of growing marijuana on her property. As a result, Fern's landlord had canceled her lease and evicted her from her home.

Wait. 'Evicted her'? From what property? When did this alleged slander take place? I read on and gasped when I found my answer. The property in question was the Happy Hills Homestead. The commune where Aunt Josephine had lived.

So, Fern believed that Edgar was responsible for the loss of the commune's land. No wonder she didn't like him. The court's decision didn't say how Fern supposedly came to possess her belated information about the alleged slander. I wondered if she'd found something back when she was trying to bug his office. According to the case summary, Fern's complaint alleged that Edgar "maliciously intended to damage her good name and reputation with full knowledge that his statements were untrue." She further alleged that he had wanted the land for himself.

I was so engrossed in reading about the case, I barely noticed when Farrah returned with our clean clothes. She walked over and plugged a charger cord into the wall outlet, then connected it to the iPad. "I borrowed this from the front desk clerk," she said.

"That's nice," I responded, still reading the computer screen. I scrolled down to the end of the court's decision and almost clicked out of the page, when something caught my eye at the very end. It was a footnote. According to the note, a third party had asked the court for permission to file an amicus brief in support of Fern's complaint. The court denied the motion. But the thing that jumped out at me was the name of the third party: Green Elf Organization, or GEO.

"Interesting," I murmured.

"What's interesting?" asked Farrah, trying to read over my shoulder.

"Green Elf Organization. I wonder if they're related

to Green Elf Energy Company. Maybe a precursor or something."

"Green Elf Energy," Farrah repeated. "I've heard of them. Don't they make solar panels and wind turbines? I know they do something with alternative energy. Like what Fern Lopez uses at her survivalist compound."

"Yeah. I'm not sure if they're a broker or a provider or what. But I know someone who would know. Zeke mentioned he worked at Green Elf Energy before getting his job at Harrison Properties."

"Figures," said Farrah. "Look at their acronym. Sounds like 'geek.'"

I Googled both Green Elf entities to see what I could learn. I wasn't sure why, but this potential connection between Zeke and Fern seemed significant.

"Hey, Kel. Are you gonna be okay on your own for a while? Tucker invited me to his private suite for a nightcap."

"Yeah, sure," I said, not looking up. "Have fun."

The first few search results I found were official websites about GEEC's sustainable energy offerings. Then I came across a comment on a message board that gave me pause. An anonymous commenter implied that Green Elf had ties to a radical underground environmental group. Following the thread, I learned that there had long been rumors about a secret network of eco-activists based in the Edindale area. Supposedly, they engaged in covert operations to further their cause.

Covert operations? That sounded right up Fern's alley. Suddenly, I recalled my suspicions about Zeke after the fire alarm went off at Harrison Properties. And that wet footprint outside Edgar's door. Had Zeke planted a bug in Edgar's office? Or was he just snooping around?

If so, he might have found something incriminating about Edgar . . . which meant, he really could be the blackmailer, as Edgar had suspected.

But something else surfaced in my memory. It was Zeke's tendency to say obscure things to me, almost as if he was dropping hints he hoped I'd figure out. Come to think of it, Fern had done the same thing. As I recalled, she'd said, "You're a smart girl. You'll figure it out."

What were they trying to tell me?

There was one way to find out.

I set the iPad on the nightstand and checked the time. It was after midnight already. I'd been surfing the web longer than I'd realized. No matter. Zeke struck me as the kind of person who stayed up late.

I went to get dressed and found that my sweater was still damp. Farrah had tossed it over the shower rod to air-dry. Instead of the sweater, I threw on my new camo nightshirt over my leggings and slipped out of the room. Moving quickly, I tiptoed down the hall, took the stairs to the first floor, and hurried up to the front desk.

There was no clerk in sight. I peeked at the computer monitor and found that it was on. Lucky for me, the screen wasn't password protected. *I wonder if this is what it feels like to be a Green Elf operative*, I thought as I snuck behind the desk and helped myself to the computer. As soon as I located Zeke's reservation, I lifted the receiver on the front desk telephone and dialed his room number.

"Hello?" he said, after the first ring.

"Meet me in the common room," I whispered.

"Who is this?" he said.

"Oh. It's Keli," I said in my normal voice. "I'd like to

talk to you. I'll be in the common room." I hung up before he could respond.

The common room was dark and quiet. Even the stone fireplace was cold and dark, the fire having died out hours ago. I curled in a chair in the reading nook, out of sight of the deer heads and stuffed birds in the main room. I'd forgotten my cell phone upstairs, but I had a feeling it was nearing 1:00 a.m. The same time Edgar had met his killer, one week ago tomorrow.

With a shiver, I kept my eye on the entryway. Still, I jumped when Zeke appeared. He hadn't made a sound.

"What's new, pussycat?" he said.

"Aren't you slightly young to be quoting Tom Jones?" I asked. I hoped a little levity would slow down my pattering heart.

"Why are you always bringing up my age?" he countered.

"Have a seat," I said.

He took the chair across from me, the same spot Ricardo had occupied a few hours earlier. I noticed Zeke was in need of a haircut. Maybe it was the rumpled clothes and visible whiskers, but his clean-cut image seemed to be morphing into that of a revolutionary.

"I'd like some straight answers, Zeke."

"Why, whatever do you mean?" he asked, batting his lashes at me.

"You know what I mean. Earlier today, in the breakroom, you said you'd tell me if I stuck around tonight. Well, here I am."

Zeke studied me for a moment without saying anything. Maybe he needed a little encouragement.

I leaned forward. "Tell me about Green Elf and your acquaintance with Fern Lopez."

Zeke's face broke into a wide smile. "Ha! I knew you were a sharp one."

"Go ahead," I said, sitting back. "I'm listening."

"I do work with Fern," he admitted. "She leads one cell in the network—you don't need to know the name. Green Elf is just one link. Anyway, our mission is simple: we aim to save the earth. In essence, we want to save humankind from itself."

I must have raised my eyebrows, because Zeke toned down his fervor. "Don't worry," he said. "We're not ecoterrorists or anything. We don't damage property or endanger any people or animals. We just like to keep our pulse on the town's leadership. We want to know what's going on and how decisions are being made, so we can influence them."

"And you do this by planting bugs and spying on people?"

Zeke shrugged. "I'm not going to confess to any criminal activity, if that's what this is all about."

I blinked, remembering what I was really after. "No. What I'm interested in is . . . information. Especially any information you may have uncovered at Edgar's office."

"Ah, yes. I miss that job. It was a bed of roses compared to other jobs I've had."

"There you go again, with the bed references! You and Fern both. She said something about politicians and businessmen being 'in bed together.' And you said something about 'making your bed and lying in it.'"

"Hey," said Zeke, barely suppressing his grin. "We're prepared to go to the mattresses, if that's what it takes."

"All right. I get it. It's about Lonnie Treat. So, what about him?"

"Okay," said Zeke, lowering his voice. "So, I was doing my job at Harrison Properties, right? Allison had instructed me to transfer Edgar's handwritten notes into the new computer system. As I was doing that, I realized a ledger book was missing. I asked Allison about it, and she searched but couldn't find it."

"What kind of ledger book?"

"One of Edgar's accounting journals where he documented financial transactions. It would have covered a particular time period from a few years back, around the time of the Cornerstone project. Have you heard of Cornerstone?"

"Yes. Go on."

"Fern was adamantly opposed to Cornerstone. She told me all about it. The development would have ruined a wetland and wiped out hundreds of trees, huge swaths of wildlife habitat."

"Did she have a hand in its demise?" I asked.

Zeke smirked. "She would have done anything to block it, but she didn't have to. It fell through anyway. But she's always been worried someone might try to resuscitate the project."

"So, what about the missing ledger book?"

"I thought it might be significant, so I looked for it myself."

"How did you get inside Edgar's office?" I asked, assuming that's where he'd looked.

"I have skills," said Zeke.

"That's what you were doing that day the fire alarm went off, isn't it? Did you pull the alarm?"

"Yes, ma'am," Zeke admitted. "I needed to clear the floor long enough to give me time to search Edgar's office."

"And? Did you find it?"

"No. When I told Fern about it, she said it must have been stolen."

I remembered the break-in Beverly had mentioned. "Was Fern referring to the time someone tried to break into Edgar's safe? I take it that wasn't her."

"No, it wasn't. But she was watching Edgar's office at the time. She knows who broke in."

Time to put this mystery to bed, I thought wryly. "Lonnie Treat?"

"Bingo."

Chapter 25

That night I had a dream about Aunt Josephine. I wanted desperately to find her. She needed my help, and I felt she was really close, closer than ever before. But I still couldn't find her.

Over the summer, I was obsessed with finding her in the waking world. My mom had unearthed an old letter Josie had sent to her parents right before she'd left the commune. She wrote that she had been entrusted with a secret undertaking and that she would return to Edindale when she had completed her mission. When it was "safe again." All summer I pored over old postcards and letters and walked the property where the commune had been. I'd tracked down all the former Happy Hills residents I could find, including Fern Lopez. But no one could help me, and the trail fizzled out.

My dream jumped to the past, when Josie was a little girl in Nebraska. It made no sense that I, at my current age, would be there with her, but in the dream it didn't matter. "I have a present for you, Keli," young Josie said. She handed me her Johnny Appleseed book. "This is the key, the source, and the power. It's the genesis and the phoenix. It's the answer."

My dream shifted again, and I saw the long-haired woman from the picture in Mila's shop. She was in the place of my Solstice vision, spreading golden seeds beneath the frozen earth. She looked up at me and smiled. "Remember the source of life," she said. "You have the answer. The alpha, the genesis."

I woke with a start. The room was pitch-black. It took me a moment to remember where I was. Farrah snored softly in the bed next to mine. I turned toward the window, peering through the darkness until my eyes discerned the outline of the curtain. As the dream faded, I recalled the information I had learned from Zeke. I had lain in bed piecing it all together, when I fell asleep.

I thought again about what I knew: Lonnie had lost a lot of money in the Cornerstone deal. He had ambitions to join the ranks of Edindale's elite and was always trying to get close to Edgar. He had stolen an accounting book from Edgar's office. And he seemed to have recently come into a large sum of money.

Lonnie had to be the blackmailer.

I would call Detective Rhinehardt first thing in the morning. God only knew how I'd explain the source of all my information. I'd have to figure that out later.

Before I'd left Zeke in the common room, I had one more question for him. "Why are you telling me all this?" I had asked. "Why help me at all?"

Zeke had leaned forward, a devilish glint in his eyes. "I don't know. Maybe you'll want to join us. You do love Mother Earth, don't you?"

In the darkness, I sighed and rolled over. I already had enough things to worry about.

An hour later, I awoke again. This time, the early morning sun shone through the curtains, casting a bright ray of light on the floor. I rolled out of bed and looked out the window.

How peaceful, I thought. The sunrise washed the snow-covered landscape in hues of pink and yellow. *All is calm, all is bright.* I couldn't help thinking of the Grinch looking down at Whoville after he had stolen Christmas. If I listened hard enough, maybe I'd hear the sound of distant singing.

I laughed at myself and started to turn away. That's when I spotted a figure emerge from the ski rental shed. It was Lonnie.

What's he up to? I wondered. He was somewhat unsteady on cross-country skis, but he soon found his stride. I watched as he maneuvered around the shed, where he met up with another person on skis. At this distance, I couldn't tell who the other person was. He or she wore ski goggles and a black puffy coat. They had a brief conversation, then headed off toward the woods.

"I have a bad feeling about this," I murmured.

Farrah groaned from beneath her pile of blankets. "Too bright," she said, throwing her arm over her eyes. "Too early."

I dropped the curtain and walked over to Farrah's bed. "Wake up, Suzie Q. Something's going down."

She burrowed deeper under her covers.

"Fine. I'll go by myself. I'm sure there's no danger."

Farrah threw her covers off and sat up. "Go where?" she asked, squinting at me with one eye.

"Just a little cross-country skiing adventure. We have to hurry, though. Before we lose them."

"Them? Them who?"

Ten minutes later we were dressed and sneaking into the unlocked ski shed. As we strapped on skis, then stole out and followed two sets of ski tracks in the deep snow, I told Farrah what I'd learned about Lonnie.

"Makes perfect sense," Farrah said. "So, Edgar confronted him, and Lonnie responded by pitching Edgar over the rail."

"And then Lonnie turned his attention to someone else," I said. "Probably Allison. I know she's hiding something. Maybe she was involved in Cornerstone, too."

"Would she have the kind of money you found in the trash bin at Ryker's Pond?"

"I'm not sure, though she does seem to be doing all right for herself. Anyway, she probably had access to Edgar's safe."

Farrah snickered. "So, Lonnie ended up with Edgar's money after all."

"Maybe."

We continued following the tracks along a wide, powdery trail. As we proceeded deeper into the forest, I was grateful Farrah had come along. The farther we ventured from the lodge, the more isolated I felt.

After a few minutes of silence, Farrah spoke up. "They must have had a big head start, huh? I don't even hear any voices."

"They must be skiing pretty fast, too," I said.

"And you don't think they're just out for a little early morning exercise?"

I shook my head. I couldn't say why. I only knew I couldn't shake a deep sense of foreboding.

"Are you thinking Allison is the person with Lonnie now?" Farrah asked.

"That's what I'm afraid of," I said. "I got the impression she didn't think much of him. If she decides to accuse him of blackmail, or if he tries to extort more money from her . . . I don't know. I'm afraid she might be in danger."

Farrah and I pushed our poles into the ground and picked up the pace. Soon, the trail sloped upward, and I started to sweat from the exertion. I unzipped my coat and removed my hat, which I stuck in my pocket. At last, we reached the top of the bluff and breathed a little easier. As we glided along the rim of the bluff, I looked down and recognized where we were.

"Check it out," I said, pointing to the split-rail fence and sprawling, manicured property below. "It's Dogwood Ranch."

Farrah paused and held her hand over her eyes like a visor. "Oh, yeah. Edgar's ranch. You and I have been there before, remember? We followed one of Edgar's security guards and wound up hiding behind Edgar's barn."

"How could I forget? We were chased by a Doberman and got lost in the forest!"

Farrah laughed. "And here we are tailing another suspect. I hope this time turns out better than the last time."

We fell silent and continued along the path, which

became woodsy once again. After a few minutes, I slowed down and stopped.

"What's wrong?" Farrah asked, coming up behind me.

I pointed at the ground. The tracks had veered off the trail and into an opening in the trees.

Farrah gave me a questioning look, and I beckoned her to follow. There was no need for discussion. We both felt we were getting closer and knew we should proceed quietly.

The terrain became rockier as it sloped upward again. It was becoming more difficult to see the ski tracks on the uneven ground. All of a sudden, the tracks disappeared.

Farrah and I halted and looked around. Then I saw something that made my skin prickle. Only one set of ski tracks emerged from the trees. It continued on ahead to pick up the path beyond.

Farrah saw it, too. "Maybe it's not what it looks like," she whispered. "The person in the rear could have followed in the leader's tracks."

"Not up here," I said. "The ground isn't flat. You'd be able to tell if two skiers had come out, even if one was following the other."

"Crap," said Farrah.

We picked our way carefully through the brush, then stopped short. We had come upon a steep drop-off. At the edge, the snow was a muddle of tracks and snow. My legs shook, as I peered over the cliff.

"Oh, God," I said.

"Is it Allison?" asked Farrah. She held back, her eyes wide as saucers.

I took another peek. It had to be at least one hundred feet to the ground below. "Hello?" I called. "Are you okay?" I already knew the answer, but I didn't know what else to do.

I shook my head, as I looked back at Farrah.

"Is she dead?" Farrah whispered.

"Not she," I said. "He. It's Lonnie Treat. And I'm pretty sure he's dead."

Chapter 26

The common room at Stag Creek Lodge was a lot less cheerful than it had been the evening before. Guests sat quietly waiting for their turn to be questioned by the police. As soon as they were given permission to leave, they checked out faster than Old St. Nick's supersonic sleigh. Farrah and I had given our statements first, but we hung around waiting to see what would happen next. So far, no one had come forward to admit being with Lonnie when he'd fallen over the cliff.

I sat in a chair with a view of the front desk and the door to the office where the interrogations were taking place. I felt sorry for all the police officers and rescue workers who had to spend their Christmas morning following up on a dead body. Detective Rhinehardt was one of the first on the scene after we'd called 9-1-1. We'd had to wait until we were back in sight of the inn to make the call, since there was no phone signal in the wilderness.

Farrah and I had sped back the way we had come. My muscles still burned from the effort. For half a second, we had considered following the lone tracks that led away from the cliff's edge, but we quickly decided against it. Neither of us had any desire to face a killer.

When Allison came out of the back office, I hopped up and went after her. I had told Rhinehardt that I didn't get a good look at the person with Lonnie, other than that they were wearing a black coat and ski goggles. However, I did mention that I thought the second person might be Allison. Since the cops had let her go, I assumed she hadn't offered up any stunning admissions of guilt.

"Allison!" I called. "Wait up."

She stopped at the foot of the stairs leading up to the private rooms. She narrowed her eyes when she saw me. "Why on earth would you tell the police you thought I went off skiing with Lonnie Treat?"

"Er, can we talk for a minute? Please?"

"Fine," she said. "Let's go to the dining room."

Farrah joined us, and we all three slipped into the quiet, empty restaurant. We sat at a table in the back. I got right to the point.

"Was Lonnie blackmailing you?" I asked.

"What are you talking about? Is this a joke?" Either she was a terrific actress, or she really knew nothing about the blackmail letters.

"You didn't receive any threatening letters demanding that you leave money at Ryker's Pond?"

"Of course not," she said. "That's crazy."

I glanced at Farrah and she nodded, encouraging me to continue.

"Allison, I have reason to believe that Edgar's death—

and possibly Lonnie's death, too—have some connection to the Cornerstone deal."

The color drained from Allison's face, as she slumped back in her chair. "How can you possibly know that?" she asked, in a small voice.

"That doesn't matter," I said. "What matters is figuring out who is responsible. Please be candid with me. Was there something illicit about Cornerstone? Something Edgar might not want revealed?"

Allison looked down at the table, then nodded her head. "I only found out about this last month," she said. "I was looking for account books for Zeke's database project, and we discovered one was missing. I raised it with Edgar, and he told me not to worry about it."

"Didn't that seem odd?" asked Farrah. "That would raise a red flag for me."

"I didn't think too much about it at first. But then, when I was pulling records for the compliance audit last week, I realized the significance of the missing ledger. I did some further searching and discovered something about the financing of Cornerstone. The primary funding source, the one that went belly up—"

"American Castle Fund?" I interjected.

"That's the one. As it turns out, Edgar had formed that fund."

"Edgar did?"

"Yes—a fact which he hid from all the buyers. The fund was no tried-and-true investment company, as Edgar led people to believe. It was something he had created. I guess he wanted to try something new. He thought he could pick some good stocks and make a go of this new venture, but he blew it. It was reckless and irresponsible, and possibly even fraudulent. At the very least, it was unethical. All those people trusted Edgar with their money, and he squandered it. I was livid when I found out."

"Did you confront him about it?" I asked.

"I did," she said. "That phone call you overheard the evening of the false alarm . . . that was Edgar on the other end of the line. He didn't deny that he had started up American Castle Fund. In fact, he didn't seem to think he'd done anything wrong. He said it wasn't his fault the real estate market crashed."

"You were still upset with him at the ball, weren't you?"

"Was it that obvious? I tried to rein in my feelings. I still cared about Edgar and supported his campaign. I just wanted him to make things right. He should have found a way to compensate the buyers who lost their down payments."

"Like Lonnie," I said.

"Yes. Like Lonnie."

I tapped my fingers on the table as I considered Allison's confession. I believed her. Everything she said added up. The problem was, we were still no closer to figuring out who the murderer was. I glanced out the window and saw Mick head for the parking lot. Seeing him reminded me of an important clue.

"Allison, as you might've heard, a witness overheard Edgar arguing with someone in the hotel the night he died. The witness thought he heard Edgar say something like 'You were never my partner.'"

"Really?" Allison frowned. "I didn't hear that part."

"Well, that part wasn't on the news. I spoke to the witness myself. Anyway, I was just thinking . . . if Lonnie wasn't the one who thought he was Edgar's partner, and you weren't the one . . . then who? Who else might have thought he was Edgar's partner?"

Allison shook her head. "Only one person comes to mind. Tucker Brinkley."

"No way," Farrah said immediately.

"Why do you say that?" I asked Allison. "Just because they were partners in the past?"

"Well, yes. But also because you said Cornerstone was the key. Tucker was an early investor in Cornerstone."

"Oh. I suppose an investor isn't exactly the same thing as a partner. And, unlike Lonnie, Tucker wouldn't likely confuse the two. Anyway, Tucker has an alibi for the night Edgar died. He was with Farrah all night."

"Well, not *all* night," said Farrah.

I turned to face her. "What do you mean? You said he spent the night with you."

"No, I didn't. What gave you that idea?"

I rubbed my forehead, trying to remember. "You said he went home with you, right? After you all went out to the nightclub and then walked back to the hotel to get his truck?"

"He took me home, but he didn't stay. I told you he was a gentleman, remember? He kissed me good night, and didn't even come inside."

"Huh."

We were all silent, as the implication sank in.

"Wait a minute," said Farrah. "So what if he had the opportunity? He had no motive. There is no way Tucker would commit murder over the mayoral election. He doesn't even want the job anymore. He has a very successful business right here." She waved her arm in the air.

I slowly nodded. What Farrah said made sense. Besides, from everything else we knew, Edgar had planned to meet up with the blackmailer that night at the hotel. I was certain Lonnie was the blackmailer. Something didn't add up.

"I don't know what to think," I said. "Last night I was so sure Lonnie was our culprit."

"Who's to say he's not?" asked Allison. "His fall could have been an accident. It happens all the time. People are careless. They don't realize how close they are to the edge."

An accident. Hearing the word was like a bad case of déjà vu. Everyone had thought it was an accident after Edgar was found dead. The police report had said it was an accident that night Wes and I ended up in the ditch.

Thinking of the ditch reminded me of Crenshaw. Suddenly, I brightened. "Maybe we won't have to be in the dark much longer. Crenshaw said he had some information for me. Hopefully, he can fill in the blanks." I pulled my phone from my pocket to check it for the zillionth time. "Come to think of it, I'm kind of surprised I haven't heard from him yet."

Farrah sucked in air, as a look of worry crossed her face. I patted her hand. "I'm sure he's fine," I said. "He probably got a ride back to Edindale as soon as the road was cleared. He's probably having a hearty—"

"Keli!" Farrah clutched my arm so tightly I winced.

"Ouch! What's wrong?"

"Listen. If there's the slightest chance Tucker is the one . . . then Crenshaw might be in danger."

"Why? What do you mean?"

Farrah's eyes darted from Allison to me. "Last night, I told Tucker about Crenshaw's call to you. I told him

Crenshaw thought he knew who the killer was, and that it was someone at the lodge."

"Oh, no," I said.

"I thought he should know. I had no idea he might be . . ." she trailed off, unable to finish the thought.

I pulled my phone out of my purse and dialed Crenshaw's number. There was no answer.

"Where is Tucker, anyway?" asked Allison. "I haven't seen him all morning."

"I haven't either," I said. "But I overheard Rhinehardt on the phone with him. So, he's aware of what happened. He must be around here somewhere."

"I should go find him," said Farrah, as she pushed back from the table. "I can talk to him, ask him a few subtle questions. I think I'll be able to tell if he's lying."

"Wait." I grabbed her arm. "Not yet. I—I have something upstairs that might help, you know, encourage the truth."

"Ah," said Farrah. "Okay. Perfect."

"About Crenshaw," said Allison. "Isn't there anyone else who might know where he is?"

"Hmm. Good point. Who was out rescuing the stranded motorists? The sheriff's department? Maybe Detective Rhinehardt would know."

"I'll go see if he's still here," said Farrah. "You run upstairs to our room and get the . . . thing. Let's meet back in the lobby in five minutes."

Allison sat back in her seat as if she didn't quite know what to make of us. "Good luck," she said.

I straightened the quilt on my bed, then dumped out the contents of my overstuffed purse. How had I let it get so full? I'd have to give my purse a good Wiccan cleansing when this whole debacle was finally over.

I moved aside makeup, keys, and wallet; Zeke's broken buckle, a multitude of beads, and assorted papers. The papers reminded me of the note I'd found in the hotel reading room. I had given it to Rhinehardt, but I still remembered the gist of the message: "Meet me at 1 a.m." Edgar thought he was meeting the black-mailer.

What if he thought wrong? It had taken me days to figure out Lonnie was the blackmailer. What if Edgar mistakenly thought it was someone else? In the beginning, he had suspected Zeke. But he had also suspected someone else he never named.

Absently, I picked through the other contents of my purse: a hairbrush, a bottle of vitamins, a big red envelope containing a Christmas card from Zeke. As I held on to the envelope, my fingers began to tingle. Wasn't it odd for Zeke to give me a Christmas card a mere three days after we'd met? Considering all his hints and innuendos, I wondered if this card was something more than a simple holiday greeting.

Using a key, I slit open the envelope and removed the card. It was small and cute, featuring a snowman and woodland creatures. Nothing strange about that . . . except that the size of the card didn't quite match the envelope. When I opened it, I saw why. The card wasn't in its original envelope, and it wasn't even meant for me. It was addressed to Edgar from his insurance company.

I turned the card over, trying to figure out what Zeke had been up to. Apparently, he had grabbed one of the cards that had been displayed on top of the filing cabinets near his cubicle. I looked in the envelope again. *Aha.*

Stuffed in the bottom of the envelope was a folded sheet of paper. I pulled it out, opened it, and smoothed the creases. It was a typewritten agreement, "by and between Edgar Harrison and Tucker Brinkley."

Looks like I won't need the truth serum after all.

I skimmed the document, which appeared to be a simple partnership agreement. Then I read it again more slowly. Under the terms of the contract, the parties agreed that they would each solicit customers to invest in American Castle Fund, a real estate investment company. Each partner would be entitled to a finder's fee in the amount of twenty percent of each investment. Profits from the fund would be split fifty-fifty. The agreement would remain in effect for so long as the company remained a viable endeavor. The paper was signed at the bottom by both men.

On its face, the agreement seemed fairly innocuous. But I knew better. There was something sketchy about the fund and the way these men handled it. My intuition told me the paper in my hands was evidence of a scam.

Suddenly, I remembered my sense that someone had been following me—not to mention the burglary at my house and the close call on the highway. Did Tucker know I had this paper in my possession? Was he after this all along?

My phone buzzed as a text came through. My heart leaped when I saw it was from Crenshaw. Then I frowned when I read his message: I'm at the SC Lodge. Have very important info. Time sensitive. Meet me at the ski shed. Bring your purse and come alone. Hurry.

Chapter 27

Of course, I knew it could be a trap. The text from Crenshaw's cell phone was highly unusual. Then again, everything about the past week was highly unusual. Regardless, I wasn't about to leave Crenshaw high and dry. If he didn't send the text, then he was in trouble.

Surprisingly, I wasn't too scared. I had gotten pretty good at bluffing lately. I could do it again. If Tucker was waiting for me, I'd play dumb and act like I didn't know he was the killer. I'd tell him the police had arrested someone else. Then he could relax and think he'd gotten away with it.

That is, assuming he hadn't already done something stupid with Crenshaw.

Well, if he tried to pull a fast one, he wouldn't get away with it for long. Before leaving our room, I texted Farrah and told her to meet me at the ski shed. I also told her to bring Rhinehardt. I knew she wouldn't waste any time in joining me.

I took the back door out of the lodge and jogged over to the ski shed. After the frenzy of activity this morning, the grounds were desolate now. I glanced over at the parking lot and saw that it was empty of all but a few cars, including mine. Then Allison marched over to one of the cars and sped out of the lot. Everyone was in a hurry to go home.

When I reached the ski shed, there was no one in sight. I started to walk around to the rear of the building when my phone buzzed. It was another text from Crenshaw. I'm at the shooting range now. Come at once.

All of a sudden, my confidence drained right through the bottom of my feet. This was definitely a setup.

I headed toward the shooting range, punching in Farrah's number as I went. The call went straight to voicemail and her voicemail box was full. *Dang it, Farrah.* I searched through my telephone contacts list for Detective Rhinehardt's number, but I couldn't find it.

The shooting range was in a long metal building, surrounded by an earthen berm for soundproofing. The door was open an inch. I pulled it open wider and called inside. "Hello?" There was no answer. I stepped inside, keeping one hand on the door, and called again. "Hello!"

A dull clanking sound came from somewhere deep within the building. I took another step inside. The lights were off in the small lobby, but the door next to the check-in counter was wide open. "Hello?" I called again.

I heard a muffled cry, then Crenshaw's voice: "Keli! For the love of—" His words broke off.

"Crenshaw!"

I ran through the door and found a long narrow

hallway. To the side was another open door revealing stairs leading down to a basement.

After a brief hesitation, I hustled down the stairs and found myself in a dank utility room.

This is crazy. It was time to go for help. I was about to turn and head back up the steps when a sharp object dug into my back. Gasping, I stumbled forward.

"That's it, Miss Milanni. You're in the right place." It was Tucker's slow drawl, completely void of any charm.

I tried to twist around, but he shoved me so hard I fell to my knees.

"Steady there, missy. I need you to do me a favor. Open up that door, will you?"

I looked up and saw a heavy steel door. I knew Crenshaw must be on the other side. In a flash, I grabbed the handle and pulled the door open. It appeared to be an old gun vault, empty of weapons now. Or possibly an ancient bomb shelter. A man lay sprawled in the middle of the floor.

"Crenshaw!" I ran forward and knelt at his side. He groaned and turned his head.

"Keli, run!" he said. *It's a little late for that,* I thought. I looked up at Tucker, who stood in the doorway. He pointed a silver handgun directly at my heart.

"Set your purse on the floor," he said calmly. "Then back into the room."

I did as he ordered. Tucker picked up the purse and frowned slightly at its heft. I had scooped up almost all the items I'd dumped on the bed and dropped them back into my purse.

"I've been quite interested in the contents of this here handbag. I surely do hope it contains a certain piece of paper I've been tryin' to locate."

"I don't know what you're talking about," I said. "Why are you doing this?"

Tucker laughed quietly. "No need to be coy. I know you been snoopin' around. I also know you were up on the ridge this morning. I was on my way back to the top, 'cause I thought I dropped something. I saw you and sweet Farrah, and figured you must've seen me."

"We didn't," I said. "We didn't know who was with Lonnie."

"Whoops. Guess you do now." Tucker backed toward the exit and reached for the door. A rush of alarm flooded through me at the thought of being trapped inside the small, dark, windowless room. I had to keep him talking.

"Edgar thought you were blackmailing him, didn't he?" I blurted.

Tucker laughed again. "You want to know the funny thing? I thought *he* was tryin' to blackmail *me* that night after the ball. He said he wanted to meet me up in the hotel reading room. Then he started talking about Cornerstone and our investment arrangement, broken promises and betrayals and hush money. I figured it was his sorry attempt at extortion."

"So you killed him."

"I got angry. And rightfully so. I stalked off, but he chased me down. He kept yammering right there in the hallway, so I grabbed his shirt and pushed him to the edge of the railing. 'Don't you dare threaten me, old man,' I said to him. Well, he lost his footing and tumbled right over. I thought that was the end of that, until I received a pretty little letter demanding sixty-K of my hard-earned cash. And it sure as hell wasn't from Edgar's ghost. That's when I realized Edgar musta got a letter, too. We each thought the other was the blackmailer. It was a regular whatchamacallit—a comedy of errors."

"So you took it upon yourself to find out who the blackmailer was."

"Indeed I did. I remembered that damn fool agreement Edgar made me sign, and I figured somebody musta found it. Well, the most logical person was one of you lawyers, who were diggin' into Edgar's papers."

"That's why you were following me."

"Naturally."

"You broke into my house, didn't you? And forced Wes and me off the road? We could have rammed into you, you know."

"Nah," said Tucker. "I had you in my sights the whole time. I sure thought you woulda flipped over, though. Or at least conked your heads."

"All that just to steal my purse?" *He's crazy. Dirty rotten, scary-crazy.*

"Well, that and to send you a message. If you were the one blackmailing me, I was gonna teach you a lesson. 'Course, then I left that stack of money in the trash bin as instructed. That's when I discovered who the culprit really was."

"How did you know Lonnie retrieved the money?"

"Why, I was watching, o'course. Hidin' in the trees. I saw you and thought I'd caught you red-handed. Then, you skedaddled and poor Lonnie come along."

"So, you killed him, too."

"He was a fool. I shoulda realized it was him all along. Sixty thousand was the amount of his down payment on the Cornerstone deal. But I'm sure that wasn't all he wanted. He would've been back for more."

"You're not going to get away with this, Tucker. Don't make it worse on yourself."

"I already have gotten away with it. Now, take a seat there next to your gentleman friend."

I glanced at Crenshaw, who appeared to be unconscious. "What did you do to him? He needs medical attention."

"Leave him be. It'll be easier that way."

"Tucker, listen to me! Just let us go. Farrah will be looking for me. The police will be looking."

"We'll see about that. You got a phone in here?" He reached into my purse and pulled out my cell phone. "I'll just shoot off a text message to Farrah, so she won't worry her pretty little head. Let's see . . . 'I left with Crenshaw. He needed some cheering up. All is well. You go home 'n have a merry xmas.'"

I shook my head. Farrah would never fall for it. *Would she?*

"Then," Tucker continued, "when I come back from vacation in January and just happen to open up the vault, I'll find the missing lovers. But it'll be too late. Everyone will think you all snuck off for a secret liaison and got yourselves locked in. Your hideaway became your tomb. So sad."

With that, he backed out and slammed the door shut behind him, leaving us in complete blackness. Fighting panic, I turned back to Crenshaw and shook him gently. "Crenshaw! Wake up. We have to find a way out of here."

I heard him groan and felt him try to sit up. Feeling blindly, I reached for his hand to help him up. With my other hand I supported his back. "How bad are you?" I asked. "What did he do to you?"

"I think I'm okay." Crenshaw removed his hand from mine to rub his head. "Tucker held me at gunpoint and compelled me to call for you, to lure you down here. When I tried to warn you, he hit me on the side of the head with the butt of his gun. I fell, landing on the other side of my head."

I cringed. "How did you end up down here in the first place?"

"Tucker showed up last night to rescue me from the side of the road. Some rescuer. He brought me to the lodge, and said he needed my help with an electrical issue. He said the fuse box for the lodge was in this basement. He led me downstairs and right into this vault, where he left me. Of course, he asked to see my cell phone first, which I handed right over. The con artist."

"So, you didn't know he was the killer? I thought you found proof in your research."

"I learned that American Castle Fund had failed to file any financial statements with the SEC. I realized any statements the company provided to investors must have been fraudulent. Putting two and two together, I assumed the blackmailer-turned-murderer was someone Edgar had defrauded—someone like Lonnie Treat."

"I thought the same thing at first. Did you tell Beverly or anyone else?"

"No. I wanted to talk to you first." Crenshaw paused. "It would seem our present situation is somewhat dire."

I tried to look around the room, but the darkness was impenetrable.

"What's in here?" I asked. "Did you look for a way to break out?"

"Of course, I looked. I combed every inch of this place and found little more than dust and cobwebs. I'm afraid our best chance is for someone to find us. I trust you didn't come here without informing someone."

I swallowed hard, and my head began to swim. My mind flashed back to the previous February when I'd found myself trapped underground with no way out. Suddenly, I couldn't breathe. Wheezing, I ducked my head between my legs.

"Keli? What's happening? Are you hyperventilating?" Crenshaw reached out his hand and jabbed me in the ear.

I lifted my head. "Ouch."

"I beg your pardon." Fumbling in the dark, he managed to pat the top of my head. "Don't fret now. You were with your friend Farrah at the lodge, correct? Based on my impression of your friendship, I'm certain she'll scour the ends of the earth to find you."

I tried to smile, but then I had a terrible thought. *Farrah's in danger.* Tucker thought we'd both seen him with Lonnie at the top of the ridge. *When he discovers the incriminating paper is not in my purse, he'll stop at nothing to track it down.*

Trying not to cry, I placed my face in my hands and forced myself to breathe slowly. I had to stay calm. I had to come up with a plan.

With my eyes still closed, I pictured the platinum-haired moon goddess from the picture in Mila's shop. She smiled at me and held out her hand. I felt a warm glow at my heart chakra. As if on autopilot, I began a whispered chant:

> Mother Goddess, save me
> Father God, protect me
> Mother Goddess, guide me
> Father God, inspire me

"Have you gone mad already?" said Crenshaw. "Where's the indomitable Keli Milanni I know so well?"

"Shh."

"I beg your pardon. I didn't—"

"Hush! I hear something."

We both fell silent and listened. There was a muffled voice. It sounded as if it was coming from somewhere within the vault.

I stood up, held out my hands, and reached to the wall for balance. Following the sound of the voice, I titled my head up. "There must be an air vent up there on the wall," I said.

"Ah," said Crenshaw. "I noticed that when the door was open. It's not even one foot wide. Not a viable means of escape."

"That's Tucker's voice," I whispered. "He must be on the telephone."

Listening intently, we heard Tucker laugh. "All righty then, Ricardo," he said. "You have a real nice holiday. I'll see you when I get back."

There was silence once more. A moment later, Tucker spoke again. "Howdy there, Mr. MacIntyre. Sorry to bug you on Christmas Day. . . . Yes, well, I wanted to catch you before you flew back to DC. About that PAC of yours—I wanted you to know how flattered I am y'all are considering me. I'm very interested in winning your support. When can we get together?"

Listening to Tucker laugh and make plans for his own bright future, after he had killed two people and left two more to die, made my blood boil. I couldn't let him get away with this. If the only way out of here was through the locked door, I needed to get him back down here to open it. And my window of opportunity was closing fast.

"That sounds just fine to me," said Tucker. "You take care now."

I peered into the darkness, trying to locate Crenshaw. "Psst. Come over here. I need you to give me a boost."

He touched my arm, causing me to jump. "A boost to where?"

I kicked off my shoes. "As close to the vent as possible. Just trust me and play along."

I stepped into Crenshaw's cupped hands and pressed my palms on the wall. Then, as loudly as possible without sounding too ridiculous, I yelled toward the vent. "Don't worry, Crenshaw! He won't get away with this. There's something he doesn't know."

Catching on, Crenshaw projected his voice as if he were on a stage. "Do go on! I'm not sure what you mean."

"I have the proof! I have that paper from Edgar's office. It's hidden in my bra."

"Oh, my!" said Crenshaw.

"When they find our bodies, they'll know the truth." I lowered my voice and tapped on Crenshaw's head. "Okay, let me down."

He complied, grabbing my arm to steady me. "Have

you forgotten our captor's advantage?" he asked. "He's armed, and we aren't."

"He doesn't want to use the gun," I said. "It's too messy. Too direct. Otherwise, he would have used it already. Think about it. We're in a firing range. He could have tried to make it look like an accident."

"True," Crenshaw conceded. "Using a firearm wouldn't be consistent with his modus operandi. However, if he's left with no other choice . . ." Crenshaw trailed off.

"We're just gonna have to overpower him. It's our only hope."

We heard a dull scraping sound from outside of the vault. It might have been the door opening at the top of the stairs. Quickly I pulled off my leggings and stretched them taut.

"Here," I whispered, handing them to Crenshaw. "Hide in the corner. I'll distract him. When his back is to you, use this around his neck. I'd do it, but you're taller."

"Good Lord, Milanni."

"Just take it!"

The door handle turned. Crenshaw retreated to the corner, and I ran to the back of the room, picking up my shoes along the way. Pressing my back against the wall, I faced the door. Besides the element of surprise, I realized we had something else going for us. Our eyes had adjusted to the darkness. I edged into the darkest corner of the room.

The door swung open. Tucker stood at the threshold, his gun held out in front of him. I needed him to come inside the room. "Forget something?" I asked.

"Come here," Tucker said.

"Why? Have you decided to let us go? Crenshaw needs a doctor."

"Stop flappin' your mouth and get over here," said Tucker.

I silently willed him to come inside: *Step in the room, step in the room, step in the room. By all the powers of the ancient universe, I command you to step into the room.*

He stepped into the room.

"Catch!" I threw a shoe at him.

Taken off guard, he fumbled to catch the shoe. It bounced off his arm. I tossed the other shoe, and Crenshaw made his move. With lightning speed, he had the leggings around Tucker's neck. The cowboy's knees buckled. I ran forward and grabbed his gun.

Crenshaw pushed Tucker to the ground and released his hold. We rushed out of the vault, slamming the door behind us.

A short while later Crenshaw and I huddled by the side of the lodge with a small but growing crowd of people, all eyes fixed on the firing range entrance. The hushed group consisted of the hunting lodge staff, including Ricardo, the handyman-turned-deejay, as well as the few remaining guests who hadn't yet checked out. I sensed a movement out of the corner of my eye and turned to see Zeke sidle over and stand next to me. I nodded at him, then turned back to stare at the solid, motionless door. It had probably been only a few minutes since Detective Rhinehardt and his officers went inside, but it felt like eons.

After locking Tucker in the vault, Crenshaw and I

had raced back to the lodge until we were distracted by the roar of a snowmobile. It zoomed toward us from the valley behind the ski shed, kicking up powdery snow in its wake. It took me a second to recognize Farrah holding on to the burly form of Detective Rhinehardt. We waved frantically at them as they sped up to us and cut the engine. The moment they dismounted from the vehicle, we all started talking at once.

"Keli, oh my God!" Farrah shouted, breathless.

"What's this I hear about—" Rhinehardt began, until Crenshaw interrupted with what was sure to be a long-winded explanation, beginning, as he did, with the night of Edgar's ball.

"Detective!" I said, cutting off Crenshaw. "Tucker is locked in a windowless room in the basement of the firing range. He admitted he killed both Edgar and Lonnie. He also attacked Crenshaw and threatened to kill the two of us." I held out Tucker's gun like it was a gift. With the slightest raise of an eyebrow, Rhinehardt took the weapon and radioed for assistance.

Farrah grabbed my arm and pulled me aside. "Are you okay? After you went upstairs for your potion, I tried to track down Rhinehardt. I found out he had left on skis to investigate the scene of Lonnie's death. I thought I could catch up to him pretty fast on a snowmobile, so I borrowed this one from the lodge. I was already halfway up the bluff when I saw your text."

"I'm fine," I said, hoping I'd feel the same when the adrenaline wore off. As it was, my legs were starting to feel rubbery.

When two police officers joined Detective Rhinehardt at the edge of the firing range building, and people started trickling out of the lodge, word soon spread about what was going on. Crenshaw took a moment to slip inside and call Beverly. By the time he rejoined us, there was quite a little crowd waiting for the officers to emerge from the firing range. At last the door burst open.

The first thing I noticed was how unconcerned Tucker appeared. With Rhinehardt in front of him and one officer at each elbow, he carried himself like a dignitary being escorted to a high-class function. Never mind that his hands were shackled behind his back. He lifted his chin high and squinted into the sunlight. But the stony façade didn't last long. As the somber procession made its way up the sidewalk, Tucker caught sight of the gawkers—including Farrah who stood front and center with her arms folded across her chest. Suddenly, the cowboy seemed to shrink before our eyes. He slumped his shoulders and cast his head downward, staring at his boots all the way to the parking lot. He didn't even look up when the officers hustled him into a waiting squad car.

"So, it really *was* him," said Zeke in a low voice.

I turned to frown at the young guy. "Are you saying you didn't know? You're the one who gave me that crude paper signed by Tucker and Edgar. Speaking of which, why did you put it in a Christmas card instead of just handing it over?"

Zeke shook his head. "I had learned someone was blackmailing Edgar and figured it must be Lonnie, but I had no way to prove it. I also knew that little paper must be important. I was afraid having it in my possession might make me look like a suspect."

Ha, I thought to myself. Little did he know that he had been a suspect anyway.

"I was aware of your reputation as a crafty sleuth," Zeke went on. "I figured you'd know what to do."

I looked back at the parking lot and noticed Crenshaw speaking with Detective Rhinehardt. When they parted, the detective went to his car and drove around directly behind the police car. We all watched as they pulled out of the lot and headed down the lane. I heard Farrah sigh and reached over to squeeze her hand.

Zeke sighed, too. "I guess this means I'm out of a job again."

Chapter 28

Five days later, I entered the lobby of Olsen, Sykes, and Rafferty fresh from my belated trip home for the holidays. After a week of homemade vegan casseroles, stews, and cakes, I vowed to drink a green juice every morning and hit the gym every evening for the foreseeable future. Now, though, my first order of business was a prescheduled meeting with Beverly and Crenshaw. I found them waiting for me in Beverly's private lounge.

"Have a seat, Keli," said Beverly, from her wingback chair by the decorative fireplace. "Would you like a cup of coffee?"

"Sure," I said, helping myself to a cup from the carafe on the coffee table.

"Welcome back," said Crenshaw. "I trust you had a relaxing vacation?"

"I did. Thanks." I sat in the chair next to his and took a sip of coffee. With the niceties out of the way, I waited expectantly for Beverly to begin.

She cleared her throat. "Keli, as I already mentioned

to Crenshaw, I want you both to know how grateful I am for your assistance and support these past few weeks. You went well above and beyond the call of duty. It means a lot to me personally. Thank you."

Crenshaw nodded modestly, and I murmured, "You're welcome."

"I also want to apologize for involving you in something that became far more serious and dangerous than I ever anticipated. I would *never* have given you the assignment to track down Edgar's blackmailer if I had known where it would lead." Beverly leaned forward, her expression earnest. "I hope you'll believe me when I say I knew nothing of Edgar's apparent wrongdoing. If I had even an inkling that he had done anything remotely outside the bounds of law, I would have advised him to come clean and make amends."

"Of course," said Crenshaw. "We know that."

"I acknowledge that my personal relationship with him might be viewed as inappropriate by some," Beverly continued, "although we were consenting adults with a long history. In any event, that's a moot point now."

"Any news about Tucker?" I asked. I really didn't want to hear any more details about my boss's love life.

"He's still in the county jail," said Beverly. "I imagine he'll enter a plea agreement, rather than proceed to trial. He already admitted his guilt to the two of you. I think he understands the evidence is stacked against him."

"I've been thinking about the scam Tucker and Edgar had going," I said. "I'm not sure I fully understand it.

Was it a Ponzi scheme? And were there victims besides Lonnie?"

"You know," said Beverly, thoughtfully, "I like to think Edgar started out with good intentions. He thought Cornerstone would be lucrative." She paused, shaking her head. "I shouldn't speculate. The truth will come out eventually. Anyway, it's my understanding that other investors did lose money due to Edgar's improprieties. Fortunately, Gretta is cooperating with the investigators, and she's promised to reimburse all of Edgar's victims from his estate."

Beverly looked down at her hands. "I'm sure Gretta didn't know anything about Edgar's business activities, legal or otherwise. She must have been just as shocked as I was."

"Of course, Edgar wasn't solely responsible," said Crenshaw. "Let's not forget Tucker. He knew very well what he had done was illegal, and he was willing to go to any length to keep the facts hidden."

Beverly looked up. "Again, I am deeply, deeply sorry for the danger you faced."

"We don't blame you," I said. "It wasn't your fault."

"Not at all," said Crenshaw.

"Well," said Beverly, "on a brighter note, Randall, Kris, and I met yesterday to discuss the future of the firm. We reached a very important decision—though, you can be assured the decision has been in the works for several months now. It wasn't based solely on the events of the past several days."

My heart started beating a little faster as I realized what Beverly was about to say.

"We'll meet with each of you separately to extend

our formal offer, but I'd like to be the first to give you a heads-up." Beverly smiled. "It would be my honor and privilege to have each of you as co-owners and junior partners in our law firm family."

I broke out into a grin. "Thank you, Beverly," I said.

I turned to Crenshaw and was surprised to find him looking at me. "Congratulations, Ms. Milanni. This is an honor you most deservedly have earned."

"Right back atcha, Crenshaw," I said, shaking his hand.

Beverly stood. "Go ahead and finish your coffee. I need to go see Julie for a minute."

When our boss left, we sat quietly for a moment, each absorbed in our own thoughts. Then I got up and set my cup on the table. "Guess I'll get to work," I said.

"Wait," said Crenshaw, standing. "How are you? That is, how have you been since our little episode in the gun vault? I hope you haven't had nightmares or flashbacks."

I smiled. "It was pretty scary, but I'm fine. No long-term damage. How about you? Have you been holding up okay?"

"Who, me? Why, yes. I've been splendid." He stroked his beard. "It was quite a remarkable turn of events, though, wasn't it? Sheana Starwalt has been after me for an exclusive interview. I wonder if you'd mind . . . ?"

"No," I said. "I don't mind. You're free to talk to her if you'd like."

He nodded. "Very good. I'm sure she would like to question you, too, if you're amenable."

"We'll see," I said.

"You know, there is one question I have for you."

"Oh? What's that?"

"How did you manage to pull yourself together down there? One minute you were hyperventilating, the next you were flying around like Wonder Woman and barking orders like General Patton. How did you do it?"

"Oh, that's easy," I said, heading for the exit. "I'm a witch."

Chapter 29

The late afternoon sun streamed through the skylights in the old civic center. The building was closed to the public during renovations, but outgoing mayor Helen Trumley had granted special permission for the use of the gymnatorium by her construction foreman, Alex Douglas. Today was his wife's initiation ceremony. She was being ordained as a Wiccan high priestess.

I glanced over at Alex, beaming with pride from the front row. I felt exceptionally proud, too—of Mila for her amazing achievement and of myself for being there. It was high time I lighten up a little, I realized, and not be so paranoid about exposing my chosen religion.

When I told Farrah I had decided to attend the ceremony, she begged to come along. She was eager for a distraction, anything to help her forget the whole Tucker affair—or, as she called it, "that time I dated a murderer." She joked about her poor taste in men, but I knew she felt hurt and betrayed, not to mention a little foolish. She also mentioned that she wanted to get to know Mila better. "I need to take a lesson or two from her," Farrah had said, "and learn to hone my own psychic abilities. Then maybe I can actually use my women's intuition instead of being duped by psycho cowboys."

I checked with Mila about bringing a guest to the event and, of course, she was more than happy to have Farrah attend. Now Farrah gazed in fascination at the altar in the center of the large room.

"What are all those objects up there?" she whispered.

"The ones up front represent the five elements," I explained. "An eagle feather, for air, a candle for fire, a bowl of water, for water, obviously, and a bowl of sand for earth. The pentagram represents the fifth element, spirit."

"Is it just plain tap water?"

"It could be," I said. "But in this case, Mila told me that her coven members each brought something special as an offering for the occasion. The water is from a stream in the woods where the group performs outdoor rituals. The sand is from a special beach, and the other items are of personal significance to the group."

"That's awesome. This is so cool."

I had to agree. The setup was beautiful, with potted white poinsettia trees on either side of the altar, a dozen white roses in a vase on a side table, and a sacred pathway delineated by pine boughs on the floor. Then I heard a rhythmic drumbeat and saw thirteen women appear all in a line on the other side of the room. The audience fell silent as the women marched up the path toward the altar.

First in line was Max Eisenberry, a university English professor I had first met when I was trying to track down a missing copy of Shakespeare's First Folio. Since then, I had become further acquainted with her through Mila. A petite woman with curly red hair, Max had been appointed as mistress of ceremonies for the initiation. She carried a stick of incense, perfuming the air with the scent of juniper berries.

Behind Max was Mila herself. In a simple white shift dress and with a flower in her hair, she looked lovely but not showy. I knew she wanted it to be clear that this was an initiation, and not a coronation. Still, she had an inner radiance that made her stand out from the others.

Eleven women followed Mila. They were a diverse group of many ages, colors, sizes, and personalities. Last in line was Catrina, Mila's young assistant at Moonstone Treasures. Catrina played the djembe in a slow, deliberate cadence that gave the proceedings an air of solemnity.

When the women reached the altar, they formed a wide circle. Max addressed the audience. "Welcome and merry meet. We're so happy you all could join us for this special occasion. For those unfamiliar with Wiccan rituals, I'll explain the proceedings as we go. First, we will cast a circle. A circle serves several functions. It delineates our sacred space, acts as a vessel for our magical energies, represents the communal, non-hierarchical nature of our religion, and symbolizes the eternal cycle of life. To cast the circle, we will call the quarters and invite our spiritual guides to join with us."

After the circle was cast, Mila walked up to the altar and stood behind it, facing the audience. Max stepped forward. "Mila Douglas, how do you join this circle?"

"In perfect love and perfect trust," Mila answered.

"And how will you accept the responsibility of High Priestess of Coven of the Magic Circle?"

"With humility, honor, dedication, and sincerity."

Max smiled and handed Mila one of the roses from the vase. She turned to the audience. "Each Circle member will now say a few words and present Mila with a rose. This is our way of expressing our confidence in her, our encouragement, and our gratitude. We'll start with Becca, who will read the Charge of the Goddess."

Around the circle they went, some women reading short poems or passages, others speaking from the heart. After Catrina had her turn, Max spoke again. "As the sun king was reborn at Yuletide, and the Wheel of the Year turns toward a new season, so do we awaken to a new dawn. Each new phase of life comes with fresh challenges and opportunities for growth, but we can be secure in the knowledge that we are not alone."

Max selected something from the side table and held it up with both hands. "Mila Douglas, I hereby present you with the silver ring of the triple goddess. May the ancestors bless you, and the Goddess be your guide."

"Blessed be," said Mila, accepting the ring. The audience broke out in applause as the two women hugged, then returned to their places in the circle. Max turned to Mila again, took her hand, and said, "Thou art Goddess." Mila echoed the blessing, then turned to the woman on her left and said it to her: "Thou art Goddess." Around the circle they went, from woman to woman, passing on their acknowledgment of the divinity within.

Farrah nudged me. "I want to be a goddess," she whispered. "Can you give the blessing to me?"

I rolled my eyes but smiled. "Thou art Goddess," I whispered.

"Yay! Thou art Goddess, too." She hugged me, then turned to watch the final part of the ritual. Max addressed the audience once more.

"Now I will close the circle by walking widdershins. That's the Scottish word for counterclockwise," she explained. "As I go, I will thank the deities and the powers of the elements."

Using a wand from the altar, Mila retraced her steps around the circle, pausing at each cardinal direction to express the coven's gratitude. Finally, she drew a pentagram in the air and said, "The circle is open but not broken. Merry meet, merry part, and merry meet again."

As the group dispersed, some lined up behind Mila to congratulate her, while others moved toward the audience to greet friends and loved ones. "Oh!" said Max, clapping her hands. "Be sure to join us in the cafeteria for cakes and ale!"

Farrah and I held back to give our best wishes to Mila. When it was our turn, Mila beamed at both of us.

"I'm so glad you came!" she said. "What did you think?"

"That was amazing," said Farrah. "Such a privilege to witness. And I have so many questions. For one thing, do covens always have to have thirteen witches? No more, no less?"

"It's not a hard and fast rule," said Mila. "Thirteen is traditional because of the thirteen full moons in the years that have a blue moon. It's also a good, manageable number. Of course, groups naturally evolve over time. People come and go. This group was together as a unit for a year and a day before we called ourselves a coven, but we sometimes have gatherings that contain more or fewer members." Mila winked at me. "Keli knows she has an open invitation."

I smiled. "I have to admit, seeing all those women in the circle was pretty impressive. I can only imagine how intense it must be when you all raise energy in ritual."

Mila nodded. "Yes. It's quite powerful."

"Still," I said, "I like my solitary practice."

"That's perfectly fine and perfectly valid," said Mila. "In fact, we should all take the time to develop a personal relationship with the Divine. This includes learning to know ourselves—as the ancient Greeks advised in the famous inscription at the temple at Delphi. You can't make magic without self-awareness. In other words, you have to spend time with yourself to gain the wisdom you need for effective witchcraft."

"Spoken like a true high priestess," I said with a smile.

"Spoken like a true oracle," said Farrah, with a tinge of awe in her voice. "I really need to book an appointment with you."

Mila laughed, a joyful sound that rang out like tinkling bells. "Anytime, dear. Anytime."

Later that evening, Farrah and I dressed up in little black party dresses and headed to the Loose Rock to ring in the New Year. As soon as we entered the nightclub, someone tossed a balloon our way. I batted it to the side and took a look around. Black and gold streamers hung from the walls, while strobe lights flashed above the dance floor. Clusters of people laughed, danced, and tossed back drinks.

I felt a tap on my shoulder and turned to see Julie from the office. She wore a plastic tiara and carried a long-stemmed glass. "Congratulations again, Madame Partner!"

"Thanks, Julie," I said, smiling.

Julie moved on, and Zeke appeared in her place. "Ladies," he said, lifting his beer glass in greeting. "Can I offer you some beads?" He pointed to several strands of colorful Mardi Gras beads hanging from his neck. *How appropriate,* I thought with a smirk. Hopefully, these beads wouldn't break like all the others he had lost.

"Sure, data boy," said Farrah. "I'll take red."

I chose green and dipped my chin to allow Zeke to place the beads over my head. As he did, he whispered in my ear. "Did you have a nice afternoon?" he asked.

I narrowed my eyes. "Yes. Why do you ask?"

"No reason." He winked at me, then disappeared into the crowd. I would have to keep my eye on that guy.

We continued through the club until I finally spotted Wes behind the bar. He had come early to give Jimi a hand. As soon as he saw me, he hung up his apron and joined us. "Hey, beauties. I saved a table for us. Are you hungry? Jimi is keeping the kitchen open late tonight."

"Maybe later," said Farrah. She grinned at Wes and squeezed my arm. "Right now I'm going to hit the dance floor and boogie my cares away. I'll catch you two later."

For the next few hours, Wes and I stuck together like the glitter glue on our candle centerpiece. It had been hard to say good-bye when I left for my trip to

Nebraska, especially coming on the heels of my close encounter with a killer. Now Wes didn't want to let me out of his sight. I couldn't say that I minded.

Every now and then, friends dropped by our table to say hello. Among them were Jimi, sporting a felt-covered New Year's top hat; Pammy and her husband; and Bob the driver. Bob told us he was offering free rides to anyone who needed a designated driver at the end of the night. He was doing it partly because he was a nice guy and partly to drum up interest in his new business. He had decided to start his own private car service, rather than work exclusively for any one employer.

At midnight, Wes and I finally left our table to join the revelers on the dance floor. We counted down the seconds, then whooped and hollered in celebration. Someone scattered buckets of confetti on our heads, while the bartender kept the champagne flowing. Wes and I kissed beneath a disco ball. Pulling back, we smiled at each other. Then, as if by unspoken agreement, we slipped out the door to stand under the stars.

The cold air was crisp and bracing. To me, it felt exhilarating. Maybe it was the champagne. More likely, it was Wes. We faced each other, hand in hand. He looked into my eyes.

"I love you, Keli Milanni."

"I love you, Wes Callahan."

Wes squeezed my hands and drew me closer. "There's something I want to ask you."

My heart skipped a beat. "Then go ahead and ask," I said playfully.

"Ah, well, it's kind of spur of the moment," he said. "I know I'm ready, but I'm not sure if you're ready."

"I'm ready for anything," I said. *Ask away*.

Suddenly, the door burst open and Jimi ran up. "Yo, Keli! I got a message for you."

I frowned at the intrusion. "A message?"

"Yeah, there was a phone call." He glanced down at a paper in his hand. "From a woman named A. J. She left her number and asked you to call her back when you can. Here you go."

He handed me the note, then tipped his hat at Wes. "Carry on," he said. He dashed back inside.

Bewildered, I read the note by the light of a street lamp. It was an Edindale phone number.

"Who's A. J.?" asked Wes.

"I'm not sure, but I have a hunch. . . ." I trailed off, then folded the note and looked back up at Wes. "What was it you were going to ask me?"

"Oh, yeah." He grinned and ran his fingers through his hair. "I was wondering . . . How would you feel about living together?"

Living with Wes? Sharing a home, waking up next to him, taking one big step closer to "happily ever after"?

"Hmm," I said, pretending to consider it. "I think I would feel . . . thrilled about the idea." I smiled at him, then laughed out loud when he picked me up and twirled me around.

"Awesome," he said. "What a great start to the New Year."

He took my hand again and we started walking back toward the nightclub door. Suddenly, Wes paused. "Wait a minute. 'A. J.' Could that be your aunt Josephine?"

Perceptive man. I was impressed. "It could be," I said. "Maybe I'll finally get to meet her after all these years. And find out what she's been up to."

Wes tilted his head as he glanced down at me. "Mystery follows you around, doesn't it? I guess I oughta get used to that."

"Yeah," I said, feeling a surge of happiness. "I think you should."

ACKNOWLEDGEMENTS

I'd like to extend a great big "thank you" to all the folks who had a hand in the creation of this book. This includes my always supportive and encouraging family, from my husband, daughter, parents, and sibs, to my beautiful Grandma Lucille—and even my amazing in-laws and far-flung extended family. You're all awesome!

And a deep gratitude, once again, to my trusted first readers: Tom, Cathy, Jana, and Jill. Although they are family, they always read my drafts with a careful and critical eye, catching all kinds of issues that I might have missed.

Special thanks to Jennifer Burke, friend, colleague, and fantastic attorney, for reading the manuscript from a lawyer's viewpoint.

Thanks to my amazing agent, Rachel Brooks, whose sound advice always makes my books stronger. And thanks to my wonderful editor and champion, Martin Biro, as well as the whole Kensington team. You all rock!

Finally, I'd like to acknowledge all the real-life Witches, Wiccans, and Pagans who have shared their views in books, blogs, articles, and videos. I'd especially like to thank Traci Logan Wood and the other lovely people who graciously agreed to be featured in an interview series on my website. My intention in writing the Wiccan Wheel Mysteries has always been to be true to life and respectful of the Wiccan religion. It has been incredibly helpful and inspiring to hear the stories of so many diverse individuals on their own magically creative spiritual paths.

Blessed be to all.

If you enjoyed *Yuletide Homicide* be sure
not to miss all of Jennifer David Hesse's
Wiccan Wheel series, including

BELL, BOOK & CANDLEMAS

Keep reading for a special excerpt.

A Kensington mass-market and e-book on sale now!

Chapter 1

The energy in the air was palpable. I could almost see it sparkling around the charred remains of the old bonfire. As I walked the perimeter of the stone-encircled clearing, I remembered the night I had learned about this place six months ago. My friend Farrah and I had stumbled upon a festive solstice celebration. We happened to be lost in the woods at the time, and Farrah kind of freaked out at the unexpected sight of a Pagan moon dance in the middle of the forest.

What Farrah didn't know was that her best friend—yours truly—was a Pagan, too. A Solitary Wiccan, to be precise. Farrah, my BFF since law school, would freak out all over again if she found out. I was sure of it.

Who would have thought? Sweet, levelheaded Keli Milanni: staid attorney, disciplined athlete, borderline yuppie. And witch.

We watched from the shadows that night a few months ago. Since then, I started coming back here on early weekend mornings, weather permitting. It was a small, secluded glade, off the beaten track. I was able to access it through the open grounds of Briar Creek Cabins, which were nestled inside Shawnee National Forest about ten miles outside of town. Lucky for me, I always found it to be quiet and empty. Perfect for my own private nature-loving rituals.

Inhaling the crisp, woodsy air, I lifted my chin and closed my eyes. A light breeze rustled the bare branches above me, where watchful birds ruffled their feathers. The pure, familiar whistle of a cardinal called out like an old friend, and I opened my eyes in time to catch a glimpse of bright red flit through the trees. I didn't know why cardinals sang all year long. All I knew was it made me happy.

Smiling, I traced a circle in the earth four times, pausing to bow in reverence at each direction. When I faced east, I raised my arms to the sky in a literal sun salutation. I breathed deeply. Rooting my feet to the earth, I envisioned myself as one of the trees that surrounded me. I murmured a prayer of devotion and thanksgiving for Mother Earth.

Then I closed my eyes, my body humming, the earth and the air humming around me. For a few moments I let it fill me up, energize me. When I opened my eyes, the world shimmered around me in an aura of golden light. I exhaled, then slowly retraced my steps around the circle to close the ritual.

Feeling light and peaceful, I walked over to the denim knapsack I had left next to an ancient white oak. I took out a small empty jar and used it to scoop some snow from the base of the tree. I would use it later, when it was time to say good-bye to winter. It wouldn't be long now before the earth showed signs of the life

stirring beneath its surface. Candlemas was less than
two weeks away.

After securely tucking the jar into a pocket in the
knapsack, I took a swig from my water bottle. Then I
grabbed a handful of candied almonds to munch as
I wandered around the woods. Each time I came
here, I explored a little more, being careful not to
venture too far afield. It was easy to get lost in the thick
forest.

I definitely felt a connection to this place. And more
than a spiritual connection; I felt a familial one as well.
I had a feeling my elusive Aunt Josephine's commune
had been somewhere around here, once upon a time.

Aunt Josephine, my mom's older sister, was the
black sheep of her Nebraskan family. When she was
sixteen or seventeen, she ran off with a guy—"a long-
haired Bohemian poet," according to the stories—who
was a few years older than Josie. Her parents were
livid. Josie left them a note but didn't contact them
again for months. Apparently, she and her man were
headed to a music festival out East somewhere but
somehow wound up here in Southern Illinois instead.
They made a home for some time, maybe a year or
two. The next postcard Josie sent was from Florida, and
the one after that was from New Orleans. Then the postcards stopped for a number of years, until out of the
blue came one from another state. A few more years,
yet another state. And so on.

I had received some of the postcards myself, on my
tenth, twentieth, and, most recently, my thirtieth birthday. It was nice to know she thought of me, even kept
track of me—like a kindly fairy godmother, if only
from afar. My aunt always intrigued me, even though I

had never met her. Her story was part of the reason I chose to come to Edindale for law school, and then stayed here to live.

Lost in these daydreams, I almost dismissed the snap of a twig some ten yards off. At first, I assumed the nearby rustling I'd heard was a squirrel. Now I wasn't so sure. Senses on alert, I looked around, squinting through the thick stand of trees and shrubbery. In my meandering, I hadn't bothered to stay on a trail. Now I realized I was only a few feet away from a winding dirt path. And there was someone coming down it, toward me.

I ran to the nearest big tree and hid behind its massive trunk. While I wasn't skyclad—it was way too cold for nudity, not that I would remove my clothes outdoors anyway—I wasn't exactly dressed for company. In my faux fur moccasins and white velvet hooded cloak, I would certainly raise an eyebrow.

Cringing behind the tree, I stood as still as possible, though I did gently lift the silver pentagram hanging on a chain around my neck and drop it into my dress. Just in case.

As the sound of shuffling footsteps drew nearer, I rested my forehead against the tree and silently begged the Goddess to shield me in invisibility. I didn't dare peek around. If someone was to see me like this, I'd die of mortification. *Why did I have to leave this darn cloak on?* I was getting too complacent out here; I should never have been so bold.

After several quiet minutes, I realized the person must be gone. Breathing a sigh of relief, I tiptoed out of my hiding place and ventured over to the path. At first, it appeared deserted. I let my eyes follow the trail as it snaked through the woods, crossed a creek, and then disappeared around a bend. I was about to scurry back to my knapsack when something caught my eye in the distance. A blob of bright purple rose from the ground, then bobbed into the trees.

I shook my head and squinted. *What in the world?*

Without thinking, I followed the trail a few feet, trying to catch a glimpse of the purple thing again. Sure enough, there it was, flashing in and out among the brown trees. After a moment, it dawned on me what it was, and I had to clap my hand over my mouth to stifle a laugh.

It was just the hiker. He or she must have been bending over, and then stood up. The vivid purple was the person's jacket.

Here I thought I was dressed strangely.

The person was far enough away that I didn't worry about getting caught anymore. I couldn't even make out the color of their hair or any other features in the camouflage of the trees. Just that crazy purple coat, waving like a banner in a parade. As I watched, it moved farther away. Suddenly, it appeared to drop straight to the ground. Cocking my head, I waited a moment. Surely, it would reappear any time now.

When the purple jacket failed to materialize, I clenched my jaw. Had the person fallen? Was he or she hurt?

I ran down the trail toward the spot where the blur had dropped out of sight. As I got closer, I realized the person must have left the path. Whereas the trail veered left, the purple jacket had been weaving among the trees to the right.

I crisscrossed the area for several minutes, even

calling out twice. I was sure this was the spot I had last seen a flash of purple. But there was no one there.

Whoever it was had completely disappeared.

Two days later, I had pretty much forgotten my little Saturday morning adventure in the woods. It occurred to me that the purple-clad hiker had probably spotted me—a suspicious, fur-footed woman in a ghostly-white riding hood—and disappeared on purpose. Who could blame them? I would have to be more discreet next time.

As I dressed for work Monday morning, I selected the polar opposite of my Goddess-worship garb: a tailored navy business suit with a straight knee-length skirt and matching blue pumps. The shoes were stylish, but comfy enough for walking—which was important, as I liked to walk to the office every chance I got. With the recent trend of mild temperatures, most of the snow had melted away. All I needed was my trench coat and shoulder bag, and I was ready for the day.

It was only a few blocks to the downtown four-story office building that housed Olsen, Sykes, and Rafferty, LLP. On the way, I strolled through well-kept residential neighborhoods, cut across a rambling public park, and passed various shops and offices until I reached Courthouse Square. In the center of the square, set off on all sides by an open grassy space lined with a smattering of benches, was the courthouse, an impressive, one-hundred-plus-year-old limestone structure fashioned in the Beaux Arts style. Complete with arched entryways, two-story Doric columns, and a center dome with a clock tower, the Edin County Courthouse was a historical landmark and local treasure. It was also the place I routinely filed legal documents and represented clients at court hearings.

Today, however, I didn't even glance at the iconic building. My attention was focused across the street where I noticed a crowd gathering toward the end of the block. Curious, I turned left at the intersection, instead of continuing down the avenue to my office, and wandered over to see what was going on. As I approached the throng, I noticed two police cars double-parked along the curb.

Maybe someone broke into the art gallery? Or the store selling designer handbags? I recalled hearing that the handbag store had been robbed about a month ago or so.

My heart sank as I realized it was the shop between the gallery and the handbag store that was cordoned off by yellow crime scene tape. Squeezing my way through a group of onlookers, I finally glimpsed the cause of all the staring and chatter around me. Two jagged gashes marred the storefront window of Moonstone Treasures, one on each side of the front door. Worse, though, was the angry black scrawl spray painted above the hole in the window. It was a single word in all caps, like a shouted accusation:

WITCH.

I froze at the sight, eyes widening. Then I quickly scanned the area for Mila Douglas, the shop's owner, and exhaled in relief when I saw her. She seemed to be okay, if a little vulnerable, standing there hugging her slender arms. Already a petite woman, Mila appeared fragile in her ballet flats, lavender skinny pants, and black turtleneck sweater. Her cropped raven shag was pulled back from her face with a girlish headband. She and her young assistant, Catrina, were speaking to a police officer near the entrance of the store. While Catrina gesticulated excitedly, speaking quickly and pointing to the officer's notepad, Mila cast a worried eye at the shards of broken glass strewn in front of her store.

Part gift shop, part psychic boutique, Moonstone Treasures was usually a welcoming place. It was a delightful destination that attracted both tourists and townies. Come in for an artsy greeting card, stay for a fun palm reading. Plus, they had an impressive collection of esoteric books and tools. As for me, I had been coming here on the sly ever since the shop opened four years ago, as soon as I discovered it carried Wiccan supplies. I couldn't believe someone would vandalize Moonstone.

"I always knew that place was bad news."

I swung around to find the source of the snide comment. A middle-aged couple walked past me, the plump woman shaking her salt-and-pepper curls self-righteously, the tall, pinched-face man staring pointedly at the storefront, his eyes glistening with great interest. My eyebrows narrowed as I watched them stalk away. I had half a mind to rush after them to defend Mila.

Before I could do anything, I felt a tap on my shoulder. When I turned, a flash went off in my face. *What the—?* Blinking, I took a step back and thrust my palm outward to block any further snapshots. As my vision cleared, the camera lowered and I recognized the smiling, dark-eyed photographer.

"Sorry about that," he said. "I forgot the flash was on."

"Wes! What are you doing here?"

"Working." He raised the camera hanging from the strap around his neck and pointed to the press ID clipped to the pocket of his wool peacoat. I noticed his usual scruffy jawline now sported a goatee, while his unruly dark hair peeked out from the edges of a gray knit cap.

I squinted at the ID. "You work for the *Edindale Gazette*?"

He nodded. "Around four months now."

Four months. About the length of time since he'd last called me. I shook my head, conflicted. On one hand, there was no denying the excited flutter I felt every time I found myself within arms' reach of Wesley Callahan. There was definite chemistry here, and I was 99.9 percent sure Wes experienced it, too. Since we first met last summer, I felt a growing connection between us. At a minimum, we always had fun together. So, what was the problem?

I thought back to our last date. After dinner and a play, we had stopped in at the Loose Rock, a fun night-club owned by a mutual friend of ours. It was over drinks that the conversation had turned to my best bud, Farrah, and her puppy dog of a boyfriend, Jake. Jake wanted to get married, while Farrah made it clear she wasn't ready to settle down.

"Good ol' Jake. He seems to have unlimited patience," I had commented, idly swirling the stirrer in my cocktail.

"Well, Farrah's got nothing to apologize for," Wes had

said. "There's nothing wrong with dating around. People have multiple friends, right? I mean, until you're married or engaged, dating around makes the most sense."

I stopped stirring my drink and eyed Wes carefully. "Um, yeah. Of course. I guess. As long as both parties are honest about it."

Wes took a drink and gazed around the room, evidently not feeling a need to respond. I wasn't ready to let the conversation go just yet.

"Anyway, Farrah and Jake *are* exclusive when they're together. They've had their breakup phases in the past, but not lately. Farrah doesn't necessarily want to see other people. She just doesn't want to be a wife right now. She likes her independence."

"Farrah's cool," Wes said. "She knows what she wants, and she's true to herself. Jake should stop pushing the issue, before he ends up pushing her away."

Hmm. I didn't say anything more on the subject, but Wes's comments had rubbed me the wrong way. He had met Farrah, through me, only a few weeks prior, yet he talked like he knew her better than I did.

Or maybe he wasn't really talking about Farrah. Maybe he was talking about himself.

The rest of the date was pleasant enough, but we were both ready to call it a night after finishing our drinks. When Wes dropped me off at my town house, he kissed me good night and said he'd call me.

A week passed—the longest we'd gone without at least speaking on the phone. So, I shot him a text, asking if he wanted to meet for happy hour when I got off work. He replied that he was tied up and would get back to me later. "Later" never arrived.

Yet, now, months later, standing on the street in the midst of the crowd around Moonstone Treasures, Wes grinned at me like he always did, as if nothing had changed. His eyes flicked over my figure, and he playfully tugged on the lapel of my jacket.

"Look at you, all conservative corporate business-woman. You look really nice."

I allowed a small smile in return. "Thanks. I need to get to work, but I wondered about all this commotion."

"Just a teenager's prank, probably."

"How could this happen with a police station right down the street?"

Wes shrugged. "It's pretty dead around here between last call at the bars and those predawn hours when some poor saps have to get up and make the doughnuts. It probably happened shortly after the three A.M. shift change when the on-duty cops were all at roll call."

"That doesn't give me a lot of confidence in our police force," I commented.

"Right," Wes said, with a wry grin. "Especially when they still haven't made an arrest in any of those break-ins that happened a few weeks ago."

I gazed down the street, trying to recall what I had read about those earlier burglaries.

"Anyway," Wes continued, "this is different. From what I heard, there was no cash in the store, and nothing appears to be missing. There's just some damaged merchandise—and, of course, the lovely graffiti." He inclined his head toward the front of the shop, where the police officer was now shooing the spectators away. There was no sign of Mila and Catrina. They had probably gone in to start cleaning up.

I would have liked to go help, but that would seem too strange. After all, why should I have any special interest in a New Age gift shop? Why would I be friendly enough with the "psychic" shopkeeper to help clean her store?

Why indeed?

As I said good-bye to Wes and headed to my office, I couldn't shake a feeling of uneasiness about the whole scene.